Right Back Where We Started: A Small Town Romance

Timber Falls

Fiona West

Published by Tempest and Kite, 2020.

This is a work of fiction. Similarities to real people, places, or events are entirely coincidental.

RIGHT BACK WHERE WE STARTED: A SMALL TOWN ROMANCE

First edition. July 27, 2020.

Copyright © 2020 Fiona West.

Written by Fiona West.

CHAPTER ONE

"HOW LONG IS THIS GOING to take?" Carter's father checked his Bulgari watch.

"I don't know." Carter kept his eyes focused on the framed diplomas behind the desk.

"I have things to do, Crash. I'm sure your job doesn't miss you, but I have people who depend on me. I can't spend all day sitting here waiting for some doctor to grace us with his presence."

"It'll only be a few more minutes. I'm hoping we'll finally get a diagnosis today; this should be the last appointment for a while, so just . . ." *Don't leave. They won't talk to me without you here.*

The office door opened, and Dr. Rose entered, running a hand down his pale pink tie. "Sorry about the wait. You must be Mr. Carpenter and Carter."

"That's right," his father confirmed, offering his hand and giving the man a firm handshake. Carter realized his palms were sweaty a fraction of a second too late to wipe them off before Dr. Rose extended a hand to him as well. They all sat back down, and Dr. Rose woke his computer.

"It looks like your wife's hemoglobin and iron came back normal, and so far, we've found no sign of tumors or acute infections that could be causing her memory loss and poor judgment."

"It's been going on for some time," Harrison said off-handedly, adjusting his watch on his left wrist. Carter hid his surprise at the comment; he wasn't aware that his father had even noticed Willow's memory issues, apart from what he'd told him.

"How long, would you say?"

"I'm not sure, I've been traveling extensively for work. More than a year." *Extensively.* That was one way to put it; this was the first time Carter had seen him in over a month. And he knew better than to ask questions about where his father went.

"I see," Dr. Rose replied. "Her chart says Carter brought her in with a fractured wrist a few months back. What were the circumstances surrounding that injury?"

When his father stayed silent, Carter sat up straighter in his chair. "She was standing on a rolling chair to try to kill a spider, and she fell. Dr. Durand assessed her for a head injury at that time, but he didn't find any evidence of one."

"Mmm. Which Dr. Durand?"

"There's more than one?" Mr. Carpenter asked, clearly surprised. "I know Evan, but not the others."

"There's three," Dr. Rose smirked. "A father and two sons."

"It was Kyle. In the emergency room," said Carter.

Dr. Rose turned more fully to Carter. "But you've noticed a difference in her behavior?"

"Yes."

"Can you elaborate a bit more on that?" *I'd rather not.* He scratched his ankle. This was awkward. He felt like he was tattling on his mom, betraying her confidence somehow. But if he didn't do something, she could really hurt herself. And there was no one else to tell these secrets; no one else cared enough.

"She forgot my twenty-seventh birthday." His leg was bouncing. He was glad his mother wasn't here for this part of the appointment; he'd sent her home with Mr. Fisher, the estate's handyman. He drove for them occasionally, so hopefully his mother wouldn't mind. But he wasn't putting any money down on a bet about what would or wouldn't upset her these days.

Dr. Rose typed something into his computer. "She didn't show up to the party or she didn't mention it?"

"Both. She was supposed to meet us at Ruth's Chris Steakhouse in Portland. She never showed. When I called her, it was like she had no idea what I was talking about." Truthfully, it had started long before that, months ago. She kept getting stuck in their conversations, a repetitive loop. She'd called her SUV a "driving machine." He had laughed before he'd realized she wasn't joking: she couldn't find the word in the files of her mind. When called on it, she laughed off her forgetfulness as a product of age. He told Dr. Rose about those moments, too.

"How's your mother's hygiene?" he asked.

"Stepmother," Harrison corrected.

Really? You have to bring that up now? Carter wanted to snap. *She's the only mother I've ever known, and you know it. And she's a better parent than you ever were.* He settled for ignoring the comment.

"I don't think she can get her contacts in . . ." Carter murmured. "She's been wearing her glasses lately, which she usually doesn't do unless she's got an eye infection or her prescription is off with her contacts. Her clothes are clean, but they're . . . simple?"

"Can you expand on that?"

"Like, she never wears anything that would require dry cleaning, nothing with complicated snaps or buttons. Does that make sense?"

"And that's not normal for her?"

Both Carpenter men barked out a laugh. "No. Not at all," his father confirmed. Carter had rarely seen her in anything but Chanel, Dolce and Gabbana, or Versace. He couldn't get comfortable in the chair, and shifting around didn't seem to help. His father stood up. "I apologize, gentlemen, but I have an important meeting to get to." It was a lie; Carter had asked his father's assistant, Nancy Buchanan, to clear his schedule all morning, and he knew she had.

Dr. Rose put down his pen. "Before you go, let me just say that early-onset dementia is a possibility, but an unlikely one, given Willow's overall good health. We'll need to rule out more possibilities first; check her thyroid, B-12 . . . let's schedule an MRI and a CT scan to rule out brain bleeds, get a feel for her brain health . . ."

"Fine. Just let me know when, and we'll get her here." Harrison shook the doctor's hand again and thanked him for his time while Carter took a deep breath and just held it. He was barely holding back his anger; this was all taking too long. This was the most inefficient process he'd ever encountered, and it was downright infuriating. These people didn't know how hard it was to get his father to these appointments, how hard it was to live with his mom right now. It was like having an ankle bracelet, the kind they put on felons; he was secretly tied to his parents' house, this heavy weight with him all the time, no matter what else he was doing. His father should be doing this. It shouldn't be his job.

"From what you've told me," the doctor went on once his father left, "there's a genuine chance that she's suffering from a neurological condition that could affect her health, possibly even her life expectancy. It's a good thing that you came in." *Affect her life expectancy. Affect. her. life. expectancy.* It was such a cold way to talk about his mother's death. She was fifty-one. She was supposed to be concerned with planning parties and receiving donations and organizing family reunions. In a few years, marrying off her boys and playing with her grandkids. Not this.

"Yeah, Dr. Durand thought it would be a good idea."

"He's right. I'm glad you listened. We'll set up those tests and have you come back in next week. And l encourage families to seek some help for themselves, too. This is a huge change in your life. You're moving from child to parent, from cared-for to caring-for. It's not selfish to start to grieve that change, to start to process it."

"Yeah, okay. I'll work on that." Never mind that he should be studying for his next actuarial exam for work. Never mind that he kept having to stop by his place in Salem just for more clothes or random books or electronics, only to lock it up again and head to his parents' estate, where he was practically living again now. Never mind that he was afraid to go out with friends, afraid she'd wander onto the highway. Bitterness began to creep in, but love swept it out. He loved his mom; their genetics were irrelevant. If she needed him, he'd be there for her.

"Do you have any recommendations for in-home care?"

Dr. Rose frowned a little. "Let's hold off on that kind of talk until we have a firm diagnosis, all right?"

Screw that. He needed help now; he'd already waited seven weeks for this appointment. Carter nodded along with him, but as soon as he was back in the hallway, he pulled out his phone.

> **Carter:** Hey, Dr. Durand. I'm at the hospital. Do you have a minute to talk?
> **Dr. Durand:** Yes. Please go to my office, I'll be there shortly.
> **Carter:** Will do. Thanks.

Kyle was only two years older than Carter, but he'd been really helpful through all of this. He had no official responsibility, yet any time Carter texted him, he always answered, never seemed to mind being interrupted. Considering he'd only seen his mom once two months ago, Carter felt he was really going above and beyond. He walked to Dr. Durand's office and waited outside the closed door until the doctor arrived.

"Good, you're still here. Sorry, I got held up by a lady who wanted to talk about her bowel movements. Come in." Carter had no time to respond to that strange greeting before he was being ushered into the small office. "What's up?"

"I just met with Dr. Rose."

"Good appointment?"

Carter nodded, then shook his head. "He didn't want to talk about care options until we had an official diagnosis. But the thing is . . ."

"You need help now."

He nodded. "I do. I need to be able to go to work without worrying, and it's not fair to ask our household staff to keep an eye on her."

Kyle leaned back in his chair and picked up a pen off his desk, spinning it between his fingers while he talked. "I don't mean to be crass, but you've got money, right?"

Carter smirked a little. "Yes." It was the worst-kept secret in Timber Falls: the Carpenters were loaded. His father was president of Timber Falls Paper Products, a certified "big deal" in the community. Half the town worked for TFPP, so the whole town knew who he was. Which made his brother Chase's drug problems all the more embarrassing.

"I don't like to assume," said Kyle. "I mean, you could still be drowning in debt if you don't manage your money well. But since cost isn't an issue, I know someone who'd be great. She's got her Master's in adult gerontology, which is technically not your mom's situation, but if Willow's got early-onset AD, she'll be an expert in that, too."

"Early-onset what?"

"Early-onset Alzheimer's Disease," Kyle clarified, not pausing to let the words land, apparently not realizing that they'd made Carter's heart clench like a fist. They were the words he'd been dreading since this began. "In the interest of full disclosure, she's also friends with my brother's best friend and my brother's fiancée, but I wouldn't let that sway me. She worked here at the hospital for a few years, so I've seen what a professional she is. I heard she went to Partners in Care just recently. See if she's available; her name's Martina . . ." He closed his eyes for a second. "Can't remember her last name."

"Lopez," Carter mumbled. "Martina Lopez."

"Oh good, you know each other." Know her? That was a bit of an understatement. She was the first—and only—woman Carter had ever loved. It wasn't just that contacting Martina was a bad idea—it was a *terrible* idea. Kyle wrote down the company's phone number on a yellow sticky note and passed it to Carter. "It would be beneficial if she knew your mother as well. It might help Willow be more comfortable with the whole situation. There's a dearth of medical professionals of this caliber in the area, so you'll want to call her as soon as possible, before she gets hired by someone else."

When Carter got back to his car, he sat and stared at the phone number for a long time, listening to the rain fall against the roof. Had she forgiven him? It probably didn't help that he'd never gotten to apologize; she'd shut him out so completely, there was no opportunity.

Who was he kidding? She'd been so bright and beautiful and full of life even in high school that he couldn't imagine she wasn't married now. It would probably be no big deal. Maybe they could even be friends again. He sighed, then started his car to drive back to work in Salem. He'd call later. *Maybe.*

CHAPTER TWO

ON MONDAY, MARTINA awoke before dawn. Snow White was singing again.

"Cat!" Martina called. "It is early, cat. It is not getting up time. Quit your yowling." There was a momentary coda in the song, a brief, thinking pause. Then the singing continued.

"Why," she moaned. "Why, cat? Why are you like this? Your breed is supposed to be quiet." It did explain why she'd been given to the shelter in the first place. Martina pried herself out of bed, yawning, feeling her way through the dark to her bedroom door. The moment she opened it, a large, fluffy Persian rubbed against her fleece-covered legs. "Yeah, yeah. Good morning, Snow." A tortoiseshell cat meowed at her from the back of the couch. "Good morning, Charming." A thin calico under the desk hissed at her as she made her way to the kitchen. "Same to you, Rajah." She got out the wet food and dished it into three bowls, taking one to each corner of the room to avoid fighting. It didn't matter; Rajah would likely ignore his so long that Snow would eat it. Charming didn't seem to know that was an option, but Snow's fluff wasn't as much fur as she liked people to think. "Greedy guts," Martina whispered to her, giving her a scratch on the head as she dug in.

She curled into a corner of the couch, pulling a knitted afghan up over her shoulders. She was too tired to go back to bed. Charming bounded up onto the couch next to her, tail twitching, curiously sniffing at her. She pulled him down next to her, letting her eyes droop closed again as she stroked his silky fur. He was a nice enough cat, but not terribly bright. In the other room, she heard her phone ding. Martina groaned.

"Rajah. Go get my phone." At the mention of his name, Rajah went scurrying under the desk again. "Snow White, how about you? You gonna earn your keep around here?"

The phone dinged again, and she sighed. "Why did I stay up so late last night?" At the suggestion of Disney Plus, she'd gotten baited into a re-watch of *The Princess Diaries* . . . and then, of course, she had to watch *The Princess Diaries 2: Royal Engagement*, not only because it had Chris Pine, but also because she liked to finish things once she started them. The books were better, but there was only so much you could do. She wasn't sure she really loved a love triangle, because someone always got left out in the cold. That's probably why she'd fallen asleep before she was halfway through it.

Martina stopped into the kitchen to grab herself a glass of kefir, then trundled back into the bedroom, carrying Charming under her arm. Her phone was blowing up, but the texts were all from different people.

Lola: Thanks for shopping with me yesterday! It was fun.

Winnie: You left your maple syrup here. We're enjoying it.

Francesca: When does your new job thingy start?

Mom: So excited for your new job today! Please let us know how it goes. :kissy-face emoji:

Dad: se acabó tu libertad, ¿sí? :smirk emoji:

My liberty is over, Dad? Really? The truth was that she was really looking forward to starting her job. Cindy Hewes, her new boss, seemed ecstatic to have someone with her education working at Partners in Care. It had been nice to have a few weeks off… she'd given herself a little vacation between finishing up at the hospital and starting her new profession in adult geriatric care. She was a little burnt out between long shifts at the hospital and long hours spent studying. It'd been nice to just have time to paint her toenails, hang with friends, and catch up on all the shows everyone was talking about on Instagram.

She picked up her phone to reply.

To Lola: Yes, super fun. Let's do it again soon. :kissy face emoji:

To Winnie: Girl, if you use up all my Grade A maple syrup without me, you and Daniel are both dead to me.

It was the good stuff: Canadian. Accept no substitutes.

To Francesca: I love you, please try to talk like an adult so people will take you seriously. Today!

To Mom: Yes, I will! Thanks, Mom!

To Dad: Gracias. Muchas gracias.

She skipped to the shower, ready to get this new job started.

SHE ARRIVED AT CINDY'S promptly at 7:30 a.m.. They had an 8 a.m. appointment with an employer. Since she'd expected to wait for a placement, Martina was thrilled. She loved this job already.

"I'll give you a ride," Cindy smiled. "Hop in!"

"Oh. Thank you. I appreciate that." Martina slid into the front seat of the woman's SUV.

"No trouble at all. I like to make sure our employees are well cared for. Though I doubt you'll have any trouble with this family. They're very well off, very well-known in the community. He asked for you specifically, actually."

Well, that's flattering. "Really?"

Cindy nodded, her hair bobbing with her head. She turned onto Highway 22. "The young man called me up out of the blue. Usually, folks do get a recommendation from someone who's been through a similar situation. Lots of word-of-mouth in this business; if you take good care of their loved one, they want to pass that blessing on to others."

"Of course." She couldn't put her finger on why just then, but suddenly she was nervous. Of course, it was her first day. Everyone must feel nervous their first day on the job. But this wasn't just first-day jitters . . . a deep sense of wrongness permeated the very air of the vehicle. It was like when you're getting sick, and you only figure out later that's why you snapped at your sister and couldn't manage to focus on your book. Or PMS. Yes, the air in the car felt like PMS. Work PMS.

"How did they know I worked for you?"

"I'm not sure, really. He didn't say. Just said that he knew you were supposed to be working for us, and if you were available, he'd pay any price to have you."

"Did you gouge him?" she smirked, and Cindy smiled back.

"No, I charged him the standard rate. He was very grateful. I guess he's dealing with all this on his own. His mother has been sick for some time."

"Well, he's got help now. I'll do everything I can to . . ." Her mouth went dry as Cindy turned off the highway into a private drive. "What did you say the name was?" She knew this lane. She knew its boxy hedges and its wrought iron fencing. She'd walked its gravel driveway, kissed a boy she loved under its cherry trees.

"Carpenter. The son's called . . ."

"Crash." Her heart was beating too hard; was she arrhythmic? She'd never had heart problems in the past, but then again, she'd never been in a situation like this.

Cindy didn't seem to notice, and she brightened at the name. "Yes, that's right. I thought it was his legal name until he corrected me. Do you know each other?"

"I thought I was going to marry him."

Cindy pulled the car to a stop in front of the stone villa. "Oh my. Well . . . " She paused, apparently at a loss for words. "Is this going to be a happy reunion?"

Pull it together, Lopez. You can't quit your first week of work. How had he even known? What was she saying, royalty was always in the know. When they bothered to check in with the peasantry, that is. Crash hadn't so much as drunk texted her in nearly five years.

"I'm sorry. I don't think this is a good idea."

"You don't even want to talk with them?"

"No, I . . . I'm sorry."

Cindy watched her for a moment, quiet. "All right, honey. I still need to meet with him in order to find out what his requirements are exactly. Is there anything I should know about working with them?

"No, they're perfectly nice people." *For some other employee to work for.*

"Do you mind waiting here in the car?"

"No, that's fine." *I'll just be here, regretting everything in my life that led up to this moment.* The massive front door opened, and Crash appeared on the threshold. Martina cursed inside her head, and she pressed herself back into the seat hard, as if that could make her disappear. As if he wouldn't be able to see her if she squeezed her eyes shut hard enough.

"Wow. He sure did a number on you, didn't he?" Cindy's voice was sympathetic. "I'll try to make this quick. Be right back." She stepped down out of the car and shut the door behind her. Martina let out a shaky sigh. She'd been able to avoid him for so long. She covered her face with her hands, trying to breathe evenly. She couldn't even watch Cindy talk to him . . . well, maybe just through her fingers. That furrowed brow, that light confusion. She knew it well; it was his *"What? I'm not getting what I want? How odd."* face. No, he wasn't getting what he wanted. Not this time. There was no way she was walking up the stone steps into that house, smiling like nothing was wrong, not for all the celebrity gossip in the universe. Smiling like paying her to watch his mom was an acceptable solution after the shit he'd pulled when they were dating. No way. Not a thing. *Uh oh*—the light confusion wasn't so light anymore; it was a deep scowl now. His footsteps crunched on the gravel driveway; *oh no*. He was coming over, he was coming to talk to her . . . she pulled her hands away from her face at the last minute and let them fall to her lap.

"Martina." He knocked on the window. "Can we talk for a minute?"

She shook her head at him, and he sighed.

"I should've talked to you before I called the agency. I'm sorry I sprang this on you, I just thought . . ."

That you'd whistle and I'd come running? Not on your life, rich boy. And yet, she knew immediately that her thoughts were unfair. High School Crash would've thrown a fit, yelling, demanding that she come inside or at least roll down the window. He wasn't doing any of that; he was asking. Politely.

"I can't help you," she whispered, and she knew he couldn't hear her through the condensation-covered glass, couldn't see her lips move through the drips down the window. Yet he read her expression well enough; he saw the pain, the unspoken regret, and he ran a hand through his hair. Now that she wasn't peeking at him through her fingers, she noticed his appearance: he was in just as good shape as he'd been when he was running track, that long, lean physique still working for him. He was wearing charcoal suit pants and a blue pinstriped dress shirt that brought out his eyes. It was open at the collar, like he'd been wearing a tie, but took it off. She looked down to confirm that he was wearing dorky loafers and blinked in surprise at his bare feet. *Doesn't that hurt? Still so impulsive, Crash . . .*

"Okay," he said, putting up his hands, as if in surrender. "Sorry. I'll just . . . I'll be in touch." These words were spoken to Cindy, who was rounding the front of the blue 4Runner in order to get back in. He stood in the driveway, hands on his hips, and he waved as Cindy pulled out.

"Well," Cindy said, clearing her throat, as they pulled back onto the highway. "That took less time than we thought, obviously. Why don't you come into the office when we get back and we'll see if we can't find another placement for you? You might have to go a bit further out, but I think we can find something . . ."

"Actually, I'll just head home. I'll come in tomorrow, if that's okay."

"Sure, honey. I understand." She glanced at her. "I've had my heart broken before, too."

TRUE TO HER WORD, MARTINA did go to the office the next morning; in fact, she was waiting outside Cindy's house when she came out to get her newspaper. In retrospect, 7:30 a.m. was probably too early . . . but, hey, now she knew that Cindy liked flannel. Maybe she could get her a new pair of pajamas to apologize for seeing her in these ones. Martina had battled guilt all night for not going yesterday, and it was after 1 a.m. when she finally fell asleep, three cats cradling her body. She only had three right now. It was usually more, but two of them had just died. She hadn't meant to take in so many; she'd just been trying to watch football at Annie's bar, since she didn't have cable. But between drinks, Annie had happened to mention that the no-kill shelter was struggling to make ends meet, and the next thing she knew, she was driving down there to save a few.

She knew it was 1 a.m. because she was still taking Buzzfeed quizzes. This one was about which unpopular Twilight character she was, and she never got to find out that vital information, sadly. So when she got up this morning, she decided to go to the library today to study, where her phone would not be welcome. Forced distance from the device was never a bad thing, but hard to get. But of course, the library wasn't open at this hour; at 7 a.m., nothing was. She wasn't a coffee drinker, so she made tea, just to kill time. She only drank about 1/4 of it before she slipped on her flats and grabbed her purse and went to Cindy's. There was a chance she'd open at eight. It wasn't that long to wait, and she always had magazines in her car. It was one of those habitual purchases now at the grocery store: she'd buy milk, bread, eggs, a magazine.

Yes, they were ridiculous. Yes, a lot of their information was inaccurate. But the way she saw it, it was better than reading something that she *knew* was fiction. But she didn't get a chance to read this morning, because Cindy let her in immediately, ushering her into the home office, sitting her in front of the large flat monitor to look at her choices while she changed into her normal clothes. Her husband shuffled by in his ratty robe and leather slippers that reminded Martina of a movie she'd seen that took place in Alaska. He shook his head, smiling, then went back to his coffee.

"Sorry," Martina called after him.

"Not your fault," he called back. "You want some coffee?"

"No, thank you, sir."

He re-appeared in the doorway. "Well, you're not the first eager beaver to show up here early in the morning to find a new assignment, and you won't be the last. Cindy's determined to make this business work."

Martina smiled, then went back to the list as he shuffled off. She paged through it, uninspired. Many were families she knew, but none particularly stood out to her. She wanted to be smart about this, start with someone who would give her a glowing review for her next job. Work like this was largely word-of-mouth, and she didn't want to start out badly. Most of these people didn't really need someone as qualified as she was . . . anyone with a strong back, a kind heart, and some common sense would be fine. Martina sighed. Reaching into her purse, she pulled out her phone, opening a notes app to halfheartedly write down a few names. She wanted to think about it first; she didn't like feeling rushed into anything. She didn't think Cindy would mind, and she confirmed as much when she came back downstairs in her work polo and khaki pants.

"Take the day and think about it. It's a long commitment with some of these folks. They're going to be around for a few more years, and we'd like to stay consistent with their caregivers, provided they're not mistreating you. I can also set up a phone call, if you'd like to talk to the family . . ."

Martina waved a careless hand at her. "Not necessary. I know most of them. Thanks, though. I'm just going to go into town and do some shopping. I'll let you know this afternoon."

"Great! Coffee for the road?"

"No, thanks, I don't like coffee." Cindy's stunned look made her laugh. "I know, I know. Everyone around here loves coffee. It's like sacrilege, but I can't help it. I don't like it." God knows her father had tried; the first time he took her to Argentina to see her grandparents, every cafe they'd gone into, he'd convinced her to try something new. Cortado? (Ew.) Café con crema? (Eh.) Lágrima? (Better . . . but still no.) Café con leche, with more milk than coffee? (Still has coffee, though, Dad.) Finally, out of desperation, he'd ordered her a submarino, a chunk of chocolate drowned in frothy milk, the best thing she'd ever tasted. Her dad laughed, kissed her loudly on the cheek as she tried to wipe the bubbles from her upper lip, hanging onto the tall glass greedily. "She's Argentinian after all," he chuckled, and later, when he finally bought her yerba mate, he confirmed that she was, indeed, his daughter. That kind of tea was just her style.

Martina got on the winding highway, letting the tall trees rush past her in the early foggy morning. A new job, she decided, was cause for celebration; she wouldn't just go to WinCo for cheap groceries today. She'd stop into Trader Joe's and get herself a few treats this week, too. She was dreaming about dried mango, turkey meatballs, and a sparkling yerba mate tonight before she went back to the library. She did her normal shopping first, put it in the trunk of her black Corolla, then hurried over to Trader Joe's with a spring in her step. She didn't skip; that wasn't very mature. But she wanted to. She'd been pinching every penny through school, and now she was ready to let loose a little.

She stepped into the boutique grocery store and sighed happily. She touched the gluten-free, vegan chocolate chip cookies by the front door. She sniffed the houseplants near the sustainably-made birthday balloons. She snagged a bottle of a cheap white wine affectionately known as Two-Buck Chuck. Chalkboard signs advertised a sale on coconut oil, and she narrowly resisted getting some, despite having at least one unopened jar at home. Dark chocolate almonds? Yes, please. Cauliflower gnocchi? Get. In. My. Cart. She was reaching for a bag of sweet potato chips when she heard a familiar voice down the aisle.

"Mrs. Sánchez, stop it! Do not put that in our cart, I *hate* Brussels sprouts."

Martina turned her head without moving the rest of her, as the older woman mumbled something to her boss.

"*I* asked for them? Oh, please. They made me vomit as a child, why would I do that?"

"I don't know, Mrs. Carpenter." The Latina woman's voice was soft, assuaging. "Perhaps it is good that you came."

Willow Carpenter tossed her straight blonde hair and held her Hermes purse closer to her chest. "I see that I'll have to from now on. You clearly can't be trusted." The look of hurt that crossed her employee's face was barely as long as a blink, but Martina saw it. Mrs. Sánchez had worked for Crash's family for probably thirty years . . . there was no way she'd make a mistake like that. Which meant . . .

Martina's feet were moving her toward the pair before she registered what she was doing. "Hola, Mrs. Sánchez. Hello,

Mrs. Carpenter," she greeted them. Willow's angry expression turned confused for a moment, then she broke into a bright smile.

"Well, hello, you! How are you, darling?" She squeezed Martina's shoulders with both hands, pulling her close for an air kiss on the cheek.

"I'm well, thank you. How are you?"

"Oh, I'm fine, just fine."

Martina glanced at the brace on her wrist. "Tennis accident?"

Willow blinked. "Pardon?"

"Your wrist," she said, gesturing toward it, as if she might not know which one. "Did you hurt it?"

"Oh, that," Willow said impatiently. "That . . . that was nothing."

"It doesn't look like nothing," Martina said, smiling, trying to keep her tone light and jovial. "Have you been cage fighting again?"

Willow laughed, pushing on her shoulder playfully. "Oh, you. You always did make me laugh. We miss having you around the house! Why don't you come around anymore?"

Martina swallowed hard. Did she really not know? Or was she saying that she'd expected them to stay friends, expected that she'd stop by when she moved back to town? She had no idea what Crash had told her about their breakup. Willow pivoted abruptly, poking around in the freezer, looking for God knows what. Martina looked to Mrs. Sánchez, whose fawn-colored eyes were sad. "Her memory, it's not good," she said softly in Spanish.

"Yes, I know," Martina murmured in reply. "I'm sorry."

"So am I," said Mrs. Sánchez. "Mr. Carter says she is sick. Maybe she will get better. But until then . . ." She gestured toward their empty cart. "Difficult."

There are things you can do, Martina wanted to tell her. *There are ways to help her be more cooperative, help her through this time with dignity.* Instead, she smiled at Willow again, a silent apology for excluding her by using Spanish. Her speech was still fluent, she was still comprehending spoken messages; she wasn't aphasic yet. That would come later, most likely. *So young.* She slipped into a diagnostic role without overthinking it.

"How old are you now, Mrs. Carpenter?"

She tittered at the question, giving Mrs. Sánchez a look that said, 'Can you believe her?' "I'm 48." The subtle shake of Mrs. Sánchez's head told Martina that wasn't quite right. If she remembered correctly, Mr. Carpenter had thrown Willow a big fiftieth birthday party last year, and Martina rarely forgot a party, especially one she hadn't been invited to.

"How did you hurt your wrist?"

"I fell," she sniffed. "It was just an accident. Nothing to fuss over."

Martina snapped her fingers. "I just remembered, I think my favorite team is playing tonight. Do you know what day it is?"

"Monday, silly." Tuesday. She was close.

Putting on a show now, she dug around in her purse. "I've been losing things lately. I can't seem to find anything. I thought for sure my phone was in here . . ." It was in her back pocket. "Does that happen to you?"

"Oh," Willow exclaimed quietly, "all the time. All the time. I swear, I'd misplace my head if it wasn't attached."

"Are you still helping out with the bachelor auction this year?"

Willow huffed irritably. "I'm going to go look for apples." She strode away before Martina could ask any more questions.

"That's a sore subject," Mrs. Sánchez told her. "They kicked her off the committee. She's so emotional, so volatile, so . . ."

"Sick," Martina finished. She watched Willow peering into open freezer consoles, looking at the frozen egg rolls and mixed vegetables and chicken breasts. "Can I distract her while you shop?"

Mrs. Sánchez's shoulders dropped, and her face lost the pinched look it'd had since Martina approached them. "Do you mind?"

"Not at all," she said with a wink, and Mrs. Sánchez smiled. By the time Willow caught back up with her twenty minutes later, the older woman had already checked out; even Martina was impressed by her efficiency. The high color on Willow's cheeks told them she wasn't happy, but she said nothing, and she didn't seem to blame Martina whatsoever. Martina knew Mrs. Sánchez would likely get yelled at in the car, but at least she'd been able to complete her shopping. They were probably afraid to leave her alone at the estate. *Which is why he was trying to hire a caregiver.*

She let the thought follow her home, dogging at her heels as she put away her groceries and drew a bath, gathering herself a bubbly drink and a book as the tub slowly filled. There was no wrong time to take a bath as far as Martina was concerned; it was her guilty pleasure. Perusing her many options, she landed on the coconut lime Epsom salts added to coconut bubble bath. It was like bathing in a piña colada, but less sticky. She shed her robe and eased into the water; it was so hot, she had to go slowly. When she'd settled into the water, the thought was still there: *He was trying to hire me as a caregiver. His mom's not doing well, and he knew I could help.* Martina let her fingers trail through the bubbles, popping the big ones idly. She wished her guilt was that easy to get rid of. No, not guilt: just sadness. Sadness for Crash and his mom and his brothers. Mr. Carpenter could take a flying leap off the peak of Mount Jefferson as far as Martina was concerned, but she hurt for the rest of them.

They'd been friends. She and Willow. Even when Crash was off doing conferences for Future Business Leaders of America or attending a track meet or at a soccer game, she'd go to the estate and poach Mrs. Sánchez's molasses cookies. They'd talk about fashion and celebrities and gossip about the town. Mrs. Carpenter had even let Martina borrow her clothes once or twice, and Martina had salivated over her wardrobe until her father said it wasn't appropriate to borrow another woman's clothes, especially a woman so much older than her. She'd felt like the daughter Willow never had, though she hadn't said as much. Still, in a family of four daughters, it was nice to feel unique.

Martina sunk down under the water with a groan, blowing bubbles, pushing her floating hair back. *What am I going to do?* Even after what he'd done, she didn't want to punish him. Well, she didn't want to punish him too much . . . a little would be okay. She broke the surface of the water, brushing the bubbles out of her hair. Martina sighed. Not even a good bath was going to solve this problem for her. She didn't need to ask what he and her mom and her sisters would think about Crash re-entering her life; they'd be firmly against it.

After several tries with her wet, pruney fingers, she slid open her phone and called her friend Winnie.

"Hello?" It sounded quiet in the background, but she wanted to be sure.

"You birthing?"

"Nope. You with someone who's dying?"

"Would I call you if I was?"

"I should certainly hope not. What can I do for you?"

"I have a work question for you . . ."

"Okay."

"It's not really an ethical question, but it sort of is . . ."

"Okay . . . consider my curiosity piqued." Winnie listened as Martina explained what had happened when she'd gone with Cindy, then what she'd seen at the grocery store.

"Well, I don't think it's an ethical question. You were asked to treat her, and you didn't feel you could. You made no commitment."

"Yes, but you know as well as I do that she'll do much better with someone she knows. And someone who knows her."

"Probably. But as I say, you made no commitment. You were honest about your boundaries."

"I feel bad."

"You do?" Winnie sounded surprised.

"What, it's so shocking that I have feelings?"

"No, you're just usually so decisive. It's unlike you to waffle over a decision like this. The only thing I've ever seen you torn over was whether to watch Prince William's wedding in real time or as a recording."

"Well, watching it was a foregone conclusion."

"Naturally." She could hear Winnie smiling. "Do you feel you're letting him down or her?"

"Both." Martina sipped her sparkling water. "We were friends, you know? When Crash and I were together, we usually had dinner with Willow on the weekends. She was so alone in that big house. And we just liked her, you know? She's a really sweet lady when you get to know her." *And she accepted my parents' dinner invitation when Mr. Carpenter refused. She raved over our empanadas and our Malbec like it was lobster and Champagne. She made me feel loved.* "It's like Maldonada and the puma."

"I don't know that one," Winnie said.

"I think a close equivalent would be Aesop's *The Lion and the Mouse*."

Winnie paused. "Let's assume I don't know that one, either."

Martina laughed. "Then I'll tell you the Argentinian version, so you can sound cool throwing it around at parties."

"Please do."

She tried to think back to all the details of the story her father used to tell her at bedtime.

"A long time ago, Spain was trying to conquer Argentina, and they set up settlements around the country. The indigenous people, the Querandi, laid siege to one of their settlements, preventing them from getting food."

"As is their absolute right against invaders."

"Exactly. A Spanish girl, Maldonada, asked for permission to go outside the walls and get food, but the captain forbade her from leaving. Being headstrong, she did it anyway, preferring punishment to starvation."

"Gotta side with Maldonada on this one."

Martina laughed. "I know, right? Anyway, our girl Mal, she sneaks out, and it's getting dark when she hears strange noises, hurting noises, coming from a cave. When she investigates, she finds a puma who's just given birth. Rather than running away, she decides to stop and help. Maldonada cleans up the cubs and stays with them while the mother goes out to hunt. She goes on like that for a few days. Then one day, she's out looking for her own food when a Querandi scouting party catches her."

"That's the people who laid siege to her settlement?"

"Right. So she thinks she's toast, right? But to her surprise, they're totally nice to her and let her come live in their village. They teach her their ways and welcome her into the community with open arms."

"I feel like something is about to go wrong . . ."

Martina chuckled. "You're so smart, Win. The Spaniards launch a counterattack, and when they discover Maldonada, they take her back to the settlement. The captain is furious about her betrayal and decides to make an example of her. He ties her to a tree and leaves her for the wild animals to rip apart."

"Classy."

"Yeah, he's a douche. But here's the thing: the Querandi go to check on her a few days later, and she's still there. The mother puma had come to bring her food every day and protect her. They untied her and she lived happily ever after."

Winnie was quiet for a moment. "So you think you're the puma in this story? Since she helped you, you want to help her now?"

"I guess so. I mean . . . I have my own mother. And she's great. But Willow, she understood my love of clothes and fashion. Taught me how to get deals on nice stuff so I could dress the way I wanted to. She knew I was kind of overwhelmed with all my family at home, being the only introvert, so she'd invite me over to paint our nails and drink sparkling cider and eat frozen pizza. Without her, high school would've been really different. She helped me figure out who I was. And when I figured it out, she made me feel like the person I wanted to be was amazing." *And I wanted to be her daughter-in-law so badly, not just because I was in love with her son.* "I think I have to do this. I want to."

"Martina?"

"Yes?"

"I think it's very admirable, what you want to do. Just don't forget that she is definitely going to get eaten, whether you protect her or not. There's no one to cut her free from Alzheimer's."

"I know," Martina sighed, watching her bubbles slowly disappear as the water suddenly turned colder. "I know."

CHAPTER THREE

CARTER HAD BEEN PACING in the foyer so long, he feared he was damaging the red Persian rug, despite his bare feet. She would be here any minute. Martina. The one who got away, she was coming. He wasn't ready. Well, he *was* ready; he'd told his mom Martina would be coming by and the other people who needed to know and the house was clean and he was nicely dressed. But when Cindy called, she'd said Martina wanted to meet with him and his mom before she accepted the job, and he sure as heck wasn't ready for *that*. Last time she'd come, it hadn't gone well, and her reaction had been what he expected on some level. This time? He didn't know what to expect. And that had his stomach twisting tighter and tighter, like an alarm clock being wound.

Tires on the driveway gravel. *They're here, they're here. Don't freak out.* He pulled back the curtains to see them. Martina wore a pale blue polo shirt with the company logo, her hair pulled back in a thick ponytail. She'd obviously straightened it first, then curled the ends. Her height was more obvious next to her boss, who wasn't exactly short. She was still beautifully curvy, and she kept tugging at the hem of the shirt, like she felt it was too short. Maybe she was just nervous. Of course she was nervous. The real question was what had changed her mind, made her come back? She hadn't even looked at him the last time she came here; now she was here preparing to accept his job offer.

They rang the bell, and he waited two seconds before opening the door. "Hello again."

Cindy smiled brightly. "Hello, Mr. Carpenter. It's so good to see you again." She stepped into the foyer, and Carter could see the way she appreciated the understated opulence. Some people needed to have a flashy house, a place that proved they'd made it. That wasn't Harrison and Willow Carpenter. Their wealth showed, of course: bamboo floors, paintings that had to be worth millions on the walls, the household staff standing by, the room-by-room environmental and stereo controls. But there were no random statues or fountains here, no marble, and he'd always found their house very comfortable, very lived-in. He and the twins, Chase and Christopher, had dumped their soccer stuff by the front door like regular teenagers, and their mother hadn't let the staff pick it up for them.

Then he turned his attention to Martina; there was a challenge in her gaze, the same look she used to give him before she dared him to do something stupid.

She stuck out her right hand. "Mr. Carpenter. Nice to see you again."

Crash cringed internally at her formal greeting, but he accepted her firm handshake, gesturing her inside. "Mom," he called up the stairs. "Your new helper is here."

Willow appeared at the top of the stairs. Her hair was thrown up into a haphazard bun, and she wore thick glasses. Her yoga pants and t-shirt from last year's Turkey Trot were clean today, thank God. He glanced at Martina for a reaction, but her face was carefully pleasant.

Willow's face lit when she saw Martina. "Darling! They didn't tell me you were coming." Carter wished he could sit down; every time his mother said something like that, he wanted to bang his head against something.

"Hello, Mrs. Carpenter," Martina smiled. "How are you?"

Willow came barreling down the stairs so fast, Carter was surprised she didn't face-plant. "What have you been up to? I want to hear everything." It lifted his spirits a little to see her enthusiastic response to the person he'd like to hire to care for her. It made him feel like maybe he was doing something right after all.

"Yes, I'd love to get caught up," she said, then glanced at Carter.

"Let's all go sit in the library," he suggested, and Willow started in that direction, then stopped.

"Who's *she*?" There was an ice to her words that Carter still wasn't used to. She was staring daggers at Cindy, who just smiled kindly.

"Oh, I'm a friend of Martina's," she said, extending a hand. "I'm Cindy." *Sort of true.* She must work with clients like this all the time; she probably had lots of tricks up her sleeve. Keeping a wary eye on Cindy, Willow shook her hand, then gestured them toward the library, as if she were in charge of this meeting. She'd always had that air about her; every party, every benefit Carter had ever attended that Willow had had a hand in, she was the one people turned to with questions. And she always had the answers. Always. It was one of the things he'd been most sure of.

Martina settled into a deep burgundy, high-backed wing chair near the window while the rest of them took the couches. This was the room where he'd introduced her to his parents, and he tried not to get lost in the memory . . . squeezing her hand, the polite pleasure on his mother's face, the unabashed rejection by his father.

"Mrs. Sánchez," Willow called, and the slender woman, dark-haired with gray highlights, appeared in the doorway. "Could you bring us some tea, please?" She nodded, then winked at Martina as she turned to go. That was a relief, at least; Mrs. Sánchez had always approved of her.

"So, tell us, darling, what have you been up to the last few years?" Willow asked.

"Well, I've been working as a nurse for a few years—"

"Have you really? That's what you always wanted to do, wasn't it? Do you remember, Carter?"

He nodded, his gaze on the unlit fireplace. He couldn't bear to see how she was reacting to all this. *Please, Martina. Please help us. Please don't walk away. I don't deserve it, but I need your help.*

"And now I've just gotten my degree in acute care to become a nurse practitioner."

Mom sat back hard in her chair, as if the news floored her. "Isn't that wonderful? I'm just so pleased for you, honey. Are you working with kids or adults or . . . ?"

"Adult Gerontology, actually," she said, and there was a strange note of apology in her tone.

"I see. Well, that's wonderful, honey." She hadn't used her name yet, and Carter wondered if she remembered it. She knew who she was, knew they were acquainted. Given how much time she'd spent here in high school, that wasn't surprising, but Carter was grateful. She was blowing up at him a lot. She knew she was forgetting. It would get easier once she didn't know, the internet and Dr. Rose had both promised. Carter wondered how long that would be. At any rate, this wouldn't be a quick assignment. This would be years. Did that change things?

"How about you, Mrs. Carpenter? What have you been up to lately?"

"Oh," she waved away the question, "you know. This and that. I haven't done many events lately. The groups have gone all to seed, those women were impossible to work with. So I've stepped back to let others take the lead for a while. I'm sure they'll realize that my way is better, eventually."

"You were always a huge asset for the Ladies' Auxiliary, I remember that. No one planned events like you."

Willow blushed, and Martina smiled at her. Mrs. Sánchez came back in with a silver tray and four steaming cups of tea. She stopped first near Willow's chair, offering her one.

"Who's that for?" Willow asked.

Mrs. Sánchez's face stayed calm, like she'd been expecting the response. She probably did at this point. "You asked for tea, Mrs. Carpenter."

"Who, me? No, I didn't. You need a vacation, Mrs. Sánchez," she giggled, making a face at Martina that said, 'Can you believe her?' Mrs. Sánchez shot Martina a pained look at that, a silent plea. *Help us*, her eyes said. *We don't know what to do with her anymore. Help us, please.* At least he wasn't the only one begging. Silently, Mrs. Sánchez moved on to Carter, who also silently refused the tea, rubbing his forehead. He lifted his head and took Willow's hand.

"Mom," he said gently, "Martina's going to be here with you during the day while I'm at work."

His mother brushed imaginary crumbs from her pants. "Why, is she shadowing me for an internship or something?"

"You know she's not."

Willow's lip trembled. "Is it because I fell? I won't get on the rolling chair again."

"No, no, it's nothing you did wrong. Remember how we talked about your memory issues? It's because of that. That's all, that's the only reason. Martina's a professional, and she can take really excellent care of you. I just don't want you to be in need when I'm not here."

"What was the diagnosis?" Willow asked, fiddling with the edge of her shirt.

"We don't have one yet, officially. When you hurt your wrist, Dr. Durand, he referred us to a neurologist, remember?"

"Doctor . . ." She swallowed hard. "Dr. Rose."

Carter felt as proud as if she were a child who'd just written her name for the first time. "That's right, Dr. Rose. And once we get you diagnosed, she can help you remember to take your medications."

"And we can get caught up," she said, casting a shy glance at Martina.

"That's right," Martina said, smiling. "It's been too long, anyway. We always had a wonderful time together, didn't we?" They did; it wasn't manipulative to say so. It was the absolute truth.

Willow's eyes filled with tears. "I'm sorry," she whispered. "I'm sorry that I'm such trouble. I'm not trying to be." He pulled her toward him and squeezed her tight into his side on the couch. She cried into his shoulder, and he pinched his eyes shut so tight, his whole face screwed shut, trying not to cry, letting her wipe her face on his nice shirt. As Willow began to wind down, Martina moved over to the couch, sitting next to him.

"Willow, it would be my honor to take care of you. Will you let me? I want to make this as painless as possible for you. For all of you." Carter's heart swelled with relief, and he took the first deep breath he'd taken in days, but the tears were threatening to fall more than ever now.

Cindy piped up. "Our company has been providing this kind of care for many years. Our employees are always professional and have the best training available. Ms. Lopez will be no different."

"Well," Willow said with a watery smile, lifting her head, "if it's necessary, I'm glad it's this one." This one; she couldn't remember her name. "I know you," she said, reaching out a hand, and Martina took it immediately, letting their joined hands rest on Carter's knees. He acutely felt the irony of being caught between them.

"Yes, you know me," Martina smiled, and a single tear slid down her cheek. That had all his self-control eroding like a mudslide. "And I know you. I'll make sure we get you dressed to your usual standards. No more slumming for you, lady."

Willow looked down at her clothes, then laughed. "I do look a little casual, don't I?"

Martina hummed her agreement. "I'll have you back in Chanel in no time, if you want. We'll fix your makeup and your hair. Get you right again."

"Maybe we could go to the Ladies' Auxiliary meeting . . . I don't know when it is, but . . ."

"We'll find out," Martina agreed, squeezing her hand. "It would be good to go. Familiar things are good right now. They'll help you feel calm."

Carter stared at her, needing to connect with her, thank her, get on his knees and kiss her beautiful feet. She, on the other hand, seemed to be pointedly avoiding his gaze. The ladies chatted for a few minutes longer, then Cindy gave them a subtle nod toward the door.

"We'll work out an official work schedule and use the pay contract we already established," Cindy said, standing from the wing back chair. "We'll be in touch, Mr. Carpenter."

"Please, call me Carter. Thank you so much, Cindy. Thank you both," he said, walking them to the door. Cindy was out the door already when he reached out to touch Martina's elbow.

"Don't," she said, her voice low. *Right.* He felt her coldness like a slap. Apparently, all the warmth she still had for Willow didn't extend to him. It shouldn't have surprised him . . . but it still hurt. But he couldn't afford to tick her off.

"I'm sorry," he said quickly, shoving his hands in his pants pockets. "I won't—I'm sorry."

"What do you want?"

"Can we talk? Tonight, once she's in bed?"

"I'm not coming here at night." Martina turned back toward the car.

"Annie's, then. Please, Tini." She visibly straightened at the nickname, and he winced. *Don't overplay your hand, Carpenter.* "I just want to clear the air before you start work. Please."

She sighed, her breath fogging in the October cold. "Annie's. Nine o'clock. Don't be late."

"I won't be late. Thank you."

"You're welcome, Mr. Carpenter." She hurried down the steps like she couldn't get away from him fast enough.

CHAPTER FOUR

ANNIE'S WAS QUIET WHEN she walked in at 8:35. She'd wanted to get to pick their spot, giving him no opportunity to choose their former favorite booth. He was already there, though, but apparently he'd had the same thought, because he sat at the bar. He still looked very nervous, and she reminded herself that his emotional state was no longer her concern. That heart was off-limits. Big ol' "do not enter" sign there. Maybe she could get him to wear a t-shirt to that effect. She slid onto a stool at the bar and signaled Annie. The middle-aged white woman came over, wary.

"This is a familiar scene . . ." she said, drying a pint glass.

"No, it's not. A ginger ale, please."

"Get whatever you want, I'm buying." Carter pulled out his wallet.

"No." She put her hand over his, and he stilled, not looking at her. "Let's establish some ground rules, right now."

He slowly put his wallet away, nodding. "Okay." Annie smirked at her, then moved off to get her soda.

"First of all, unless I am working at your house, I will provide my own food and drinks. This will not be a weekly or even monthly occurrence. I know there will be times when we need to discuss things about your mother's care; those meetings should occur at the house during work hours. There will be no cutsie nicknames," she said, ticking the items off on her fingers, "there will be no incidental touching. There will be no discussion of the past unless it benefits your mother. What happened between us is ancient history."

Crash was spinning slightly on his stool, a power move that showed his abs off against his shirt, but his voice was small. "So I'm not allowed to call you Tini?"

"No. You may call me Ms. Lopez at work. And I'll call you Mr. Carpenter."

"Can I say something?"

She gestured for him to go ahead as she accepted her drink and took a sip.

"I just . . . I just really appreciate you doing this for me. I should've talked to you about it before I requested you through the agency. I was just afraid you'd say no."

"A heads up would have been nice," she agreed. "But having seen her in the grocery store . . . I understand."

"I needed you. She knows you, likes you. And I know we can both trust you completely." He lifted his ice-blue gaze to hers, and she saw how sincere he was. It was quite the switch from the brash, bossy young man she'd known before.

"How do you know I won't exact my revenge for our breakup?" She drew circles in the condensation on her glass with her thumb, letting it trickle down the glass.

"Because I know you, Ms. Lopez. You're a professional. You wouldn't do anything to hurt my mom." Crash's easy smile was missing. She realized she hadn't heard him laugh even once since she'd seen him at his house. Where was his mile-a-minute humor, his way of elbowing into every decision, his golden boy posturing?

"True." She kicked a foot gently against his stool. "Do you have any conditions?"

Was that surprise on his face? Why shouldn't this go both ways? She shouldn't be the only one who got to dictate how things would be.

"I . . . I'm just so relieved you agreed to take the job, I don't think I deserve to put any conditions on it."

She lifted her hand to place it over his, then remembered her own rule: *no incidental touching*. Harder than it looked, really.

"Of course you do," she said, flipping her part to the other side of her head with the hand she'd lifted. "Come on. There must be something you want or don't want."

"Honestly, I . . . I don't know. I don't think so." He was staring down into his lager, which bubbled quietly. "I'm fine with whatever." Crash, with no opinion? Going with the flow, stammering through his sentences? This felt wrong.

"It's been a hard few months for you, hasn't it?" Geez, they'd been together twenty minutes, and she was already plowing through the caution signs she'd set up for herself. *Stop it. Stick to the plan. Stop . . . caring.*

"I can't talk about this with you." His gaze was dead, shut down.

"You can if it's part of your mother's care."

"Ms. Lopez," he began. Oh, that name sounded awful coming from his mouth. When someone's lips have kissed you, your professional name suddenly became repulsive falling from them. "I asked for you because it would comfort my mother. I

need your help, I do. And I knew you would want to help us if
you could, because that's the kind of person you are. But honestly, I don't think I need to draw a lot of boundaries around
our professional relationship, because I won't be around much.
I'll pay you on time, through the agency. I know that the relationship we had is gone now. I don't like it, but I know it." He
took a long pull on his beer. "My therapist says it's good to accept things as they are, not as you want them to be. So I'm not
trying to trick you or mislead you; I just need your help. And
lucky for me, I can afford it." He turned to her more fully. "But
if this is going to make you uncomfortable, I understand if you
want to turn the job down."

"No . . ." He'd never been a bad guy at heart, even if some
of his choices were very immature; they'd just wanted different
things. Different things that he hadn't bothered to clarify when
she was talking about their future together . . . had he been selfish? Yes. He was still being selfish, really. Only a selfish person
would ask their ex for such a personal favor. "No, it's all right.
I'll take the job." Because that's what it was: a job, not a favor.
What was the worst-case scenario? He'd make a pass at her, and
she'd have every right to tell Cindy that she wanted a new assignment.

No, her mind commented loudly, *the worst case is that he
makes a pass at you, and you don't stop him, because you're lonely
and you're still in love with him.* A new boyfriend would be es-
sential, she'd already decided, just so she had more incentive
not to get with Crash, and she already had one picked out:
Greg Trout, one of the interns from the hospital. He seemed
like a nice guy, and she'd never been unfaithful to a boyfriend.
She wasn't going to start now. But ending up back in a rela-

tionship with him, as her employer? Cindy had already made it clear that was not an option. So she'd find another outlet for her romantic intentions . . . just a fling. Something to keep her mind off him.

"Here's the thing," he said, reaching for his wallet. "I want someone with real medical knowledge; lots of people can make sure she doesn't fall in the bath and wipe her mouth. I want someone who can make medical decisions, treatment decisions. I don't want her going back to the hospital; I mean, she can go see her neurologist when needed. But people are much more likely to die from a secondary infection during a hospital stay than those who can rehabilitate at home, and I don't want her to have to be hospitalized. So your role is going to be preventative as well."

"Well, I do have my Master's—"

"I know. And here's the last thing: I'm going to pay you what you're worth."

She sat up straighter. Her debts weren't drowning her, but she was treading water a little. Her father had paid for her undergrad, but she'd refused him for her Master's out of pride. It was a decision she was proud of, looking back. But the way he was talking now made her nervous.

"What does that mean?"

"It means Cindy and I came up with a number, and you're not going to argue about it."

"But I don't have any real experience yet . . ."

"I don't care. Her pay scale was too low, based on my research. You have the experience I care about: a relationship with my mom that has positive associations for her. And your education makes you very valuable to me as an employee."

"I see. And what number is this?"

He did smile then, just half of one, just a hint of it, really, the left side of his mouth hitching up. "You'll find out when you get paid." He drained the rest of his drink and dropped a twenty on the bar. "Thanks, Annie," he called, then turned to Martina. "Can I walk you to your car?"

"No, I think I'll stay for a while."

Crash frowned a little, then shrugged. "Suit yourself. See you Monday."

"Okay." As she watched him walk away, she couldn't help but shake her head. She'd walked in here so ready to lay down the law with him ... and now, all that fire was gone. Dust. Cold.

"Didn't think I'd ever see you two back here together again ..." Annie said, her voice low under the chatter of the game on the TV.

"Me neither." Martina wiped her mouth. "But it wasn't a date. This is just business."

"Uh-huh. Is that why he paid Gray and Booker $20 to move somewhere else?"

She sighed, letting her head fall to her arms. "This is a mistake, isn't it?" Martina was all about learning from experience, she just preferred that it be someone else's experience. Making her own mistakes wasn't her first choice, or even her fourth or fifth choice.

"Couldn't say," Annie mused. "Though I do see a lot of people make mistakes here. You'd think I'd be an expert by now."

Martina snickered. She'd take a distraction right now, and her imagination was sent spinning with that thought in mind. "What's the most romantic thing that's ever happened here?"

The barmaid dried her hands, her gaze thoughtful. "I don't know that romance is really happening around here. Not like you mean it, anyway."

"Oh, come on," Martina pressed. "No engagements because they had their first date here? No long-lost loves finding each other again?"

"You read too much People magazine," Annie said, grinning. "Well, I take that back . . ."

"Yes?" She pressed forward, putting her chin in her hands and her elbows on the bar like Annie was about to tell a fairy tale.

"I'm pretty sure Darby Ferris and Shane Billingham hooked up in the back of her 4Runner a few months ago."

Martina stuck out her tongue. "That's old news, she delivered their baby a year ago."

Annie's eyebrows shot up. "Oh, really? Last I heard, we didn't know who the daddy was . . ."

Martina pulled her lips to the side. Her friend Winnie had delivered the baby, which is the only way she knew Shane had been there.

"Well, let me rephrase that: he was there when Bailey was born. I guess I don't know for sure she's his."

"Seems pretty likely, though."

"Don't tell anybody, okay?"

"Tell them what?" Annie asked innocently, then gave Martina a wink as she moved down to the other side of the bar where Gray was signaling her. Martina brushed away the guilt she felt about spreading gossip; it wasn't a HIPAA violation or anything, but she should know better. Sometimes the news was just too good: it was just too tempting to let secrets spill out. And even this bit of juicy gossip had her thinking . . . she didn't know Darby was still seeing Shane. Last she knew, she was trying to do the single mom thing all by her lonesome, and it wasn't going all that well. She had moved back in with her mom a few weeks ago. Darby and Shane's relationship, if it could even be called that, was volatile at best . . . it reminded her more than a little of how she and Crash had been. Martina felt her gaze drifting to the TV.

"Oh, come on," she yelled in unison with half the bar as a 49ers defender took down a Browns cornerback in what was clearly a flagrant horse collar. "*That's* a no call? Seriously? You've got to be kidding me . . ." She wouldn't mind if the Browns won, since it would weaken the 49ers' record against the Seahawks in November. Then again, they were going to meet the Browns next week in Cleveland, so it wouldn't hurt for them to be demoralized. The Seahawks historically didn't do as well on the road.

Right now, any distraction was welcome. Anything so that she didn't have to think about what working for her ex was going to be like.

CHAPTER FIVE

AT 12:58 P.M., HIS mother was scrolling through her phone in the waiting room of the hospital, seemingly unbothered by the people and noise around her. That, at least, was something to be thankful for. The rest of the situation was stressful enough as it was. Carter checked his phone again: no messages from his father, and it was two minutes until his mom's appointment was supposed to start. Once the hospital had realized who they were (i.e. the family who'd funded most of the new pediatrics wing), they'd moved up her CT scan and MRI, and now they were ready to finally get the results, and hopefully, a diagnosis.

He hated that his father had thrown his weight around to make that happen, but progress was progress. He wondered obliquely what this process was like for people who didn't have his family's influence. 12:59. Carter wanted to pace or bang his head against the wall, but it wouldn't do any good. His father showed up when he wanted to. He pulled out his phone to text his assistant.

Carter: Is he on his way?

Mrs. B: As far as I know. I canceled the appointments that overlapped.

Carter: Okay, thanks. Sorry to bother you.

Mrs. B: Oh, were you bothering me? I didn't think
so.

Mrs. B: I'll make a note for future interactions: in-
quiries into his father's whereabouts when he's due
at important appointments are bothersome.

Carter smiled in spite of himself; he liked Nancy.

"Willow Carpenter?" The nurse, a thin black woman with braids, stood at the doorway smiling. Carter nudged his mom, who stood up and followed him back into the offices. He couldn't help but look over his shoulder, in case his dad showed up. But when they got to the office door, his anxiety melted away as he heard his father's laugh through the door. Melted and re-formed into anger as it hardened. He didn't have ten seconds to shoot him a text and let him know he was already here?

The nurse gave a cursory knock, then opened the door for Carter and his mom.

"Ah, here they are," Dr. Rose said, as if they were late. "We were wondering."

His mom gave a gracious smile, the kind that told him she didn't know what she was doing here. Carter guided her to the chair next to Harrison, and then leaned against the wall, since all the chairs were taken.

"Carter, you can grab a chair from the nursing station if you'd like . . ." Dr. Rose said.

"No, no. I'm fine. Please, go ahead. I don't want to put you behind schedule."

The doctor sighed. "Well, Mrs. Carpenter, as far as I can tell, we're looking at early-onset Alzheimer's as the source of your memory issues."

"I'm dying?" she asked, her voice shaking, and Carter leaned forward to offer her his hand, which she took immediately.

"Well, no. Not any time soon. This condition can go on for years, but it does deteriorate a person's mental capacity as well as their muscle tone. But there are some wonderful new drugs out there, and we're going to find the ones that are right for you. Your new medical staff member has been in contact with me, and she and I will discuss some possibilities, but for now, just know that you're in good hands."

Willow sat silently, just staring at the desk. Harrison reached out to touch her shoulder. She jerked away, leaning closer to Carter, and he watched his father's expression harden.

"I want to go home," she whispered to Carter.

He knelt next to her chair. "Can we stay just a few more minutes? I have some questions for Dr. Rose . . ."

"I'll wrap up for us," his father broke in. "You two go ahead."

But you don't know what my questions are . . . He nodded anyway, giving both men a smile as he led his mom back out into the hall. Maybe Martina could help him understand more about the condition, now that they had an official diagnosis. He'd been surprised to hear that she'd already been in touch with Dr. Rose . . . but then again, she was good. He should've figured she'd be on top of things.

THAT NIGHT, AT ELEVEN o'clock, Carter woke to the sound of a piano. He stumbled out of bed and down the hall, not bothering to put a shirt on. Willow sat at the big black Steinway, eyes closed, playing a slow, mournful song he didn't recognize. He leaned against the doorway, listening, watching her. He'd never known his biological mom; Harrison didn't talk about her or have any pictures. From what he knew, Harrison had cheated on her, paid her a big old settlement to leave quietly, and then hired Willow to care for the three boys. Since Willow and Harrison eventually married, and Willow and the boys looked so alike, people assumed she was their mother. And more than that, she'd always been his protector from his father, as much as she could. She'd pled his case on more issues than he could count, and he knew it was the same for his brothers. But now it was his turn to protect her, to try to take care of her, if he could.

"Crash." His father's voice startled him, and he turned to see him still dressed in the same gray suit he'd left the house in that morning. Harrison gestured him down the hall, and Carter followed him into his father's bedroom, which was not also his mother's bedroom. They hadn't slept in the same room for several years, and he didn't want to know what that meant.

"What did Dr. Rose say?"

"Oh, nothing, really," Harrison said, waving a careless hand. "Empty promises. We'll look into a better neurologist."

"No, I like Dr. Rose, and he's close by. Since I'll be the one getting her to her appointments, I'd like to have some say . . ."

His father held up his hands, as if in surrender.

"Why were you there before us?"

"Ted and I had lunch together. Turns out we're members of the same golf club." He put a heavy hand on Carter's shoulder. "That's how you get things done in the world, son. Take notes."

Carter crossed his arms. "When do you leave?"

"Tomorrow morning. And I still need to pack." He gestured toward the music room. "See if you can get her to keep it down, will you? I'd hate to have to get rid of the piano. The movers are outrageously expensive."

Never mind that it's the one thing that makes her happy . . . Carter shuffled back to the music room . . . she'd shifted to "Clair de Lune," an homage to the moon, which happened to be almost full, lighting up the white carpet with its glow.

"We played this song at our wedding," she said, her fingers still moving steadily over the keys. "Sometimes I wonder if he married me just so he wouldn't have to pay me to watch you boys."

Carter went over to the black, padded bench and sat down next to her, facing away from the piano. "He's a jerk. Always has been."

"I didn't think so. Not back then."

"Why didn't you have kids with him?" That was probably too personal, but she seemed so present tonight, and he'd always wondered.

She smiled at him. "Oh, but I did. I had you. You three were more than enough for me. You filled up my heart. Still do."

He returned her smile, nudging her with his shoulder. "It's late, Mom. You should go to bed."

"I can't sleep. When's he leaving?"

"Tomorrow."

"Good." She kissed the top of his head. "I'm sorry, I'm keeping you awake. I'll stop."

He hadn't even gotten back under the covers yet when she started up again, and he wondered if she'd forgotten or if she just needed it that much. He recognized the song, and he grinned; his question was answered. Apparently, it was neither. Carter fell asleep to the muted sound of "Brahms's Lullaby" coming through the wall.

CHAPTER SIX

"ALL RIGHT, FIRST THINGS first," Martina started. They sat at the kitchen table on Friday morning, papers spread out in front of them. "Do you have medical power of attorney for your mother?"

"No, but I was wondering if I should," Carter answered. "My father hasn't been around much lately. Do you think I should?"

"I don't know what the situation is with your father, and I'm not trying to probe, but if she's hospitalized, it would be good to be able to make decisions without having to consult him. A medical power of attorney would solve that problem."

"Right. Yeah. I can contact our lawyer." He pulled out a leather journal and made a note. Martina tried not to be impressed that he was so organized; he'd always blown off his work in the past. Clearly, High School Crash and Adult Carter were two different people.

"I'd also discuss with her sooner rather than later if she'd want a DNR or DNI and what her wishes are for her remains. And while we're on the subject of legal documents, did you receive a copy of our contract?"

He nodded, still writing. She'd sat down with Cindy yesterday at the office to go over it, and some of the language was still on her mind. *Signatory agrees that their behavior will be professional toward the patient and their family at all times. This includes not entering into intimate or romantic relationships with patients or those residing with the patient. Such behavior will be grounds for immediate dismissal.* She really needed to get Greg's number and give him a call. Getting fired was the last thing she needed.

Martina slid him one of the handouts she'd prepared. "Here's a list of online classes and seminars about Alzheimer's, if you're interested. Since she's so young, some of it won't apply to her, but it would still be good information for you and your family to have."

He looked at the paper, wide-eyed, still silent. Martina hesitated; this was her first meeting with a patient's family. Maybe she should've asked Cindy to come with her. "Would it be possible to get me a copy of her schedule?"

He grimaced. "I don't have one. I know she kept a Google calendar; I think she shared a link with me once, but I don't think I ever opened it up. Mrs. Sánchez would probably have one; she always seems to know when to have dinner ready."

"Okay, I'll ask them both. Are there more of her affairs you'd like me to help manage?"

He was looking at the handouts again, his expression tense and defeated. "I mean, if you can get her to her hair appointments and stuff, that'd be really helpful."

"Of course. Does she know she's not allowed to drive anymore?"

"Is that necessary?"

Martina nodded. "I'm afraid so. Since Alzheimer's patients have a tendency to wander, we want to make it as difficult for them as possible. Not having wheels slows them down so we can catch up more easily."

"Okay. I'll explain it to her . . ."

"No, I can talk to her about it. We'll blame it on me; you don't have to be the bad guy all the time. I'm sure you've done plenty of that."

His lips were pressed together. He looked so much older than twenty-seven.

"Now, as far as patient-proofing the house, how much latitude do I have?"

Carter waved a hand. "As much as you need. Make it Fort Knox."

"Okay. There's some sensors we can put on the doors to alert us on our phones when they're opened and closed." *We.* It felt so very strange to be in a "we" with Carter Carpenter again, of any kind. "I'd like to at least get all the medications under lock and key, including the ones in your bathroom. Do I have your permission to go through your medicine cabinet?"

"Um, yeah. That'll be fine."

"I'll also be putting her on a schedule for exercise, showering, stuff like that. Her bedtime will be pretty early, probably no later than 8:30. Patients do better if they know what to expect most days."

"She'll also have a night nurse . . . but she reports to you. Cindy hasn't found anyone yet, but . . ."

"Okay, we'll cross that bridge when we come to it." She shuffled the papers until she found the next one. "I would also like to make a visual cheat sheet for her, with people's names and roles. Can I get a picture of you?"

He looked up at her. He didn't smile, his face tense and stoic.

"Okay, but it's not a mug shot, so could you maybe smile?" He snorted quietly, and she could tell he was trying, but the forced smile didn't reach his eyes.

As soon as the camera was off him, Carter sunk his fingers deep into his hair and went back to reading the page in front of him. The one entitled 'late-stage Alzheimer's,' that depicted the end of the disease, when patients could no longer do things like swallow or use a toilet. It was hopefully a few years off, but it was coming.

"Let's put that away for the moment," she said gently, flipping it over. "It can be pretty overwhelming, getting so much information about what's to come."

Carter said nothing, still staring at the table. That's when she noticed the wet spots, tears that had fallen like polka dots on the paper, letting the letters on the other side show through. Crash was broken. And if there was anything Martina couldn't stand, it was watching someone she cared about be broken.

"Mr. Carpenter . . ." She felt like such a terrible person, calling him that, just watching him cry. She leaned forward across the table, extending her hand toward him as a show of sympathy. "This is really hard for everyone. But I promise, it'll get easier. You've got help now. That's a good first step. Once we get her on some medications, get her on a routine . . . it'll help."

"Thank you, Ms. Lopez." To her surprise, he reached out and took her hand, the one she hadn't realized she was offering. That small connection; it assuaged her conscience. She gave him a small squeeze as she continued.

"I know some of her favorites, but it would be helpful to have a list of favorite activities, foods, scents, etc. Can you get that to me? Doesn't have to be today, just sometime this week."

"Yeah, that shouldn't be too hard."

"Well, take your time. We don't have to push this. These are just things that'll help as we all get used to each other again."

"Thank you again for doing this." He pulled his hand back, turning his head to wipe his eyes, as if she wouldn't see. "I have to get to work."

"Of course. See you tonight."

"Right."

FOR A FIRST DAY AND with no medication yet, it had gone pretty well. Martina had tried to start Willow on some herbal supplements that she thought would help, but she wouldn't take them. Willow had gotten a frustrating phone call from someone that she didn't want to talk about or let her handle. Martina was just sitting at the kitchen island, writing out her report to Carter when a soft voice interrupted her.

"Martina? May I speak with you?" Mrs. Sánchez was dressed to go home, her tan raincoat buttoned, her hair under her plastic bonnet, her shiny black purse over her arm.

"Of course, Mrs. Sánchez." She gestured for her to sit, but the woman shook her head, glancing around. She turned and disappeared down the dark hallway toward the back door. Martina followed her, curious. Why all the secrecy?

"Is everything all right?" she asked her in Spanish. Mrs. Sánchez stopped by the back door.

"I need to know: can you fix her?"

"Fix her?" It dawned on Martina slowly, what she meant. "Oh, Mrs. Sánchez . . . it doesn't work like that. Her mind, it's failing her. She most likely has Alzheimer's." Had Carter not talked to her about this? She'd gather the staff tomorrow and make sure they understood. "There's no cure. She will be sick for a long time, years maybe, forget all of us, then die."

Mrs. Sánchez put a hand on her arm. "Mrs. Carpenter, she is a nice lady. But this lady? She slaps my hand. She curses me. Says I steal things. I don't know her. Not the same lady I worked for these thirty years. Not the same lady who sponsored me when I became a citizen, helped me learn English, helped me when Diego passed away." A tear fell on her soft cheek, running through her mascara. Martina closed her eyes, trying to keep herself together. Mrs. Sánchez could've quit. She could sue them. Instead, here she was, asking for hope.

"Mrs. Sánchez, what's your first name?"

"Yesenia," she said softly.

Martina took her hand. "I'm so sorry that happened, Yesenia. You should not have had to go through that. Did you tell Carter?"

"How can I? He is crushed with grief. I see it. He carries too much alone. I did not want to burden him."

"But Carter cares about you. He would want to know."

Her lower lip trembled, but she nodded. "And sometimes, she doesn't know me. She asks me, what am I doing in her house? Me!" she said, thumping her chest indignantly. "Like we're *strangers*."

"It hurts, doesn't it?" Martina murmured, squeezing her hand. "She treats me the same way. This morning, she thought I was you, twenty years ago. Then some moments, she's fine. She's here."

Mrs. Sánchez nodded vigorously. "When she's here, it's good. Like before."

"There will probably be more good days once she starts her medication. But I can't promise it." She took both Yesenia's hands. "What I can promise is that if she's violent or abusive, I can keep her away from you. You don't have to endure that."

"Endure?" Her confused stare told Martina it was a vocabulary issue. She hadn't meant to switch back to English; it was harder to speak Spanish when she'd been thinking all day in English. Some days, they both felt like second languages.

"Um, put up with. Live with. Suffer through."

"Ah, sí. Of course." Her lower lip trembled and another tear fell. "But Mr. Carter. I don't want to leave him. He is losing her. He loses me, too? He is alone. His brothers, they have big problems. His father, he's too busy for everyone. Mr. Carter needs me."

"It's a hard choice. We would hate to lose you, both of us. But we would understand. You must do what is right for you. If you can't work here anymore, we will support you, help you find another job, if that's what you want."

"At my age?" The woman laughed, wiping her tears. "It would not be easy."

"No. There is no easy way now. For any of us."

"I want to be here. Mrs. Carpenter, she . . . she needs me."

"That's incredibly generous of you," Martina said. "But do what's right for you. I mean it. We'll find our way through."

"And that is why I will stay for now; you are in our corner now."

CHAPTER SEVEN

ALMOST ONE WEEK IN, things were going pretty well. The night nurse was running thirty minutes late, citing a 'personal emergency.' Martina didn't like to judge people; she loved it. And this gal had a lot of personal emergencies. Martina wondered how long she was going to last in this job if she couldn't commit to being on time. It's not like she could leave Willow alone . . . she wouldn't be alone alone, Mrs. Sánchez and the others were there, but still. What if something happened? Martina was also concerned that the girl wasn't that qualified for the work. She, on the other hand, was very overqualified. Maybe that's why this gal's qualifications seemed lacking . . . everyone's did, by comparison. But lots of nurse practitioners were doing more personalized care now, and that's what Carter had said he wanted at the bar. He wanted her expertise.

She'd just helped Willow take a shower, and when her hair was done she'd either call Cindy for a relief nurse or maybe the other gal would've arrived by then; the other gal never did a good job with Willow's hair anyway. Martina felt like a Victorian-era maid, combing and drying Willow's thick blonde hair as she sat on a cushioned stool in front of her vanity, watching her in the mirror. Her hair was pretty, but Martina could see that her highlights were growing out. She made a mental note to make her an appointment with Farrah Durand at Shear Brilliance.

"Your hair's so pretty," Martina called over the noise of the hot air, spinning it around the round brush so it would curl under at the bottoms.

"What?" Willow called back.

Martina turned down the hairdryer. "Just said your hair's pretty, that's all." She smiled at Willow in the mirror, and Willow smiled back. "Doesn't it feel good to be clean?"

"Yes. I feel more like myself when you help me." Willow put a hand over the hand that held the brush and gave it a light squeeze . . . a wordless thank you. Carter did that, too, she remembered. Martina could see the way that it calmed Willow. Was it the feeling of connection to another person? The older woman didn't get much physical affection from anyone but Carter, and even he was hardly ever around. Martina felt a little puff of anger flicker to life; he should be here more. Willow needed him. Who knew how much time she really had left before she didn't remember who he was?

And yet, selfishly, when Cara finally showed up, puffing out apologies, Martina breathed a sigh of relief as she walked down the front steps, because she hadn't seen him again today. But yesterday, he'd left her a note: *Thanks for this. Appreciate you. – C.* Not appreciate *it*, meaning her work. Not appreciate *that*, meaning her report. Appreciate *you*. And he'd signed it just like he'd signed their love notes, passed back and forth in AP Chemistry behind the back of a particularly clueless teacher. The fact that she hadn't trashed the note, tucking it instead into her back pocket, meant it was definitely time to find that stay-

out-of-trouble temporary boyfriend. And she knew just who to
ask for help.

> **Martina:** Hey. What are you up to tonight?
> **Winnie:** Just finishing up at the hospital. You want
> to come over?
> **Martina:** No, let's go out. Let's go to Annie's. Bring
> Greg and Daniel.
> **Winnie:** Greg who?
> **Martina:** Greg Trout, the resident.
> **Winnie:** Oh, that Greg. Sure, I can ask him. Is this a
> double date, then?
> **Martina:** I'll explain later.
> **Winnie:** Okay . . . no backing out this time.
> **Martina:** I won't. I swear on my stack of Cosmos.
> **Winnie:** LOL, that is pretty serious. Okay.
> **Winnie:** Annie's, half an hour?
> **Martina:** Fabulous. Can't wait.

Wait, if this was a date, she needed to go home and clean
up. She was about to start her car when Carter pulled up in his
black Tesla. Even in her Corolla, they were more or less at eye
level. He stopped next to her and rolled down his window, so
she cranked hers down as well.

"Hey."

"Hey."

"How'd today go?"

"It went fine. I left you a report on the kitchen island."

"I saw that yesterday; thank you." It wasn't for him, really.
She felt it was good to have records of the things that happened

with her patient, and she didn't want to have to talk to him. That limited her options. She particularly didn't want him to have her phone number . . . he could probably get it through the agency, but it felt like protection, the way it was now. That extra layer of effort was valuable. She couldn't do any late-night texting if she didn't have his number, either.

"I have to go, I have a date." She hadn't thought his face could fall any harder; she was wrong. He looked crushed. *Why did I say that?* It made her angry that she could still hurt him . . . she wanted him to be indifferent. Needed it. If she wasn't going to be able to get over him, he could at least do her the courtesy of acting like he didn't care. *I will get over him. I will.* It hadn't helped that she'd never seen him with anyone else in the nine years they'd been apart; they'd both left for college immediately after their break-up, and then he'd been mostly absent from the Timber Falls social scene. He'd moved to Salem a few years ago; he probably hit trendy bars there or in Portland instead of Annie's.

His expression had mostly returned to normal, but there was still a tightness to his jaw that she didn't care for. "Okay, sorry to keep you. See you tomorrow. Thanks."

She didn't leave. She could drive away now, go get ready for her date, the one she'd just callously announced to her high school boyfriend that she was going on. Her mind released a string of curses that she'd have to confess at church the next time she went. *Drive away. Just start your car. Go.*

His kicked-puppy gaze had attached itself to her heart. He was going home to an already-cooked dinner, his laundry was done, his bookshelves dusted . . . but no one was going to shoot the breeze with him over spaghetti and meatballs. He would eat alone, rinse his plate, put it in the dishwasher and go to bed.

"How was your day?"

"Oh, you know." He put his elbow on the open window of the very expensive car and rested his chin in his hand.

"No, I don't know. I don't really know what you do, except that it makes ginormous amounts of money."

Carter chuckled. An actual laugh, not a humorless scoff or a broken snicker. It was soft, but it was there, and her heart went gooey. *Laugh again. You should laugh every day, even now, even when your mother is sick. Someone should be around to make you laugh.*

"Well, since you asked, I'm an actuary at Greenfield Insurance in Salem."

"I thought you worked for your dad?"

"I tried. I . . . it didn't work out."

"Oh, I'm sorry." She tucked her hair behind her ears. "What does an actuary do? It sounds like somewhere birds live."

He laughed again. "That's an aviary, Tin—Ms. Lopez. The Society of Actuaries, to which I belong, defines an actuary as 'part super-hero, part fortune-teller, part trusted advisor.' So I'm basically magic."

"That must be why they pay you so well," she said, stroking her chin as if she had a beard. "I knew I picked the wrong profession."

"I don't think so. Mom seems happier than she has in a long time. Seriously."

"She just likes the way I do her hair . . ."

"I offered to buzz it for her, but she declined," he said, straight-faced.

Martina gasped. "You wouldn't dare! Her hair is so gorgeous. She'd look like Demi Moore in that war movie."

Carter cracked a smile, then sobered. "Have a nice time on your date, Ms. Lopez."

"You have a nice evening, too."

Fat chance, she thought, cranking the window back up, flicking her headlights on, driving back down the long sandy lane to the highway. She'd told Winnie half an hour; she only had fifteen minutes to get there now. Going home was out of the question; she'd just touch up her makeup in the car. Not ideal, but she'd noticed Greg watching her a few times at the hospital. Okay, he was looking at her backside, and he wasn't subtle about it. She had one of those rear ends that just . . . popped. It wasn't her fault she was curvy . . . and it wasn't her fault that her scrubs didn't really hide anything. And to his credit, he always blushed when she caught him staring.

He was laughing when she walked in. Winnie was telling a story that apparently had both men in stitches; it surprised her. Winnie wasn't usually such an entertainer, and Greg wasn't usually so easily amused. He seemed to keep to himself, mostly. He had no intention of staying in Timber Falls, that much she knew. He was from a small town in Washington, up near the Canadian border, she thought. Bluecreek? Chewelah? Something like that. It was nowhere she was interested in living, that was for sure. There was no Walmart up there. She needed Walmart.

"Hey, Martina," Greg greeted her, standing as she approached the table, one hand on his flat belly. *Well.* That was gentlemanly. She was a fan of that. He pulled out a chair for her, and she lowered herself gratefully into the worn wooden chair. "How was work?"

"It was good," she sighed. "Willow was in a good mood today. But I was ready to get out for a bit, thanks for meeting me."

"Sure," said Winnie, "we were just saying that it's good to hang out outside of work." Winnie's phone rang. "Excuse me."

"Uh oh," sighed Daniel. "I know that tone." He turned to Martina. "Don't suppose you could give me a ride home?"

"No problem at all," Martina assured him. She hadn't really come out to drink, just to socialize. It was nice to be with people. Young people. And it was nice to be putting her plan into action to use Greg. She winced internally as he smiled at her. Using him was the wrong word . . . well, maybe it wasn't. Maybe she shouldn't really be doing this. Still, he'd likely get some fun dates out of it, and she'd work her job for Carter until Willow died, and then Greg would move on. Problem solved. She didn't need a fairy tale prince, just someone to be faithful to until she got over Carter. So he was useful, but maybe she wasn't using him, exactly . . .

"How was your day?" she asked him, and he let out a long sigh.

"Dr. Baker gave us another one of her infamous pop quizzes. None of us did too well."

"Oh, I'm sorry," she cooed, as she slid her hand over his and gave it a squeeze. "Would you like a study buddy? I could probably find some time for you over the weekend." There. It wasn't subtle, but neither was Martina. She knew what she wanted, and she didn't mind asking. Greg's eyes widened a little, then he smiled, a slow smile that implied he knew what she had in mind.

"Yeah, I think . . . I think that'd be good. Thanks."

"Great, let me give you my number." She held out her hand for his phone, but she could see Daniel smirking at them out of the corner of her eye. She liked Daniel; he was good for Winnie, who was much too uptight despite being a very capable provider and a good friend. But he'd better not mess with her plan, or she'd have to put him in his place. Greg brushed her fingers with his as he passed it over to her, and it gave her a pleasant tingle on her skin.

"How about you, Daniel? How was your day?"

"Good, no, it was good. Well, okay." He put his forehead down on the table. "I'm okay," he said into the scratched wood. "Just fine, everything's fine." The other two chuckled.

"I felt the same way when I was working on my Master's," said Martina, feeling sympathy for him. "It'll get better. Once you're just working and not trying to study all the time and plan a wedding, too."

"I hope you're right," Daniel said, sitting up, but Winnie was approaching the table with a grimace.

"So Evelyn's headed to the hospital . . . I couldn't talk her out of it, I'm so sorry."

"It's okay," Daniel said, sitting up, giving her a winning smile. "Go! Care! Reassure! And don't forget your cape." Winnie smiled back as she tipped down to give him a kiss.

She glanced at Martina. "You can give him a ride home?"

"For sure. I'm sticking to water tonight." They waved to her as she hurried off.

"How's your new job, Martina?"

"It's pretty good," she said, choosing her words carefully. "I still can't figure out how he even knew to ask for me. I mean, I just started working there. I don't think I was even on the website yet."

Daniel raised his hand guiltily. "I have a theory about that . . ."

"I'm listening."

He leaned forward, lowering his voice. "Kyle treated Willow when she came into the ER with that broken wrist. He was the one who referred them to Dr. Rose. I know he's stayed in contact with Crash; he felt bad that he was dealing with all this on his own. He's always thought highly of your medical skills; he probably told him you'd be available for hire soon."

Well, that explains it. Martina let her gaze fall to the table, fingering the scratches thoughtfully.

"I'm sorry," Daniel said. "He's not always so socially aware, so he probably didn't realize that he was doing anything that might be uncomfortable for you."

"No, no. It's fine. How could he have known? I appreciate him trying to help both of us. It's a great job, for the most part." She glanced at Greg, who was listening with interest. She didn't want him to know she was still hung up on Carter, so she smiled and changed the subject. "So Greg, do you like football?"

"Yeah, I guess."

"Wrong answer," Daniel laughed into his glass as he took a sip.

"Wrong answer?" Greg asked, perplexed. "Most women don't care too much for football. They want to do stuff on Sunday."

Martina sipped her sparkling water. "As far as I'm concerned, Sundays are for leftovers, a hot bath, football, and sex. Not necessarily in that order."

"A woman who knows what she wants. I'd be happy with that. I hate shopping."

"Oh no, you misunderstand: I still go shopping. I just do it online at half time, unless I'm otherwise occupied at half time." She winked at him, and both men laughed.

"How long is half time, anyway?" Greg asked, popping some peanuts into his mouth.

"Twelve minutes. Don't ask how I know that."

They laughed again, and Martina slid her foot against Greg's under the table. His gaze darkened a little, and she just smiled at him.

"How's your new house?" she asked Daniel.

"Great," he sighed. "I just wish I had more time to do all the little projects that need to be done."

"Like what?" asked Greg. The two men dragged the conversation off toward home repair. It was a direction Martina couldn't follow, which was fine with her, since the Chiefs were playing the Broncos. She watched the game over Greg's head, nodding occasionally when it seemed like they wanted her agreement. After an hour, the game was over, her drink was gone, and Martina was tired. Daniel read her fidgeting and finished his beer in a giant gulp.

"Ready, pretty lady?"

"Ready," she confirmed, then turned to Greg. "I'm so glad you could come out with us. I'll see you this weekend, right?"

"Yes, me, too." His gaze was warm and affable, not aggressive or lecherous in any way, and her conscience started poking her with a pointed stick. Saying it wasn't polite to use such a nice man. Saying she should just deal with her own emotional baggage without stringing Greg along. She slapped the thoughts away and smiled at him, pressing a friendly kiss to his cheek as she left. Daniel nudged her with his shoulder as they walked to her little car.

"So, you and Greg, huh?"

"Yup," she said, popping the p. "Me and Greg. Greg and me."

"I'm surprised. He doesn't quite seem like your type."

She turned to meet Daniel's gaze. "And what is my type?"

"Fast, brash, confident. Alpha in the streets AND the sheets." *In other words, High School Crash.*

She waved a careless hand. "That's old news. Those guys never stick around. I'm ready to try the nice-guy thing. It worked for my friend Winnie."

He ignored her attempt to distract him with compliments. "But you know Greg's not sticking around. So why start something? Itching to leave Timber Falls?"

Horror gripped her at the very suggestion. "No! Of course not. Daniel Durand, how dare you."

He held up his hands. "I'm just asking. Sure sounds like you're trying to hitch your wagon to a horse who's leaving town. You were laying it on pretty thick back there. Don't usually see you go after someone like that."

Martina pursed her lips, her tires crunching over the gravel. She wasn't sure if she should trust Daniel with this. Then again, Winnie already knew, so he would likely find out eventually. "I just need a stand-in."

Daniel was quiet for a moment. "Like, for a movie?"

She laughed. "No. I need a reason to stay away from Carter. And I won't cheat."

Daniel stroked his beard thoughtfully. "So Greg is what? Insurance?"

"That's a fair assessment."

"Just don't play with his heart, okay? Keep it light. Greg's a really nice guy. I don't want to see him get hurt."

"I promise I will show him a good time, no strings or hearts attached." She smiled, but privately, his comment troubled her. She was afraid of the same thing. *But better that than me losing my job or worse, throwing it all away for someone who doesn't really care about me.* "So," she queried, "when are you two going to make a baby?"

"Seriously? We haven't even gotten married yet, Martina."

"I know. And it'll all be perfect and beautiful, but now it's time to talk about snuggly little bundles of joy. I request three."

"Three?" Daniel laughed. "And are you going to come over and feed and change these little bundles of joy?"

"Gladly. I love babies. They remind me that life goes on, that nothing can stop the world from turning." *Not even death, not even heartbreak.* It was a fact she wanted to be reminded of frequently in her line of work. She loved working with geriatric patients, but it wasn't easy emotionally. Holding babies was her self-care.

"Hmm." Daniel seemed unconvinced. "I think babies are a bit down the road for us. I'd just be happy if the lawn was mowed and the washing machine worked right."

"You know, you could *pay* someone to do these things for you."

He sighed. "It may come to that."

She pulled onto his road. "Thanks for coming out tonight. It was nice."

"It *was* nice." He held up his fist for a bump, and she touched their knuckles together, then they both made soft explosion sounds.

"Oh! Before I forget, can I get your mom's number? I need to make an appointment for Willow."

"You can just call the salon."

"I'd rather have a moment to explain what Willow's going through. It'll help the appointment go smoother."

Daniel nodded slowly. "Right." He pulled out his phone. "You ready?" Rather than reading it, he turned the screen so she could see it, and she copied the numbers into her own phone. *Dyslexia strikes again.* At least he had good coping skills.

"Thanks. Have a good night."

"See you."

"Bye." Martina waited until he'd gotten inside the Craftsman home. She let a little twinge of jealousy sit in her stomach instead of pushing it aside. She'd love to be married, starting a family. Owning a house. Her career was great, but she felt like she was starting over every time she leveled up. Expectations; she'd expected to feel more settled by this time in her life. And she'd expected to feel more fulfilled by her job than she did. On a deep level, a soul level, it wasn't enough.

CHAPTER EIGHT

ON FRIDAY, MARTINA parked her little Corolla on Hoover Avenue in downtown Timber Falls at a spot with an open meter, then came around to open the door for Willow. A giant pair of scissors was painted on the sign for Shear Brilliance, the salon Farrah Durand had started a few decades ago. As she'd promised, Farrah was waiting for them at the front rather than the normal receptionist.

"Willow," she greeted her warmly, "how are you, lady?"

Her patient beamed at the greeting, but said nothing. Martina was glad she'd warned Farrah, because she didn't miss a beat.

"Farrah, I'm Martina. It's nice to see you again." They had met before, of course, but it didn't hurt for Willow to hear her stylist's name, and the last time she'd been in was for prom, and she didn't expect Farrah to remember that.

"Nice to see you, too, Martina. Come on back, and we'll get you girls right." She gestured to an older lady with wetted brown hair, gray at the temples, getting a haircut. "You remember Hattie?"

"Of course I do," Willow smiled, stooping to give the woman an air kiss on the cheek. "How are you, Hattie?"

"Oh, just fine, just fine. And you?"

"I'm doing well, thank you."

"Your husband's keeping things running smoothly as usual at TFPP. I barely even have to attend the board meetings."

"Yes, he's always been a whiz at business," she replied graciously, and Martina worked hard not to roll her eyes. She thought it maybe didn't work, because Hattie turned her attention to her next.

"And how are you, Ms. Lopez? Martina, isn't it?"

Martina opened her mouth, but no sound came out. "Yes. I'm fine, thank you," she finally whispered. She wasn't normally intimidated by anyone, but she had no idea Mrs. Meyer-Bagsby, the unofficial mayor of Timber Falls, even knew who she was. This woman was kind of her hero: she'd survived the unexpected death of her husband and gone on to take the reins of Timber Falls Paper Products herself, learn all its ins and outs, and yet she'd never become corporate or cold. She was a maven. Her silence didn't seem to faze Hattie.

"Your father's Christmas trees look lovely this year; I drove by the farm the other day on my way to Mr. Powell's.

"Thank you, I'll tell him. He'll be pleased to hear it." In fact, he'd be so tickled, he'd probably use it in the promotional literature. Hattie approval was big in Timber Falls.

"So what are we doing today?" Farrah asked, securing a cape around Willow's shoulders. "Same as usual?"

"That sounds good," Willow nodded. Both women were glancing at Martina for confirmation, and she smiled at them.

"Go for it."

"Including color?"

"Of course," Willow sniffed. "I can't have my roots showing, even if my mind is going." It was the first joke Martina had heard Willow make about her diagnosis, and she took it as a positive sign. As she'd requested, Farrah turned Willow's chair so that she wasn't pointed at the mirror, so that Martina could sit in Willow's line of sight in a hard plastic chair. She picked up a magazine and pretended to read as the women around her chatted and gossiped.

When Farrah and Willow came back from getting Willow's hair washed, she looked so relaxed, Martina was tempted to ask Carter to invest in one of those sinks for the estate. It was a cool, cloudy day outside, but the salon was warm and bright.

"How are your boys?" Farrah asked lightly, combing out Willow's long tresses.

"Oh," sighed Willow, "about the same. Carter's around, but I never see the other two. They're all so busy with their own lives. How are yours? Plus Maggie?"

"Oh, the boys are okay, but Maggie . . ." Farrah gave a deep sigh. "Don't get me started on Maggie."

"What's she up to now?" Willow asked, dutifully tipping her head down, and Martina noticed several women seemed to be listening in as well.

"Oh, nothing in particular, she's just so secretive about everything. She entered a contest for her art, and then she didn't even tell us when she won! The only reason Evan even found out is that she was trying to get her brothers to cash her winnings for her, since she didn't have a checking account, and Kyle ratted her out."

"Let me guess: she didn't tell him it was a secret," Willow smiled knowingly. Martina felt the richness of the many years of conversations they'd had together, and she reminded herself to try to find out who else Willow had been close to. There was no reason they should be lost.

"You got it in one," Farrah laughed. "I just wish she felt like she could confide in me like the boys do. She talks to Evan, she talks to Daniel and Philip and Kyle, even to Winnie, but not to me. She's even started a sibling night, but Evan and I aren't invited."

"I think that's quite normal, though," Willow said. "I used to feel a bit hurt when the boys did things without us, but whenever I felt left out, I just told myself that it was a blessing to have children who got along so well. They'll still be friends long after I'm gone." That hit Martina right in the chest for two reasons: first, she knew that would likely be earlier than Willow had originally planned, and that sucked; second, she used to have that kind of relationship with her older sisters. But when they married, something had fundamentally shifted for them. It wasn't just that they had kids now and she didn't; they still hung out, but it was harder to confide in them now. She felt self-conscious talking about her single girl problems when those were so firmly in the past for them.

"You're probably right. Still hurts, though," Farrah admitted.

"For what it's worth," Hattie offered, "my kids did the same thing. I expected them to form secret clubs when they were kids, not when they were grown-up."

"Exactly," Farrah said, pointing with the scissors. "And she still has no idea what she's going to do after graduation." Martina couldn't relate to that at all; she'd always wanted to be a nurse. "I can't even get her to look at the promotional literature for any of the nearby schools. When I try to talk to her about it, she just goes into her room and shuts the door."

"Does she have a computer in there?"

"No, but she has her art supplies, and that's better than the internet, as far as she's concerned." She sighed. "And she has zero interest in her looks. I thought we could at least bond over that, now that she's older. But all she wants to do is read Terry Pratchett, paint, and be alone. She's never even gone on a date."

"Carter used to, but now he just stays home all the time. I don't know if he's depressed or what." Willow didn't seem to realize the irony behind her words, that her mental decline might be responsible for both his depression and his staying home, but thankfully, no one pointed it out to her.

"Are you organizing the bachelor auction this year, Willow?" Hattie asked as her stylist ruffled her hair and tried to even out the layers. Martina frowned slightly; did Hattie not know about Willow's diagnosis? Had Harrison not told anyone at work? Some things were private, yes, but surely he'd at least told the board. How else was he explaining his absences for her appointments?

"No, I wasn't available this year," she said, somewhat vacantly, and Martina wondered if she even knew it was a lie.

"I heard Tina Gross was organizing it," Farrah said, and Willow huffed.

"She couldn't organize her way out of an Hermes bag," she quipped, and several of the other women laughed.

"You put on such a wonderful event last year," Hattie said. "Highest donations in five years. Of course, having your youngest in the line-up didn't hurt . . ."

Martina put her gaze back on the magazine. She didn't want to think about women clamoring for a shot with Carter.

"He's a keeper, that's for sure," Willow said softly, and something in her tone made Martina look up. The older woman was staring at her, her gaze almost wistful, intimate, like they were sharing a secret. Martina painted a smile onto her face, then ducked her head again.

Color took an hour, and then Farrah insisted on drying Willow's hair, so it was lunchtime by the time they were done. Farrah seemed unconcerned by the time, and as Willow got hugs goodbye, Martina breathed a sigh of relief that it had all gone so well. She opened the car door for Willow and made sure she got her seatbelt buckled. When she straightened to go to the driver's side, she jumped. Hattie was standing next to her, looking concerned.

"Do you have a moment, Martina?"

"Of course," she said, tossing her hair. She smiled. "What's up?"

"I assume you're working for the Carpenters; is that correct?"

"For Carter, yes."

Hattie nodded slowly. "Do you mind if I ask why Willow needs your services?"

"I'd prefer you talk to Harrison or Carter about it," she said. "Privacy and all that."

She nodded again. "Understandable. Just please know that she is always welcome at town functions. We will accommodate her however she needs us to. Every one of those women today has missed her and was genuinely glad to see her. I hope you'll bring her around more often, even if her hair doesn't really need a trim."

Oh dear. That had Martina tearing up a little, and she blinked the tears away. "Thank you, Mrs. Myers-Bigsby."

"Please, call me Hattie." She smiled. "I'll see you around town."

"Okay."

CHAPTER NINE

MARTINA GOT UP EARLY to get ready for her hangout with Greg on Saturday: she blow-dried her hair and straightened it instead of just slapping it up into a wet ponytail. She didn't want the ends to wave. She kept her makeup light but intentional, and she put on her black fleece-lined leggings (the best invention ever) with a checkered black-and-white collared shirt (for a bit of flair) and a tan cable-knit sweater (because it was warm) over the top. Her nude heeled boots completed the ensemble. She knew she'd probably have to take them off the moment she got inside, but she never got to wear them to work, and she didn't want them to feel neglected. Plus, it made for a heck of an impression at the front door. She wasn't a short girl, and the added height put her close to eye-level with Greg. There was something sexy about eye contact.

When she looked up the address online, she blinked. She knew that place; that was Mildred and Dennis Wilson's house. Millie was in the quilt guild with her mother, and she often quilted large projects on the long-arm machine she owned as a side business. She wasn't sure what Mr. Wilson used to do; he was retired now. A teacher, maybe? She couldn't remember. He was outside watering his roses when she pulled into the driveway a little while later, and he waved at her. She waved back and gave him a big smile. Not that she ever tried to be rude, but it didn't hurt to be extra friendly with old people; they were her future clients, after all.

"Hola, Martina!" he called as she stepped out. Oh yes, she remembered now: he was the old Spanish teacher at the high school, before she'd been there.

"Good morning," she called back in Spanish. "I'm just here to see Greg." Her heels wobbled on the gravel, and she paused to make sure she didn't turn an ankle.

He gestured with his free hand to the garage. "Yes, their apartment is just up there." She paused, confused. Was he conjugating wrong, or was there more than one person living here?

"Their?"

"Oh yes, it's just the two of them. Greg and Tharushi." *Oh?* How had she not known that Dr. Udawatte lived here, too? It made sense; they were in the same residency group with Daniel, and there wasn't a lot of high-density housing around Timber Falls. She was lucky to have her own apartment; she'd inherited the lease from her sister Augustina when she married Stephen.

"Oh, sure. Thanks. Have a nice weekend."

"Careful on the steps in those fancy shoes!" he called, and she smiled. *You're just jealous. I bet Millie never wore heels this awesome in her life.* Martina mounted the wooden stairway to the upper-level apartment over the garage and despite her annoyance, she did use the handrail. She was stylish, not stupid. She checked her hair and makeup with her phone camera, snapped a selfie for good measure, then knocked quietly at the door. Greg opened it almost immediately; in his black polo shirt and khaki pants, they looked like they'd planned it. Too bad they weren't going out; she wouldn't mind being seen as part of a couple who has it together.

"Hey, Martina. You look great!"

"Oh, thanks," she said, stepping inside and unzipping her boots. "So do you. We look like we planned it."

"Yeah. Weird coincidence, eh?" Was he Canadian? She didn't think so. Maybe his parents were. She took a moment to look around the place; it was sparsely furnished, but it looked comfortably lived-in. The kitchen was clean. That mattered. Time would tell on the bathroom, but men's apartments weren't known for cleanliness in that arena. At least he didn't have a male roommate; that lowered the odds considerably. "Thanks for coming over. I was flattered that you offered."

"You're such a sweetheart," she said, taking a spot on the couch. "I'm happy to help."

"Can I get you anything? We might have some orange juice or something." He mumbled the last bit as he stuck his head in the fridge. Most commercially-produced juices had little nutritional value; she'd already purged the Carpenters' fridge, much to Carter's dismay. She grinned a little as she remembered his annoyed face when he discovered her "improvements." Pastor Kellan had been glad to get all that junk for the food pantry at the church. Then she noticed Greg was watching, his head cocked. Oh right, a drink.

"I'll take some water. Thanks." She picked up the textbook next to her on the couch. "Addiction, huh?"

"Yeah," he said, handing her a glass of water. "Dr. Baker wants us boning up on it. Been seeing more opioid cases lately."

"Ooh. That's not good." She opened the book. "Do you want me to quiz you or just read to you?" She'd done that with

Daniel, too, in her down time at the hospital, once he'd told her about his dyslexia.

"Quiz me."

"You got it."

The front door opened and Tharushi came in wearing black nylon tights and a black jacket and running shoes, looking at her phone, her dark hair in a high ponytail, her chest damp and heaving. She froze for a moment, then removed her wireless Bluetooth headphones slowly. "Hi."

"Hey." Martina waved. "How are you?"

"I'm fine." Her voice was flat. "How are you?"

"Oh, I'm great, thanks. Just helping your roomie study."

"Uh-huh. Well, I won't keep you, then."

"Why don't you join us?" Greg offered. "You know, after your shower?"

She looked at both of them, her gaze narrowed, assessing something Martina couldn't begin to imagine. "No, I don't want to intrude. Thank you, though." She strolled through the living room and through the kitchen to the bedroom on the far side of the apartment and shut the door.

Martina looked at Greg; he was blushing so hard, his ears were like strawberries. "I-I'm sorry," he stammered, staring after his roommate. "She's not usually so rude. She's a very warm person once you get to know her." Martina's BS detector was going off loudly, not because of Tharushi's slightly odd interactions with them, but because of Greg's response to them. But she didn't really know him well enough to press him, especially about another woman. Especially since she needed him to be interested in *her*. Martina put a hand over his, and his head snapped back to her.

"Don't worry about it," she purred. "I'm just happy to be here with you. Let's get back on track." He smiled gratefully, and she picked the book back up. They studied for another hour before they paused for lunch; Tharushi still hadn't re-appeared. Did she have her own bathroom? Was she just going to sit in there all sweaty because Martina was here? That didn't make much sense. Someone else might've felt guilty, but Martina had always been of the opinion that people were free to share their grievances like adults. If Tharushi didn't want her here, that wasn't her problem, especially if she left it unexpressed. It was Greg's home, too. Greg apologetically brought her a ham and cheese sandwich with a dill pickle on the side.

"Sorry, I don't have much in the way of lunch food. I usually just hit the cafeteria at work."

"Why wouldn't you?" Martina asked, nibbling on the pickle. "It's so convenient. Especially when you're single."

"Exactly," he said, and he seemed relieved that she understood. It was impressive that she noticed, because she was distracted by this pickle. She was something of a connoisseur of fermented foods, and this pickle was excellent; it was definitely not your run-of-the-mill grocery store pickle.

"Can I ask who made this pickle? It's very good." It was crunchy, bright, and not overly salty or soggy like so many. She favored carrots for that reason, but she'd consider trying cucumber pickles again if they could come out like this.

Greg grinned. "My mom, actually. She keeps sending me things she canned from her garden. I appreciate the pickles, but I could do without the stewed tomatoes and the roasted beets."

"Oooh, you have beets, too? I'll take them off your hands, if you want. I'll bring back the jars." Lies. If they were nice jars, she was totally keeping them. Good jars were hard to find, and there were so many ferments she still wanted to try. She already had kefir and a sourdough starter that kept going moldy in the damp environment of her kitchen, but she wanted to try a pear and ginger sauce that sounded like it would be amazing over coconut milk ice cream. And as soon as summer hit, she was going to convince someone to give her fresh tomatoes for a fermented garden salsa.

She must've sounded too eager, because Greg made a face. "Really? You're welcome to them. She thinks I'm not eating enough vegetables."

"I think most mothers have that opinion." Except hers. That'd never been a problem for her; her mom was a great cook, and she loved vegetables of almost every variety. Her pocket dinged. "Speaking of mothers . . ." She glanced at the TV, cued up with the show she'd picked for them to watch. "Go ahead, I can listen and text at the same time." Greg pressed play and took a huge bite of his sandwich.

> **Mom:** Your dad is missing you lately. Would you come home for dinner sometime this week?

> **Martina:** Sure. What night?

> **Mom:** Well, we have the town meeting on Friday, bunco on Wednesday, and your dad has his Elks meeting on Thursday.

Martina rolled her eyes. Her mom had a habit of offering information without actually making a decision.

Martina: So . . . what day?
Mom: Whatever day works for you. We can make anything work.
Martina: Monday?
Mom: Great, Monday it is!

When she re-pocketed her phone, she subtly scooched herself closer to Greg, close enough for their arms to touch. He did not seem to notice, his eyes trained on the screen. Martina ate her sandwich and watched the show, her mind elsewhere. Did she need to be more direct with him? How could she arrange to see him again? She needed to lock this down ASAP. When she finished her sandwich, she put her plate on the coffee table and scootched closer still, letting her whole right side rest against his body. Still no response. She didn't know what hackles were, but hers were up. What was it going to take to get this guy interested? They sat snuggled until the show ended, and then she stood up. "Can I use your restroom before I leave?"

"Oh. Yes. It's through that door." He pointed to the right corner of the kitchen. She peered into the small room. No laundry. That sucked. All the plumbing seemed to be on this side of the building. It was an odd layout, as afterthought dwellings often were. She looked into the medicine cabinet without guilt; he seemed all squeaky clean, but you couldn't be too careful. Drug addicts were definitely not her thing, but they were usually better about hiding it. The medicine cabinet looked very normal except for . . . was that an epi pen? Interesting. She wondered whose it was and what their allergy might be, but there was nothing else that gave any clue. She closed the cabinet quietly and flushed the toilet without using it, then washed her hands for real. There was another door in the bathroom, so that confirmed it: Tharushi must have used the bathroom and gone back to her room without coming back to the living room.

Martina got her purse and Greg walked her to the door.

"Thanks for coming over," he said, his hands stuffed deep in his pockets.

"Thanks for having me," she said with a wink, and he chuckled, looking down at his feet. "Let's do it again this week."

"I'd like that," he said, giving her his green gaze again. "We'll go to Annie's this time."

"Sounds great," she said. And quickly pressing another chaste kiss to his cheek, she turned to precariously work her way back down the wooden steps outside. At least she'd gotten a real date set up. That was enough.

For now.

CHAPTER TEN

CARTER CAME HOME EARLY on Friday to do some studying for his fourth exam. He'd claimed his father's office months ago out of necessity, but now he found he quite liked being near the front door. No one could come in or out without his knowledge, which was handy when your mom sometimes thought she'd walk ten miles to the grocery store. No, no one escaped his notice. Not even the hot nurse practitioner currently attempting to tiptoe across the foyer. Her suede, chunky heeled boots weren't exactly conducive to quiet. His mouth went dry when he saw what she was wearing: it was a far cry from the baggy scrubs she usually wore. Her thin maroon cowl-neck sweater dress hid nothing of her curves, and the fringe at the bottom played peekaboo with her long legs.

"Where are you off to, Ms. Lopez?" Carter winced internally. He wasn't her dad, for heaven's sake. He hated calling her that. He had to keep from spitting it out of his mouth every time. He'd actually spent time practicing while he was brushing his teeth last night, trying to remind himself. Since their windows-down conversation outside the other night, it had gotten even harder. Every time he looked into her eyes, he was right back in his teenage bed, snuggled with her against his chest, kissing her, touching her . . . Carter averted his eyes before she

could see what was happening in his head. She was too shrewd
sometimes.

"Just meeting a friend for drinks," she said, but the rapid
flutter of her eyelashes showed the statement for the lie it was.
She's seeing someone. The jealousy that reared up inside him was
foreign to him, like being picked up from Oregon and dropped
on a desert island. His heart was beating out a war drum pattern, ready to annihilate whoever it was. *No,* he reminded himself. *She's single. I'm single. We're just two single . . . friends.*

"A friend, huh?"

"Friends," she amended quickly. "Just friends."

A wicked thought entered his head, and he grabbed onto it
with both hands. "Oh. Well, you look amazing. Have fun."

The side-eye glance she gave him told him she wasn't buying his "too cool" act. "Thanks. See you tomorrow."

"Mmm." He put his gaze back on his laptop, enjoying her
hesitation at the front door, her long stare. He waited until
she'd been gone ten minutes, then he put on his shoes and
grabbed his keys.

"Mrs. Sánchez," he called into the kitchen. "I'm going out.
I'll be back late; see you tomorrow." Carter took his black Lexus
SUV; he'd heard it might be icy this evening. Unusual, but not
unheard of this time of year. He hoped it wouldn't kill the daffodils in the front; his mom had planted those herself, years
ago. They were always the first sign of hope that winter was almost over. When he pulled in and saw those daffodils, he knew
it was going to be okay, even if he couldn't feel it yet.

He found the highway quiet and empty at this time of day.
The parking lot at Annie's was full, however, so he parked in the
back of the building. Inside, the room was warm and smelled

like pizza and beer. She did an Italian thing on Fridays . . . and there was Martina. She was sharing an appetizer with a man Carter didn't recognize . . . mozzarella sticks, from the look of it. She laughed as she stretched the warm cheese, sucking it off her fingers seductively. He'd pay anything for it to be his fingers. Then again, money wasn't going to fix this problem. He strode into the bar, feeling a little of his old bravado, ignoring her as he went by like he hadn't noticed her there. As if that was even possible when she lit up the room like that. Like his soul wasn't drawn to her like a moth to flame.

Annie smiled at him and slid him a Cascade Lakes Secret Weapon stout. "Saw you coming," she winked as she passed someone a napkin and nodded at another customer who wanted to order.

"Thanks, Annie." She really was the best. Some kind of mind reader. It wasn't like he always got the same thing . . . was it? Dang. He did always get the same thing. When did he get so *boring*? He needed to get some of his old spark back. He used to take off and drive to the coast just to watch the sun set over the ocean. Stow away in a freight car just to see where it was going. Jump off the top of waterfalls for the heck of it. Okay, maybe that last thing wasn't very safe. But he was sick to death of being safe. Playing it safe hadn't gotten him what he wanted at all. His mom was still dying. Martina was still here with someone else.

"Your favorite nurse is here again." The strange voice behind him was too far away to be speaking to him.

"Heard he hired her." The stranger had a companion, apparently.

"Who?"

"Carpenter."

The two men behind him weren't speaking as quietly as they probably thought they were. His ears perked up at his own name, even as his shoulders pinched with stress. He used to love being talked about: for his soccer championships, his hot girlfriend, his academic prowess. This gossip had a different bent to it. He didn't care for it.

"No. No f'ing way."

"It's true. Hired her to take care of his mom. She's got dementia or something."

Apparently, they didn't see him sitting a few feet away from them. He pretended he couldn't hear them. He wished he couldn't. His brain began replaying his mom's best hits: all the birthdays she'd made special, all the times she'd shown up to cheer him on, helped him study, quietly encouraged him to be his own person, been his ally. Who better than she understood how it felt to be on the other end of a Harrison Carpenter agenda? He'd owed it to her to get the best care available. And that was Martina.

"Figures. They want something, they just buy it."

"Must be nice."

"I know, right?"

Who were these muttonheads? He hazarded a glance over his shoulder. Ranger Zane and his brother Dirk sat at the small table, each with several empties in front of them. *Whatever.* He hadn't bought her; if they thought that was even possible, then they didn't know her at all. He peered past them to see her, just for a second. Now she was feeding him a bite of her pasta? Ugh. Why had he come here? *Uh-oh.* She'd noticed him. She was coming over, carrying their wine glasses. *Nice cover, Tini.* He grinned at her.

"Fancy seeing you—"

"Save it. What are you doing here?"

"Can't a guy just enjoy a drink at Annie's on a Friday?"

"Some guys can. You can't. Not if you're here to spy on me."

He sipped his beer, enjoying the notes of chocolate, considering. "Spy on you? But you said you were here to meet a friend. That's not something I'd care about, right?"

She gave her high-heeled boot a kick against the rough wood floor like she couldn't help let out her frustration somehow. "You know what I meant."

"Yes, I did," he smiled, turning on the stool so that his elbows rested on the bar. "So who's Friday-worthy?"

"Huh?"

"Fridays are a prime date night. Why does this guy rate?"

"His name is Dr. Trout, and he's a very nice man."

Carter nodded in agreement. "He *looks* like a nice man. Look at the crease in those chinos. He even put product in his hair. Looks like a keeper."

Martina folded her arms. "What's gotten into you tonight?"

"Me? Nothing. Nothing but this delicious stout and the feeling of being out on a Friday night for once, I guess."

Out of the corner of his eye, he could see a blonde woman approaching him, but he kept his attention on Martina until he felt a hand on his arm.

"Hey, Crash," Jennie Wallace cooed. "Don't see you around here much."

"That's because I don't come here much anymore," he said, leaning toward her a little bit, grinning. He enjoyed the way Martina's eyes widened a little and she rolled her lips between her teeth like she was afraid of what she'd say if she opened them. "How've you been, Jennie?"

"I'm better for seeing you," she said, leaning on the bar, sliding onto the stool next to him. Then she paused. "Oh. Hey, Martina. Didn't see you there."

"Well, here I am." Her tone was slightly salty, and Carter hid his smile. "I'd better be getting back to my date. Excuse me." Martina walked away without the wine glasses that Annie set down on the bar, her thick hair flying as she whipped around quickly. He turned back to Jennie, who seemed oblivious to the subtext of what had just happened.

"When do you think she'll remember her drinks?" Annie asked, leaning forward on the bar in a rare moment of non-movement.

"I'm not sure she's going to," Carter answered, sipping his beer. "This really is so good, Annie. Thank you for introducing me to it."

"My pleasure," she said, stepping away to help James carry a large box of beer bottles and using her phone to restart the music playing through the restaurant's speakers.

"Jennie, would you excuse me for one second?"

"Sure," she smiled. "I'll be right here."

Carter picked up the two wine glasses and took them over to Martina's table. She looked none too happy to see him; in fact, he wanted to touch his face to see if her glare was leaving burn marks on his face, but his hands were already full, unfortunately. "Here you go, two glasses of seedless red for Table Seven."

"That's a *M*A*S*H* quote!" the man exclaimed, and he seemed delighted by the fact.

"Yes, it is," Carter smiled.

"You've got good taste, man. I love that show."

"Me, too. I'm Carter Carpenter," he said, extending his right hand.

"Greg Trout." The man had a firm handshake. Carter could respect that. At least he wasn't one of those wimpy, limp fish handshake people. He hadn't learned many useful things from his father, but that was one of the things he'd insisted on. Eye contact and a firm handshake.

"Sorry to interrupt your date, but Ms. Lopez ran off before she could claim your drinks."

"Hey, thanks. You want to sit down?"

"No," Martina said sharply, but she softened a little under the surprised gaze of both men. "No, I just mean . . . this is a date. And Mr. Carpenter is my boss. I see him all the time." She reached out and took Greg's hand across the table. "Tonight's just for us. I can see him any time." Carter stood there, staring at their joined hands, wondering what he could do to make him stop touching her. Probably nothing. That knowledge wasn't doing much for the feeling of too much acid in his esophagus. He didn't want her to be unhappy and alone . . . but that's what it amounted to, didn't it? He couldn't be self-ish like that again, asking her to be alone just because he was. It wasn't fair. Carter forced a smile.

"Enjoy your evening, you two." He shuffled back to his stool, quite forgetting that Jennie had wanted to talk to him, until she cuddled up against his side. "Sorry about that. How've you been?"

"Oh, not bad. My cousin had a baby in my bathtub a few weeks ago. That was pretty great."

Carter tried not to show his disgust. That didn't sound great, that sounded like a household cleaning nightmare. He wasn't a neat freak by any stretch, but bodily fluids in his bathtub? Hard pass.

"How interesting. You still working at the Falls?"

She nodded, sipping some kind of pink drink that smelled sweet. "Yup, sure am. We just had another tour group come through today. Thirty people."

"I haven't been up there for a long time." He wasn't much of a hiker. If he was going to be outside, he preferred to be engaging in some kind of competitive sport. His rec soccer league hadn't started up yet, but it would soon, as soon as the weather improved for more than five seconds. Maybe he'd play indoor this year.

"Oh, you should come! The new visitor center is so nice! And we've got local artifacts and taxidermy from all over the county. It's really neat. The kids especially like the owl pellets."

Carter leaned down to scratch his ankle, and out of the corner of his eye, he saw Martina sit up straighter. What was she . . . *Oh. She thought I was going to kiss Jennie.*

Jennie Wallace. She'd always been a flirt. It wasn't inconceivable.

"Owl pellets, huh?" he asked, leaning closer to her, and Martina's face went from its normal tawny to more of a rosy glow. She definitely wasn't paying attention to Greg Trout, whose back was to him, and appeared to be telling some sort of very animated story that involved a lot of gesturing with his hands.

Jennie smiled at him. "Yeah, you can see all the little bones from the food they ate. It's pretty neat."

"Sounds like it." Carter gave her a super-fake grin. "Can I buy you another drink?"

"Oh, sure," she said, tucking her hair behind her ears. "But it's just a Shirley Temple. I have to work tomorrow. Saturday's our busiest day."

The work part of Carter's brain chimed in to wonder whether insurance companies should be charging more to tour groups that took people out on Saturdays . . . if the parks and attractions were more crowded, did it make them more ripe for an accident? Less supervision over more people might be a factor, too. Fewer staff to remind people to stay on the walkway, not climb the fencing, etc. He realized he was staring at Jennie, and she'd stopped talking, her eyebrows doing a cute little dance that told him that she was somewhat perplexed by his spacey behavior.

"Shirley Temple. Got it. I happen to be a fan myself," he teased, and he lifted a finger to signal Annie. She brought Jennie another one, and Annie looked between the two of them. Her meaning was clear: "What the frack are you doing?" Carter gave her a one-shouldered shrug, tilting his head subtly toward Martina, who was stiffly watching their interactions. Annie rolled her eyes and rather than leaving immediately, she decided to make conversation.

"How's your mom?"

Two-shoulder shrug this time. "A little better, actually. Ms. Lopez has been a great addition to her medical team."

"Martina's the best," Annie agreed.

"I love Martina. She's so fun when we go out," Jennie agreed. "Once, we went skinny dipping in Detroit Lake, right by the highway. Full moon and everything."

"Full . . . moon?" Annie asked, cocking her head, as she dried a load of glasses with her white towel. "You wanna rephrase that?"

Jennie looked at her blankly, then laughed. "Oh, how funny! That was a total coincidence."

Carter nudged her with his elbow good-naturedly, and he didn't even need to see Martina's response.

"Excuse me," Martina said sweetly. Before he knew what was happening, she was squeezing between the two of them, and Carter had to scoot back, lest she knock him right off his stool. "Annie, can we get a dessert menu? I think we want some of your Death by Chocolate cake, but I want to see what else is available."

Annie gave her a nod and scurried off to meet her request. Martina made no attempt to step back, her hands braced on the bar like it was going to fall down if she let go.

"Cake," he mused. "That's a good idea. You want to split a piece, Jennie?"

"Sure!" she bubbled. "I love cake!"

Martina's hands tightened on the polished wood, her knuckles going white.

"Everything okay, Ms. Lopez? You seem . . . tense."

"Just been a long week. I was looking forward to relaxing tonight."

"So why don't you?" he asked softly, waiting for the moment she'd turn to face him. "I bet Dr. Trout would rub your shoulders." As usual, her big brown eyes look his breath away. Forget the cake; that honeyed gaze was so sweet, even when she was mad at him. And make no mistake, she was mad at him. But it was something real. Something more than that 'Mr. Carpenter' BS and having a professional relationship and clinical indifference toward him. *Yes,* he thought, *give it to me. Let me have it. Yell at me. Shout. Make a scene. Just don't ignore me. And don't pretend you feel nothing for me. We both know that's not true.* He held her gaze until Annie came back, then Martina shook her head a little like she had a leaf in her hair she was trying to get rid of. Instead of giving him a morsel of truth, Martina turned without a word and went back to her table, leaving him hungry. Thank God Jennie remembered to order a large slice of carrot cake; he'd completely forgotten about it. Something about those big brown eyes had wiped his mind clean of any thought that wasn't about her.

He ate it quietly; he'd planned to tease Martina some more, feeding bites to Jennie. Instead, he just listened to Jennie talk more about the wildlife at the state park and how she was planning to hike Timberline this summer as soon as the snow melted enough. He nodded through stories about her sisters and her cousins. At ten o'clock, since he was starting to yawn, he put on his coat and walked her out to her car. They passed Martina and Greg, who were still sitting at their table. He tried not to notice their entangled fingers, and the way his thumb swept back and forth over the back of her hand.

"This was really fun," Jennie said, rolling the edge of her shirt in her fingers as they crossed the parking lot. "We should do it again sometime."

"Yeah, maybe," Carter said noncommittally. "See you around, Jennie."

"Crash, wait." She trapped him by his jacket sleeve, and he turned back to her patiently. "Do you want to . . . I don't know, come back to my place?"

"Oh. Wow." He hadn't been expecting that. He scrambled to answer in a way that wouldn't hurt her . . . it wasn't easy when her wide blue eyes were staring up at him, all trusting and vulnerable. He felt like he was talking to a human incarnation of Bambi. "I don't know if that's such a good idea," he said gently, pulling her hand away from his sleeve, then sheltering it in both of his. "But it's not you. Seriously. I'm just . . ."

"In love with someone else," Jennie finished with a sheepish smile. "I can tell. Sorry, I shouldn't have asked. I just hoped that if she was moving on, you might . . ." She shook her head.

He gave her a rueful smile. "I'm sorry if I gave you the wrong impression."

"No, you were a perfect gentleman. Just wishful thinking on my part." This smile was all sympathy. "I hope you guys can work it out. I really do."

Carter brought the back of her hand up to his lips for a grateful, innocent kiss. "You're a sweet person, Jen." His eyes snagged on movement across the parking lot; Greg and Martina had just exited the bar. Greg was trying to help Martina with her coat, holding it open for her, but she was standing stock-still, her fists balled at her side, watching him and Jennie. *Not over me, either, are you, beautiful?*

He shifted his focus back to Jennie. "Have a good night. Maybe we can hang out again sometime."

"That'd be fun," she agreed. "See you, Crash."

"It's Carter, actually."

She cocked her head. "Pardon?"

"My name. Crash is kind of an unfortunate nickname for an actuary, so I'm trying to shake it."

"Oh, yeah. I don't even remember how you got it . . ."

"I landed an airplane with the gear up in high school." *Because I was so busy showing off, I couldn't be bothered to do my landing checklist. How idiotic is that?* At least that had been pre-Martina. He couldn't live with himself if he'd hurt her.

"Right. Carter. Sorry. I forget stuff sometimes."

"Me too," he joked, then he opened her car door for her, shutting it behind her once she slid inside. Once she was gone, he looked around for Martina, but she was gone. He'd screwed this up. He never should've come here. Carter raked his fingers through his hair with both hands, yanking on the ends a little. And what in the world was he going to say to her on Monday? Carter shuffled back to his SUV, now dreading the forty-eight hours that stretched before him like a prison sentence.

CHAPTER
ELEVEN

ON SATURDAY, CARTER went into the office. Normally, he wouldn't on a weekend, but his mom wouldn't leave him alone to let him study, and he was already behind. He figured he could get in a few hours and be home for a late lunch to spend time with her this afternoon. Assuming, of course, she remembered she'd wanted to hang out with him . . . The fluorescent lights above him hummed approvingly, and the rain fell steadily outside, dripping down the windows. Carter sighed with contentment. It would knock the leaves down, but he'd missed the rain; it had been a dry fall so far, and it just felt wrong.

Around 10 a.m., he got a text message.

Chase: Hey.
Carter: Hey.
Chase: How's your day going?
Carter: Busy. How's yours?

He wasn't trying to blow his older brother off. But he wasn't trying not to blow him off.

Chase: It's going good.
Carter: Good.

And after that exhibition of their stellar conversational skills, Carter was out of things to say, and he went back to his practice test. But Chase wasn't done.

Chase: I wanted to see if you'd bring Mom to see me again.
Chase: If you have time.
Chase: I know it's a long drive.

Chase was acknowledging that his behavior affected other people? That was new . . . and not unappreciated.

Carter: I'll try. I might send her with her new caregiver. So she'd bring her on a weekday.

Chase: Oh, you hired somebody?

Chase: That's great, man. I'm really glad you did that.

Chase: Is she hot?

So not everything about Chase had changed. Carter went with the simplest explanation.

Carter: She's a qualified professional.
Carter: Found her through an agency here in TF. She was well-vetted.

That probably sounded defensive. He wasn't used to Chase taking any interest in his life or Willow's. He'd just been the little brother who lived in the twins' shadows, doubly large for there being two of them, both very successful and well-liked.

Chase: So that's a 'no' to her being hot. Check.
Chase: You seeing anybody?
Carter: No.

I shared a drink and a piece of cake with Jennie Wallace last night. Does that count? And if I tell you I only did it to make my ex jealous, does it still count?

Chase: Why not?

Carter had a much better rein on his temper than he used to, but when he just wanted to study and no one would leave him alone and when brothers who barely existed started asking personal questions, once in a while, he let an arrow fly in warning.

Carter: I don't know, Chase, maybe because I'm constantly worried that our mom is going to wander off or hurt herself or forget who I am while I'm gone? Could it be that?

Chase: Hey, I wasn't trying to be critical. I just don't know much about your life.

And whose fault is that?

Carter: I have to get back to work.

Chase: Wait, you're working on *Saturday*? Is nothing sacred?

Carter snorted. He just now realized it was Saturday? The days probably blended together a bit in rehab. He was lucky he'd gotten away with just rehab again. The first stint he'd done clearly didn't take . . . it was hard not to be frustrated with him. Having his help right now would be amazing, allow Carter to breathe a little easier instead of feeling like his mom's health and happiness was all on his shoulders. Instead, Chase was just adding to his problems.

Carter: You used to work Saturdays!
Chase: I know. But I shouldn't have. Boundaries, man.
Carter: It's just too noisy at the house.
Carter: It's not a big deal.
Chase: Yes, it is. You should prioritize your own mental health.

Carter bristled. That was easy for him to say. As far as he could tell, Chase sat around and did art, helped cook, and talked about his feelings all day at this rehab place. Considering they were getting his brother's free labor, Carter couldn't believe how much it cost.

Carter: How much longer are you going to be in Bend?
Chase: I'm not sure yet.

So his help would not be forthcoming. Check. Tired, Carter gathered up his stuff and left the building. He flicked his hood up as he walked through the parking lot to his Tesla. It was a fun car to drive, but he missed flying airplanes; up until his accident, it'd been one of his favorite activities, especially on a Saturday. He'd gotten his license at sixteen and been up there ever since. There was something almost meditative about it. It made him feel vulnerable and powerful and alive all at once. He peered up at the thick clouds through his windshield, the wipers whipping across his vision. Not today, but maybe another day. Maybe he'd get back behind the yoke and reclaim that piece of his soul. His love life, however . . . that was a crash he wasn't sure he'd ever recover from . . . but he was willing to try. He just didn't know if she was.

Carter drove to his condo and let himself in. The place felt empty now despite not having removed any furniture. He wasn't having it cleaned while he lived in Timber Falls, and it smelled like dust. This had been his sanctuary, once. Man, he missed being in his own space, uninterrupted, no one monitoring what he was doing or having to consider how it affected anyone else. He grabbed a book he'd been wanting for work, and while he was at it, he grabbed his private pilot book, just to brush up. A concert ticket fell out, and he picked it up. After he'd turned down his old friends so many times due to his mom's condition, they'd just stopped calling; he used to go out every weekend. Apparently, if you couldn't go out on the weekend, it wasn't worth texting you any other day of the week. He flicked on the light in the bedroom, then opened the top drawer of his dresser; there it was, her pink flip-flop. He touched the rhinestones she'd tenderly glued to the straps. He probably should've tried harder to get it back to her, but there was no point now. He tucked it safely back into the drawer, gathered up a few more clothes, then locked the place back up and started the drive back to Timber Falls.

CHAPTER TWELVE

"THAT'S JUST HOW I HURT my wrist." Willow's matter-of-fact tone and her unexpected volume were startling. Martina wobbled on the wooden chair for a moment, grabbing onto the grandfather clock for stability. It was Monday evening just after dinner, and she'd blown off her parents, explaining that she had to work. It was mostly true . . . but she also didn't want another lecture on why she shouldn't be working for Carter. She and Willow were in the upstairs hall, near the top of the stairs. She had no desire to roll down them for the sake of her prank. She'd decided over the weekend that Carter needed more fun in his life. She'd come to this conclusion in the bath, after replaying their confusing interactions at Annie's on repeat all day Saturday. This morning, she snuck into the back door before he left, calling up the stairs that she'd arrived, but made a point to stay out of his way until he left for work. He'd be home any minute now, so she needed to work quickly.

"It's okay, mine doesn't roll. That was your mistake, right?"

"Right. Mine rolled. That wasn't the best idea."

"No," agreed Martina, "but I bet you won't do it again. Live and learn, right? Besides, if you see another spider, I'll gladly kill it for you."

"Oh, you," she smiled. "You take such good care of me."

"I'm doing my best," Martina said, stretching to skootch the Troll a little farther back. "Tell me, can you see this pink-haired doll from where you're standing?"

Willow craned her neck a little. "Not really. But I don't have my contacts in."

"You wear glasses?"

"Yes. But I can't find them."

"Willow," she sighed. "That's not good, lady." She moved the doll forward an inch. "Can you see it now?"

"Yes! Well, a little bit. It's blurry, but that's not your fault."

Martina giggled. "Right." She jumped down off the chair and moved it back into Carter's room, lest he be tipped off immediately. "Let's go find your glasses." They had a good search in Willow's bedroom, Martina putting away earrings that she found in the toothbrush holder and facial cream that had ended up in the closet somehow. No glasses.

She put her hands on her hips. "Okay. Where else could they be? Where do you take them off?"

"I take them off when I play sometimes. I don't need them with my eyes closed."

"Play?"

Willow smiled and gestured for Martina to follow her down the hall. She trailed after her patient, past the guest rooms, back toward the top of the stairs. Willow entered the music room, and she let out of a sigh of relief. Like she was finally home.

"This is where I play." She sat down at a black baby grand piano in the center of the room; the bookshelves all around were filled with sheet music, CDs, and black cases of different shapes and sizes and there was a large bay window with a window seat. Willow started to play, a light piece, and Martina guessed it was probably a waltz or some kind of dance based on the timing. Martina felt her fingers tapping on their own against her leg, and she went and curled up in the window seat, just listening. It was too light inside and too dark outside to see out the window, but she could watch Willow's reflection in the glass. That's when she realized; Willow wasn't using any music. She was just playing. And as she'd said, her eyes were shut, and her body swayed lightly; she was putting her whole self into the music.

She'll probably be able to play until she dies, she thought, and it gave her some small comfort. Brains were weird, but at least even sick, they could hold onto some important things, even if it wasn't names or dates. The music stopped, and Martina applauded with gusto.

"Lady, we definitely need to add a music time to your daily routine."

"I'd like that," Willow said softly, touching the keys affectionately. "I haven't played much lately. I don't know why. I still love it."

Martina came over to lay a reassuring hand on her shoulder. "You just forgot. It's okay. Forgetting is going to happen. We're here to remind you. And look!" She grabbed the black glasses that sat on the piano, camouflaged against the black paint. "We found your glasses!"

"Oh," Willow sighed with relief, putting them on. "Oh, that's much better."

"Well, funny enough, it's time to take them off again, because it's time for bed." They both laughed. She laid out two pajama choices for Willow, and she chose the lighter, white sleeveless nightgown.

"Have you been too warm at night?"

"Sometimes. Just hot flashes, I think." Martina shook her head; women who were slowly losing their cognitive function should be exempt from menopause.

"Have you been able to read?"

"Yes, I can still read some things. But I like shorter books, ones where I don't have to remember so much. No more thrillers or murder mysteries. Otherwise, when I get to the end, I can't remember whose murder we were trying to solve." She laughed, and Martina laughed, too. She put some toothpaste on the toothbrush for her and handed it to Willow. Then, since she'd seen to all her hygiene needs, she left her alone. She was on the stairs to go down and get her bag when a voice startled her.

"Martina?" Mrs. Sánchez's voice was so quiet, she almost missed it.

"Yes?" She motioned for her come into the music room, where she was dusting with a large brown duster made of ostrich feathers. Martina jogged back upstairs and into the music room.

"She is in bed? Already?"

Martina smiled. "I wore her out today. Patients tend to sleep better when they have things to do. True for all of us, actually."

Mrs. Sánchez took Martina's face in her hands, apparently not noticing how the duster tickled her ear. "You said the medication would help; it does help. But you, you help, too. Nuestro ángel."

"What?" She scowled. "No, Yesenia. I'm no angel, it's just good care."

"Care that comes from your heart, because you are full of love for others." She poked her in the chest, over her heart. "Yes. Our angel. Before you came back, we had no hope. Anger, fear, pain; those we had. Now, we have hope instead. She has dignity. You are a blessing to us."

Martina couldn't listen to any more of this, even though she knew it came from a genuine place in the older woman's heart. She was no angel; she was making too much of something she'd do for anyone who meant as much to her as Willow. It was nothing to fuss over in such high and lofty spiritual terms. "Thank you," she mumbled, her face burning with embarrassment.

"No, mi ángel, thank *you*." Mrs. Sánchez turned abruptly and went back to her work. Martina stood there staring at her back, confused for a split-second, until a man cleared his throat behind her.

"Ms. Lopez? May I speak with you for a moment, please?"

"Of course. Excuse me, Mrs. Sánchez." She followed Carter into the hallway, wondering what was happening.

"Just wanted to touch base with you."

She stared into his ice-blue eyes. "Okay? About what?"

Carter shifted his weight, looking past her into the music room, as if to see if Mrs. Sánchez was listening. "About Friday." He paused. "I wanted to apologize."

"For ruining my date?"

"Ruining?" He scratched his chin. "I was going to say 'impacting.'"

"Ruining." She crossed her arms. She wasn't going to let him off easy. "Ruining is the correct word in this situation. When your boss shows up to crash your date, no pun intended, that's ruination." Also, she liked watching him squirm a little. He had been wrong to screw things up for her. Even if they were fake and weren't going to end in anything more than a goodnight kiss at her door anyway. *He* didn't know they were fake.

"I see. Well, then I owe you even more of an apology than I realized. I'm sorry I *ruined* your date."

"I accept your apology, Mr. Carpenter."

His gaze narrowed as she passed him for the stairs again. "You do? Just like that?"

"Of course. Have a nice night, Mr. Carpenter."

She heard his footsteps behind her on the stairs, steadily following her down. "Because you seemed pretty upset at the time. Not just that I was there, but that Jennie and I were . . ."

At the other woman's name, Martina spun to face him. "You can flirt with whoever you want, Mr. Carpenter. I haven't given it a second thought. I don't give you any space in my head or my heart anymore."

He leaned on the railing, crossing one ankle over the other. "That's not what it looked like to me."

"Then you weren't seeing things for what they are, Mr. Carpenter."

"Please stop calling me that. I hate it."

Yes, I'm aware. I'm only doing it to remind you what we are to each other, since you seem to be forgetting. Just like I forgot a few days ago when I let your antics get to me.

"I'm sorry, sir." She gave him a very insincere frown. "What would you like me to call you, sir?"

"Why can't you just call me Carter?"

"Fine, I accept your apology, *Carter.*"

"Thank you."

"Can I go finish my report?"

"Of course. I'm sorry I kept you."

Martina walked down the stairs, trying to pretend she wasn't wondering whether he was checking her out from behind. He followed her into the kitchen.

"Is there something else I can do for you?"

"No, I just wanted the plate that's in the fridge for me."

She checked her phone. "You haven't eaten yet? It's nearly eight o'clock."

"I don't see how those two things are related. I eat when I get home. I just got home. So it's time to eat."

She sat at the kitchen island and pulled out the report she'd started earlier. He sat down at the kitchen table behind her, and she wished he'd sat somewhere she could at least see him while she worked. He didn't have to sit with her, but he didn't have to sequester himself like that, either . . . irritating.

"You could get fast food."

"I hate fast food."

"So do I." *Danger! Danger! Stop finding commonalities! Stop bonding, darn it!*

"And speaking of food, when do I get orange juice back in the fridge?"

"Any time you like, *Carter.* But Mrs. Sánchez won't find it on her list." It didn't have the same impact, using his first name, even when said with appropriate attitude. She was kicking herself for agreeing so easily. Then again, he was paying her. "Your mother should be limiting her sugar intake. It'll help her mood, her immunity, and perhaps the disease itself."

"Yes, I read the article you left me on the link between blood sugar and Alzheimer's. But that doesn't explain why *I* can't have orange juice."

"It runs in families. I'm doing you a favor."

Carter went very still. "She's my stepmom, remember?"

She hadn't. He loved her so well, it didn't seem to matter. "No, I forgot." And darn him for reminding her, because it just made all this sacrifice that much more meaningful.

Martina worked to finish her report, getting data from her phone that she'd collected throughout the day, noting her possible issues with body temperature particularly and the found glasses, as well as the recommendation to get a second pair of glasses. She left it on the counter just as Carter got up to put his dishes in the dishwasher. He paused, cocking his head to read the report, as she gathered her things from the cupboard where she'd stashed them.

"Thanks for finding her glasses." His voice was soft. She was coming to recognize it as his "feelings voice." Time was when his voice would just get louder and more excitable when he had feelings. Now it seemed to go the opposite direction.

"You're welcome, Carter." Dang, she said it without attitude. It sounded too tender, said like that. She'd do better next time.

"If I make an appointment with her optometrist, can you take her?"

"Of course."

He nodded. "Have a good night, Martina."

"Ms. Lopez," she corrected gently. "You too, sir."

CHAPTER THIRTEEN

Chase: Hey bro. How's it going?

CARTER SIGHED. TODAY had not been a good day at work. He'd found an error in one of his formulas that meant he'd not only had to go back through and fix a bunch of reports, but also go to his coworkers and ask that they also recalculate based on the new data.

Carter: Fine. How are you?
Chase: Oh, you know. Another day, another counseling session.

He'd just put his work bag up in his room when he saw Martina crossing to the front door down below.

"Hey. Ms. Lopez. I was wondering . . ."

"Report's on the kitchen counter. Sorry, I can't stay, I've got a date. Have a good night." She was gone before he could even get out 'goodbye.' He sighed. She'd been weird around him ever since their tiff about him crashing her date, avoiding him, leaving as soon as he came home.

Carter: Sorry. That sounds boring.

Chase: Some of it's not. Some parts of are interesting.

Chase: I was thinking maybe I could get a pass for Thanksgiving.

Something caught his eye that didn't belong. Good grief, was that . . . ? It couldn't be. There, on top of the grandfather clock: it looked just like the troll they'd hidden in the house for two years while they were dating. He used to tear the place apart looking for it after she'd left. Then when he went to her house, he'd leave it somewhere for her to find, and back and forth, on and on. She'd had it in her possession when she left nine years ago . . . could it be the same one? Her sister had informed him that she'd burned everything when they broke up.

Striding into his room, he grabbed a wooden chair that sat near the window and climbed up next to the grandfather clock. Theirs had had his initials written on its backside with a pen. *Not very mature, looking back.* He turned it over and laughed out loud: "MAL." *Martina Annaliese Lopez, you crack me up.* He looked around; no one had seen him. He couldn't hide it at her house, but he could hide here. Somewhere she'd find it . . . surely Mrs. Sánchez would remember the game and leave it alone. He snapped his fingers: the medicine cabinet. Carter stuck it in his pocket and jogged downstairs, lighter than he'd felt in months.

Carter: Good idea. Do you need me to send a car?
Chase: Yeah, that'd be nice. Thanks.
Chase: I might not get the pass, but I just wanted to check with you first.

Carter: Okay.

He went into the kitchen and unlocked the medicine cabinet just as Mrs. Sánchez was coming in to do the dishes.

"Oh," she laughed. "Not this again."

"She started it!"

Her eyebrows went high. "Did she? Hmm."

"Hmm, what hmm?"

"Nothing, nothing. Just hmm. I think it's nice. She wants to be friends again."

"That is nice," he agreed, tucking the doll carefully into the cabinet and re-locking it. *And it's the most I could possibly hope for.*

"Do you want hints, if I see it?"

"Mrs. Sánchez, are you saying you're Team Carter?"

"Of course!" she exclaimed, shaking her head, as if the question were ridiculous. He crossed to the fridge and took out his plate.

"Also," she whispered, motioning him over, "I hid some cookies from mi ángel. When it comes to treats, she is ruthless."

Carter chuckled. "Yes, she is. Thanks for looking out for me."

Out of nowhere, he felt himself being hugged from behind. "Always," she whispered. "You're a good boy. You're good to your mama. You're good to live here, instead of leading a young man's life. I'm sorry it's so heavy on you."

He had no free hand to respond physically, but he smiled. "Well, you make it lighter. Thank you."

"My pleasure." She went back to her dishes like nothing had happened.

"Oh, Mrs. Sánchez? Do you remember the name of that flight instructor I used to use? I'd ask my mom, but she doesn't . . ."

She paused, shaking the bubbles off her gloves. "Robinson?"

He snapped. "That was it. Dale Robinson. Like the helicopter. How could I forget?"

Yesenia chuckled. "Perhaps it's catching."

"Don't even joke," he laughed, starting on his dinner. "One memory patient is enough. More than enough."

"Are you going flying?"

He nodded.

"Good. It has been too long. We have more help now, we don't need you. Go. Enjoy yourself."

"What, right now?" he mused, pretending to peer out into the night. "It's kinda dark out right now, and the airstrip's not very well lit . . ."

"Oh, oh. He's funny now. He's going to joke with Mrs. Sánchez. Fine, fine. I can take it. Who do you think taught you how?"

"You did," he admitted.

"You do a little more joking with Ms. Lopez, maybe she'll joke back." She winked at him. "You like to see her laugh, sí?"

"Sí," he agreed emphatically.

CHAPTER FOURTEEN

SHE WASN'T LYING; SHE did have a date. Because doctors worked weird schedules, Monday had been the only day Greg had free. And this time, she was taking no chances on his roommate interrupting things; he was coming over to her place. She rushed around the kitchen, putting the final touches on the meal she'd put in the crockpot this morning. The recipe had called it Greek chicken . . . she wasn't sure what was so Greek about it beyond the olive oil and the oregano, but it smelled good. She'd just finished tossing the salad when there was a knock on her door. Rajah hissed and hurried under the desk. *Just as well. I don't need him getting scratched the first time he comes over. It might be the last, and we can't have that.*

She checked her makeup in the mirror by the front door before she opened the door. "Greg! Come on in."

"Thanks," he said, blowing on his hands.

"Chilly out there?"

"Mm-hmm," he said, and he proved it when his cold nose brushed against her cheek when he gave her a chaste kiss in greeting. It left a funny feeling inside her which was shaped suspiciously like guilt. Especially since the kiss, while sweet, had made no impression whatsoever on her heart.

"Brr!" she said, hurrying back into the kitchen where it was warm. "Oh—you can just toss your coat on the couch."

He took off his scarf with a quizzical look in her direction. "Not hang it in the closet I'm standing next to?"

"Well," she said, taking salads to the table. "It's your funeral if you want to try."

Greg smiled as he carefully laid the coat on the back of the couch. "Is there a man-eating creature in there?"

"No, Rajah's under the desk."

Greg bent at the waist and peered into the darkness, only to step back quickly at the hissing. "Oh, you weren't kidding."

"No," she smiled. "Rescues come with some extra baggage, and Rajah's is heavier than most. Don't take it the wrong way; he doesn't like anybody."

They sat down, and the conversation flowed easily as Martina pressed Greg for all the new dirt on what was happening at the hospital. Winnie was a good friend, but her gossip left much to be desired. Martina had tried to reform her many times, but it was no use; her friend just refused to even try. *Quitter*. Greg, on the other hand, had no such qualms.

"I heard Kyle Durand is dating Ainsley, finally," Martina said, cutting her chicken.

"Not just dating . . . he bought a ring. I saw it in his locker."

Martina spluttered into her wine. "He brought it to the hospital? Why?"

Greg sneezed. "As far as I can tell, he carries it around everywhere with him. He pulled it out the other day when he was looking for a script pad." Martina wondered if Ainsley knew he was that serious about her; she hadn't caught up with her friend in a while.

"This is good stuff. What else?"

"I think you've heard enough about me . . . what about you?" When she paused, unsure what to say, he took the opportunity to look around. "You live here alone?"

"Yeah . . . why?" Greg was a perfectly nice guy, so it didn't come off as creepy.

"Just wondering whose artwork this was." Wiping his mouth, he stood up and walked over to the art print. "'Never let your wings be stolen from you?'"

Martina nodded, sitting back in her chair. "For a villain, Maleficent is surprisingly wise."

"So you have a real fairytale thing happening, huh?"

"I guess so." She knew how it probably looked to him; childish. But she'd never believe that true love was just a fantasy. She was going to hold out as long as it took. "You have time to stay and watch something?"

He paused, then sneezed again. "Sure, as long as I get to pick."

"You're claiming the remote in my house? Bold, Trout. I didn't think you had it in you."

"I'm full of surprises, I guess." He scrolled through his options before settling on a sitcom she'd seen before. Which was fine, because he took her hand as soon as she sat down and held it the whole time, and that was distracting as heck. Her conscience was a woodpecker, continually pecking away at her moral center. It felt nice to be touched, his thumb stroking the inside of her wrist where it was sensitive. *He started it, though. He took my hand, not the other way around.* When the show finished, they both looked at each other.

"You wanna fool around a little?" he asked, sniffling, and Martina couldn't tell if he was nervous or what, but he didn't look all that excited about the prospect.

"Sure," she said. He started off slow, but his technique was okay; a slow slide of firm lips against hers, and she felt a shiver go down her spine. When he gently encouraged her to lie down with his hands on her shoulders, she went willingly.

"You're a good kisser," she whispered as he moved to her neck.

"So are you," he said between kisses, still sniffling.

"Why didn't we do this last time?" She hadn't exactly meant to say that out loud, but he was making her brain a little fuzzy. Her heart, however, could not be reached for comment; she felt like it was giving her a busy signal. *Nothing to report.* At least her body was more on board . . . she didn't want him to think she wasn't having fun. She was. Sort of.

Greg turned his head to sneeze, but he managed to catch her in the head with his elbow in an attempt to cover it.

"I'm so sorry," he said, but she waved him off. It was just as well; the longer it went on, the more she felt guilt ruining it for her. She tried to focus on Greg, but there was an owl outside distracting her. Her apartment building was out of town a ways on Mr. Ramona's land. A four-unit, rust-red building, but it was quiet. Her downstairs neighbor was hardly ever home, and she never saw the guy across the hall.

He shifted so he was more on top of her, and she felt a stabbing pain in her hip; she must've left her keys in her pocket. She wasn't going to say anything, though; she let her hands wander over his strong back and tried to get back into it, but her conscience was still ruining things. Nice Guy Greg probably thought this was leading to a relationship . . . a good night kiss at the door was one thing, a heavy make-out session was something else. She couldn't let him get invested. She'd promised Daniel, and she never broke a promise.

He sneezed again, this time being more careful with his elbow.

"Are you allergic to something?"

"Cats," he sniffled. "I have meds, I can take them next time beforehand. Sorry." Well, that was a perfect segue to not making out if she'd ever heard one.

"I just remembered," she said, gently removing his hands from her hips. "I got dessert. You want some?"

"What kind?" he asked. Okay, he seemed perfectly happy to give this up for pie. So maybe she was blowing it all out of proportion.

"Apple pie. From Riverside Coffee."

"Ooh." He sat up, running a hand through his hair. "Yes, please." He reached out a hand and helped her up, too. *Such a gentleman.*

"With vanilla ice cream?"

"Is there any other way to eat apple pie?"

Martina smiled, hoping her relief at being a little farther away from him wasn't obvious. "Some people like whipped cream, I think."

"Fools."

She laughed. This would be way easier if he were a jerk . . . it was just her luck. Why did he have to be such a nice guy?

CHAPTER FIFTEEN

A FEW WEEKS LATER, the house looked the same as it always did when Martina climbed the stone steps in front of the house. The same boxwoods in pots flanking the door. The same raked walk. The same eagle door knocker . . . it was all the same. But something was not the same. Martina felt it, like the house had been cursed overnight, and when she put her hand to the doorknob, static electricity gave her a tiny shock, and she gasped. She didn't like being superstitious, but . . . she was. She didn't even foster black cats; it was bad luck. Martina wanted to turn and leave, but she pushed her premonition aside as silly and hurried into the house.

Mr. Carpenter sat in the study to the right of the entryway. Not her Mr. Carpenter, Willow's Mr. Carpenter. She didn't even know his first name: he was just Mr. Carpenter to everyone, Dad to his kids, honey to Willow. Even when she was dating Crash, she'd never learned his father's first name. Not that he'd spent a lot of time with her when she and Carter were together; he found her unsuitable. He'd cornered her in the hallway to tell her so once, on her way back from the bathroom. It had been so humiliating, she'd fled from the house shortly afterward, claiming to have a stomachache.

He looked up when she stood there, mute, staring at him. "What are you doing here?"

She crossed her arms. "I work here. What are *you* doing here?"

"I live here." *Not that I've observed.* He must be back for Thanksgiving; it was only two days away.

"Where's Carter?"

"I assume he's at work."

The man sneered. "I told him to be here to meet with me at nine a.m. sharp."

It shouldn't have surprised her, but it did. His selfishness knew no bounds. Yes, why not demand that your son skip work in order to talk to you when you'd done nothing but ignore his mother and make his life difficult for the last few months? And that was only the months that she knew about; it could be a lot longer.

"As far as I know, your son is at work, Mr. Carpenter." She turned to go to the kitchen and check for Willow's night reports, put her purse away . . .

"Young lady, I wasn't done." Oh good, he had more to say . . . Martina bit her tongue hard, a silent reminder to herself that this man might be the one actually paying her checks, and she should be polite to him. Even if he wasn't reciprocating.

"Where's Chase?"

"I believe he's in Bend at the moment." Chase's drug problems were not her business. She liked collecting gossip, not spreading it to people who would misuse it.

"Doing what? When I talked to his boss, he said he hadn't been to work in weeks."

"I'd encourage you to talk to Carter about the situation. Now if you'll excuse me . . ."

Mr. Carpenter rose from behind the desk like a wave, seeming bigger somehow than his six feet, and the sense of premonition she'd had earlier returned, tugging at her like an undertow. "I will not excuse you. What job is it you've been hired to do?"

"I've been hired by Carter as your wife's personal health care provider."

Mr. Carpenter gaped at her, then caught himself. "*You're* the nurse he hired?"

"Yes." Her mother would've wanted her to add a "sir" to the end, but villains did not deserve respect.

His low chuckle made her spine tingle in an uncomfortable way. "Of course you are. Poor fool. He's never gotten over you. Of course he'd use his mother's illness to bring you back into his life."

"It wasn't like that," Martina gritted out. "I'm extremely qualified to help Willow."

"Oh, I have no doubt that you are, young lady."

"Martina."

He cocked his head. "I beg your pardon?"

"You've been referring to me as 'young lady,' and I'm letting you know that I'd prefer you use my name. My name is Martina Lopez."

"Of course, Martina," he said, rolling the 'r' obnoxiously. Eyes shut, she turned back toward the kitchen when he called to her back. "Don't get comfortable, Martina. You won't be here much longer. I'm having my wife placed in a residential program for people with Alzheimer's. She'll be much more comfortable there."

She whirled to face him, all semblance of calm bled from her like he'd stabbed her with a hypodermic needle and sucked it out. "You shouldn't do that, Mr. Carpenter. She'll be much more comfortable *here*, surrounded by the people and places that she loves."

"Don't you want to know which facility I chose?"

"It doesn't matter," she snapped, storming toward him. "It'll be far away from here. Your wife's mental health is very fragile; she needs stability and familiarity. My care has been exceptional, I really don't think—"

"I don't remember asking for your opinion," he said, tossing the papers he held to the desk. "You may work for today. Don't worry, we'll provide you with a generous severance package."

"It's not about the money!" she shouted. "God, why is everything about money with you? Is that all you care about? I've never met anyone so shallow and self-absorbed in my entire life!"

Mrs. Sánchez appeared at the top of the stairs. "Oh, thank God you're here. Come quick, she's having a terrible day today, and we can't get her calmed down. She's practically climbing the walls."

Without giving Mr. Carpenter another scrap of her attention, Martina surged up the stairs. She could hear Willow's voice, coming from her music studio. She took a deep breath, ditching her purse in the hallway as Mrs. Sánchez and Mr. Fisher trailed behind her anxiously. If they'd called Mr. Fisher inside, this was serious; he much preferred the garden and the garage.

"Good morning, Willow," she said quietly. "I heard you're having a hard day. Is that right?"

Willow was pacing back and forth in front of the window, her arms wrapped so tightly around her middle that she looked waif-like, no thicker than the piece of sheet paper that sat on the piano.

"I'm not happy about this, Martina. And it's your fault."

Smoothly, Martina moved to the stereo and shut off the piano music that someone had started; it wasn't helping. She sat on the end of the piano bench to face her, keeping her body language predictable and calm. "I'm so sorry. Please tell me what's troubling you, and I'll do what I can to help."

There was venom in her voice. "That man."

For a moment, her professionalism slipped, and Martina felt grief well up inside, thrashing, searching for a way out like a salmon caught by a hook. Willow might not be sure who her husband was, but she knew she didn't like him. And Martina could not find it in her heart to blame her one bit.

"What about the man?" she asked gently.

"I don't want him here." It would do no good to ask why; she probably didn't know. Her mind could probably invent reasons, but that wasn't going to help the situation.

"I hear that. But unfortunately, he owns this house."

"He . . . he owns my house?" Deep creases etched Willow's forehead in confusion. "No, this is my house. I live here, not him. I don't want him here."

"You know what," Martina said, trying to keep her voice conversational, "I thought it might be a good day to go visit your son, Chase. Would you like to come with me? It takes about two hours in the car. Maybe the man will be gone by the time we get back."

Willow stared at her, her body tight. She swayed a little on her feet, self-soothing as she rocked. When she didn't respond, Martina went on. "Or we could just go for a walk. Maybe you'd like to visit the falls with me, hike up to the top . . ." It wasn't good weather for walking up the paved path to the falls, but it would get her out, away from the source of her

agitation . . .

"No, I want to go see my son."

"Wonderful. Let me get some food and things packed up, and then we'll go." She looked over Willow's clothing; someone had put her in khaki-colored dress slacks and a white silk blouse. She should grab her a sweater, though . . .

"Thank you." Willow's words were soft, and Martina turned back to her. She held out a hand to her, and Willow grabbed it, holding on as if for dear life. "Thank you."

"It's okay, Willow. We've got you, okay? We've got you. We'll take good care of you." She squeezed her hand, and Willow took a deep breath.

"I know you."

"Of course you do. I'm Martina."

"Yes, Martina. I know you."

"That's right," she soothed. "Let me go get ready for our trip, then we'll take a little drive, just you and me."

Willow nodded, letting go with clear hesitation. Martina started out of the quiet studio, then paused next to Mrs. Sánchez and Mr. Fisher.

"Just keep reassuring her that she's safe here," she murmured.

"But is she?" Mrs. Sánchez replied, her voice a tense whisper. "I hear what he says, he says he will take her to a facility.

Mrs. Carpenter would not want that, Mr. Carter, he would not want—"

"I'm going to text Carter right now and let him know what's happening. I'll take Willow to see Chase, and hopefully, by the time we get back, this whole mess will be straightened out." She pulled out her phone. "Do you have his number?" Martina felt her face heat under the sudden scrutiny of the two older people; her plan to keep him at a distance seemed so stupid right now. As if not having his number was going to keep her from loving him.

Mrs. Sánchez read out the number, and Martina texted him right away.

Martina: Hey, it's me, Martina. We've got a situation here at the house.

Martina: Your dad is here, and his presence is really upsetting Willow.

Martina: I'm going to take her to see Chase; can you send me the address?

Carter: Yes. Take my car, the black SUV.

Carter: The keys should be hanging in the garage.

He sent her the address, and she threw some snacks, drinks, Willow's stuffed cat, and the chick lit she was currently reading into a paper grocery sack. Martina brought Willow down the back staircase to avoid seeing Mr. Carpenter again, who, based on the sound of typing coming from the front hall, had gone back to work. She didn't start breathing easy again until they hit the highway; Martina kept checking her mirrors, trying to make sure he hadn't come after them. Willow was staring out the window, her breath fogging the glass, silent as she watched the world slip by.

CHAPTER
SIXTEEN

MARTINA WOUND HER WAY east down Highway 22, relieved to be away from Mr. Carpenter. His venomous gaze still felt like it was on her . . . she turned on some music to try to shake the feeling. Willow gave a little smile when she landed on the classical station, and she decided to leave it there, at least until it went to something too intense or too sad. Willow was humming along to the song, and Martina relaxed marginally. Carter's response to the crisis had been . . . calm? She didn't want to be disappointed, but she admitted to herself that she was, a little. She'd hoped for a little more support, a little feelings or something. He wasn't a drama llama anymore, but was he really so blasé about the whole thing? Maybe she didn't really deserve to know that side of him anymore . . . she'd been the one to push for strict boundaries. Did he want that? He'd said that he didn't feel like he could ask for anything, when they met at Annie's. When did he become so emotionally impoverished? The Crash she'd known thought he was worth everything at any time. He'd had the world at his fingertips. *He'd had you at his fingertips,* the voice in her head reminded her. But it couldn't be just that. Surely their breakup hadn't devastated him that much. He hadn't even seemed that upset at the time.

She let herself fall back into the memory of that day; she didn't usually, but today, she would make an exception.

They'd stayed out all night for an end-of-summer bash at Detroit Lake, and they were both exhausted. Mrs. Sánchez was making them pancakes and bacon, and Martina was devouring it greedily. She lounged against Crash, her back against his chest, her bare feet up on the bench tucked into the kitchen bay window that looked out over the front gardens.

"I'm going to eat bacon every day when I'm in college," she announced, taking another crispy bite. "I've heard the cafeteria has it every morning. That's what Lola said."

"Isn't she at Western, though?"

"No, she's at Oregon State." *Which you'd know if you'd been listening the first four times I told you . . .* She shook her head and reached out to sneak a sip of his coffee.

"I was thinking," he said, nudging her. "About college."

"What about it?"

"Well, I'm going to be at Duke, and you're going to be here . . ."

"So?"

"So I thought we might see other people."

It was a miracle that she held onto the ceramic mug. An actual miracle. She had no idea how she managed to keep her fingers curled around the handle of it when every other muscle went suddenly slack as if she were having a stroke.

"What?" she whispered, and even Mrs. Sánchez looked alarmed, even though she was trying hard to act like she wasn't listening.

"Come on, Tini. You haven't thought about it? Aren't you going to be lonely without me?"

"Well, yeah, but—"

"So why deprive ourselves? We can see other people when we're apart and see each other when we're together. We'll spend the whole summer together. We'll still be together."

She put her feet on the tile and turned to see his face. "You're not joking?"

He reddened a little, then took his coffee back from her. "I just don't see how else it's going to work. We're going to be hundreds of miles apart, thousands!"

"Yes. And we'll write emails and call and video chat. Send letters. Figure out visits."

"But that's not enough," he complained. "That's not going to matter."

Excuse you? Why isn't it going to matter? Martina stood up under the auspices of refilling her own coffee, taking her time adding the creamer. She fought hot tears. "Are we not getting engaged?" She didn't mean for it to come out so angry, so unhappy.

"Engaged?" Crash sounded shocked. When she turned, his face was as white as Mrs. Sánchez's apron.

"Yes, I kind of thought . . ."

"No. No way. I'm not ready to be tied down. There's going to be a lot of people to meet at college. We're both going to change a lot the next few years, and besides, we're way too young for that kind of thing."

"Don't want to be tied . . ." She shook her head in disbelief. No, they hadn't talked about it, exactly, but the implication had been there, in vague terms. That they would be together; that they were soul mates. Meant for each other, now and always. She would gladly chain herself to him like a protester at a construction site and throw away the key. "I thought you wanted to make this work."

"We'll still see each other. I'll still call you."

"Between dates with other women? You honestly thought I'd be okay with that?" Her tone of voice had apparently driven Mrs. Sánchez from the kitchen, because the pancake pan now sat smoking lightly on the extinguished burner, and the woman was nowhere to be seen. "Do you know me, like, *at all*?"

"I don't care if you see other people," he said, gesturing widely. "Have at it."

"I know you're not a jealous person, but . . . seriously, Crash? Why can't you see how hurtful you're being right now?" she whispered. "Do these past two years mean nothing to you? Are you really this selfish?"

"I'm not being selfish, Tini. You're the one who wants to keep me from enjoying college. Four years is a long time. A really long time. You can't expect me to wait for you until summers and breaks."

"So this is about sex."

He said nothing, but the set of his jaw confirmed it. Without a word, she set down her mug and moved for the front hall as fast as she could without running.

"Where are you going?" She could hear him pounding after her.

"I'm not gonna stand in your way. If you don't care about me, don't care about our relationship, go for it. You want to sleep around? Now you can do it with a clear conscience, since you don't have a girlfriend."

"Martina, don't—just calm down." He put a hand on her arm, but she wrenched it from his grasp so hard that he gasped. "God, you're being such a baby about this."

"Oh, yes," she drawled, livid. "I'm the immature one, not the boy who can't keep it in his pants. Goodbye, Carter." She snatched her backpack from the bench in the entryway where she'd left it.

"You'll be back. Just wait and see. You can't go months without sex, either. I know you."

"Well, now I won't have to, will I?" She slammed the front door behind her, tears blurring her vision as she took the slippery stone steps faster than was prudent, losing one pink flip flop in the process. By the time she got to her car, heaving sobs were billowing from her chest. She let her forehead rest on the steering wheel and put her arms over her head, trying to help herself breathe, when it felt like panic was squeezing all the air from her lungs. *First things first.* She went to block his number and saw that he'd already texted her.

Crash: Come on, Tini. We're not over. You know we're not.

That's what you think, idiot. As soon as she got home, everything he'd ever given her was going into a bonfire in the backyard. Her sisters plied her with chocolate and got the whole story out of her that night. They were gratifyingly incensed. A few days later, he'd called her sister Augustina, who yelled at him in Spanish until he hung up. A week later, he came to the house, but her father met him at the front door, putting a fatherly arm around his shoulders, turning him back toward the driveway as he talked with him quietly. She'd made herself stay away from the window, so she never knew what her father said to him. She'd been too chicken to ask him after the fact; she didn't think he'd have told her, anyway. Probably would've said something about how it was advice not meant for her ears. But she knew her dad was on her side, even without all the details. It was fairly possible that her sisters had passed information to her mother, who'd passed it to her dad. She sent his daily emails to spam. She avoided his normal hang-out spots, like Annie's and Subway. She kept most of their mutual friends, though a few of the male ones sided with him.

When Crash resorted to letters, she finally texted him: *I don't want to hear from you again. Ever.* He stopped after that. It was a relief and heartbreaking at the same time, knowing for sure that it was really over. She'd really lost him. The two years they'd spent together was just a happy memory, soured by his selfishness and shortsightedness.

Martina pulled her mind back to the present as the cloud layer broke and she and Willow drove over the summit of the mountain pass; she pulled out her sunglasses. They'd cover the tears at the corners of her eyes, too.

CHAPTER SEVENTEEN

WILLOW WAS RESTLESS by the time Martina pulled up in front of the rehab building. It was more like a house than she expected, its three stories towering above them, the building itself seated on a large piece of land with a barn in the back, a large vegetable garden, and not much else around. Willow had her seatbelt off and the door open by the time Martina put the SUV in park.

"Hang on, lady. Wait for the caregiver, please."

Willow ignored her and hurried up the steps of the lodge-like house. Thankfully, she rang the doorbell, and the time it took for someone to come to the door allowed Martina time to catch up with her. A white-haired woman in a cozy orange sweater smiled at them.

"Hello! And who are you here to see?"

"Chase Carpenter," Martina supplied, and the woman nodded.

"Chase!" she called. "Your day just got booked up." She disappeared, and Chase appeared in the doorway. He blinked. "Martina? Mom!"

"That's us," Martina smiled. "Can we come in? I really need to pee, and your mom probably does, too."

"I do," Willow confirmed. She air-kissed Chase on the cheeks as they came inside. "How are you, darling?"

"I'm good, Mom. I'm Chase, remember?"

She sighed impatiently. "Yes, of course I know. You're my *son*. The one who lives nearby, but not with me. I haven't forgotten *everything*, you know." She was in a *mood* today, and Martina was 100% blaming Mr. Carpenter for that.

The left side of Chase's face tipped up in a half-smile. "Being a twin, I'll take it."

"Is that an insult?" she asked, largely unemotional, checking her reflection in the large brass-framed mirror that hung on the wall of the entryway. "I *can* tell you and your brother apart, you know. I always could, even when you switched clothes." She looked around. "Is he here?"

"No, Christopher lives in New York now. Bathrooms are down the hall, straight back." Martina started to follow Willow down the hall, but Chase put a hand on her arm. "It's one at a time."

"Oh, it's okay. She'll do better if we go in together. I turn around to give her privacy unless she needs something."

His gaze bounced around the entryway like he was trying to do long division in his head, then finally landed on her. "You're the nurse."

"Right." She pulled away from him gently. "Be right back." She barely got to the door before Willow locked it. She wasn't great about remembering how to undo locks, unless they were locking things they didn't want her getting into. Funny how that worked. Once Willow was done, she deposited her back with Chase, pausing just a moment to appreciate the bright, matching delighted smiles they gave each other when they were reunited, then saw to her own needs. It gave her a moment to wonder a few things: why didn't Chase know she was his mother's nurse? Why wouldn't Carter have told him? He wouldn't bother hiding the fact, so there must be another reason. He was probably just busy. When she came back out, they were still chatting in the entryway.

"So Carter's moved back home?"

"That's right," Willow said, shrugging. "I think he must be having financial problems. Quite sad, really. But I'm happy to have him there."

Martina kept her face impassive, but she pulled out her phone.

> **Martina:** Your mom is telling everyone here you moved home because you're broke.

> **Carter:** Then tell them it's not true!

> **Martina:** For all I know, it could be. I don't think I should.

> **Martina:** I'll need to see some bank statements first.

> **Carter:** Listen, if I'm living at home at 27, it would only be for the family's sake. I'd rather live in a cardboard box, truth be told.

> **Martina:** I saw Mr. Fisher getting rid of one this morning. We could put it out back for you.

> **Carter:** Great. I'll put it in front of the back door so Mom can kick me as she goes by at midnight.

Martina: Don't even joke. I don't want to be called out for a patient-hunt at that time of night.

Carter: Is she having fun?

Martina: Yes. They both are. But he was surprised to see me.

Carter: I told him I hired a nurse. He doesn't pay attention.

Martina: No, he knew she had a nurse, just not that *I* was the nurse . . .

Carter: Well, I'm sure I mentioned it.

Martina: Uh-huh.

She put her phone away, since she was being rude, ignoring the two of them.

"Martina," Chase was saying, "we're going to go horseback riding. Do you want to come along?" *I should definitely not have zoned out on that conversation . . .*

"Oh. You know, I'm not sure that's going to work, because Alzheimer's patients don't have great muscle tone, and it requires a strong core to stay on a horse. Also, if she were to get confused, it'd be hard for me to get to her in order to help. But I think feeding or grooming the horses is a wonderful idea."

"Young lady." Willow had her ornery voice on. "I've been riding horses for years."

"I'm sure that's true, but today, we're just going to look at them."

"I'm sorry," Chase said to Martina, his eyebrows pulled together. "I didn't realize she wouldn't be able to . . ."

"I can! I grew up riding horses!" Willow protested. "I know how to ride a horse."

Chase looked chagrined. "I don't want you to get hurt, Mom. Let's just walk them around."

"Or maybe," Martina said, touching Willow's arm, "you could let me lead you around? So I'd be close by?" She'd offer to get up there with her, but she was crap with horses.

"I *know* how to ride a horse," she muttered, still clearly perturbed.

"I know you do," Martina said, giving her shoulders a squeeze. "Come on, let's go pick your mighty steed."

Willow rolled her eyes. "Fine."

"I'm sorry," Chase mouthed, but Martina waved away his apology. How could he have known? She was glad she'd worn her cowgirl boots rather than her regular tennis shoes; it was a little muddy in the corral.

"So, are you single?" That was the Chase she remembered. His name had been a double entendre ever since he knew what girls were.

Martina grinned. "Why, you gonna drive to Timber Falls to see me on weekends?"

"You've never heard of an LDR?"

"I have, but I'm not a fan of long-distance relationships, sorry. Also, I'm seeing one of the doctors at Santiam. But even if I wasn't, you're not my type, handsome."

"Shame. I always envied Crash a little. I wouldn't have tried to steal you, of course, but still."

"Well, if that's not genuine brotherly affection, I don't know what is."

"Ha."

Martina looked at Chase, trying to figure out what was so different about him. He looked a bit scruffier than usual; his blond hair wasn't styled particularly, and he needed a shave. It wasn't even his T-shirt and jeans lazy Saturday type attire. No, there was something deeper to the man that was fundamentally changed.

"Sure you're not into me? You're kinda staring."

"Sorry." She actually blushed a little. "You just seem really . . ."

"Different."

"Yeah."

"I am different." He dusted off his hands. "So when I get back, I expect you to introduce me to your friends."

"Ha," she said, echoing his earlier response. But her nature got the better of her . . . she liked playing fairy godmother. "Like who?"

"I don't know. Got any freckled, red-haired friends who're single?"

"Just one," she said, "but she—" Martina paused. Willow was standing dangerously close to that horse's rump, and she did know enough about them to know that they didn't like having people behind them.

"She what?" He nudged her with his shoulder.

"She seems pretty busy. She doesn't come out with us much." Deputy Lizzie Painter mostly kept to herself, Martina thought. Maybe she thought it undermined her authority in town for them to see her drinking at Annie's. Either way, she'd never gotten to know her as well as she would've liked to. She seemed like a sweet gal. Unless you were a criminal. Then you should run. Deputy Painter did not tolerate that in her town.

"Hmm." He seemed strangely pleased with this news for reasons she couldn't quite piece together, but she lost her train of thought as Willow continued to wander closer to the horse's backside.

"Hey, let's go inside, shall we? It's cold out here, and I bet there's coffee inside."

"But you don't like coffee," Willow said, in an almost scolding tone of voice, and Martina felt a little flicker of pleasure. Too soon, Willow wouldn't even remember her name, let alone her drink preferences. But today she did.

"Thanks for remembering that. But I know you like it, so I was thinking of you."

Willow smiled and took Martina's arm through her own. "This one takes good care of me," she informed Chase.

He nodded as he led Apple Blossom back to her stall. "Glad to hear it. I wasn't sure how you'd take to her, given their messy break-up."

"Break-up?" Willow gave him a thousand-yard stare, her eyebrows twitching, like she was trying to coax her brain into cooperation. And Martina hoped for the first time that Willow wouldn't be successful.

"Let's go get that coffee," she said gently, moving them back toward the house. "Where did you get that hat, Willow? It's so lovely, I'm kind of jealous of it."

She touched her colorful intarsia knit hat. "I got it at the Christmas Bazaar . . . can't remember when. I think Rhea Devereaux knitted it."

"Mmm. I didn't know Rhea was a knitter."

"Oh yes, she's an accomplished knitter. I believe she sells her goods on that craft site . . . what's that called?"

"Etsy?"

"Yes, I think she has a store on Etsy. Beautiful hand knits—in local wool, too. She gets her wool from Mr. Powell. She did a scarf for me, too, in the same pattern. I couldn't find it this morning." Man, her memory was good today. Too bad she was feeling so ornery.

"Next time, ask me. I'll help you. You can always ask me."

Willow patted her hand affectionately, but said nothing.

"I know her son Sawyer; he's Ainsley's cousin, and he hangs around the library a lot."

"Yes, I've heard rumors about him. He spends all his time working on motorcycles on that property of his, renting the big house, living in the cabin. Hardly ever comes into town. Strange for a young man who had so much promise."

"Hmm." Martina didn't know much about what Sawyer had done after college; he was older than her. "He's not much of a talker at the library, unless he's talking to a certain reference librarian . . ."

"Oh, really?"

Chase was giving them both a strange look as they continued their gossip as they all walked back inside. Mother and son sat and chatted in the library, and Martina wandered away under the auspices of getting a cup of tea. She leaned against the wall in the entryway, listening to them. Chase's questions were polite, but probing: he was clearly trying to figure out how extensive her memory loss was. She chided herself for not sending him and Christopher the same resources she'd given Carter.

She'd just assumed he'd pass them on . . . but this family was not the same one she'd known nine years ago. They'd been close, at least the brothers had. Or maybe she'd gotten it wrong. She reflected, not for the first or last time, that it was a shame she couldn't separate memory from perception . . . she'd like to be able to look back on her life and know if she was really seeing things the way they were. Bored, she pulled out her phone.

Martina: Hey.
Dad: Hey is for horses.

She rolled her eyes. Someone had taught him that joke years ago, and he still thought it was the funniest thing.

Martina: Actually, I just pet some, and all they said was 'neigh.'

He switched to Spanish.

Dad: Is this my daughter or an imposter? My daughter doesn't care for large animals.

She switched to Spanish, too.

Martina: Very true. But I can make exceptions. Willow wanted to see them.
Dad: They're lucky to have you.
Martina: I'm lucky to have them, too, Dad. They're paying me very well.

He was still grumpy about her decision . . . but more than that, she suspected that he was grumpy that he hadn't been consulted first. She was struggling to know how to make him feel included without being patronizing or obligated to take his advice. Especially when there was just so much of it . . .

Dad: You're coming tomorrow, right?
Martina: Yes.
Dad: And you won't leave when all the kids show up?

She shifted her weight uncomfortably. Of course he would bring this up. Augustina was a good sister and seemed happy in her marriage, but her kids . . . her kids were so badly behaved.

Martina: I will not leave, but I'm also not going to let her kids smack me. They're old enough to know better.

Dad: That's fair. Do you want me to talk to Gus?

Martina: No. But thank you.

Dad: Your mother said to tell you that Gus and Stephen are taking a parenting class at the church, and she thinks it's helping.

Martina: Glad to hear it.

Martina: Love you, Dad.

She sighed. This family stuff was getting out of hand. They all loved each other; they should be able to work this out without needing a United Nations mediator. She peeked at Willow and Chase again; they were laughing over a game of Scrabble, and Willow leaned over the board to give her middle son a hug. Martina was already dreading the moment she had to take her back to Timber Falls.

CHAPTER EIGHTEEN

CARTER WAS IN A MEETING with one of the more senior actuaries when his phone rang. *Harrison Carpenter.* His father had sent him a message earlier, saying he wanted to meet this morning, as if Carter didn't have anything better to do. He sent his father's call to voicemail, put it on vibrate, and apologized to his co-worker. When it rang again, he didn't take it out of his pocket. When it rang a third time, Marco paused their discussion.

"Do you need to get that?"

The phone dinged plaintively.

"No, it's just my dad."

"Seems like it might be important," Marco said, leaning back in his chair.

"He gives that impression constantly," Carter remarked dryly, and his coworker laughed. To appease the man, he pulled out the phone and looked at it.

Unknown: Hey, it's me, Martina. We've got a situation here at the house.

Unknown: Your dad is here, and his presence is really upsetting Willow.

Unknown: I'm going to take her to see Chase; can you send me the address?

He debated briefly whether he should go try to intervene, but Martina was a professional. She was good with his mom; he could probably handle her better than he could anyway. He wanted them out of there, as quickly as possible. He didn't know what his father was up to, but it seemed like nothing good.

Carter: Yes. Take my car, the black SUV.
Carter: The keys should be hanging in the garage.

"Everything okay?" Marco asked, clearly curious.

"Yeah. Sorry. I'll call him back later."

Later ended up being lunchtime. Carter sat in his car with his tuna sandwich and put his father on speaker.

"We had a meeting this morning." His father sounded annoyed. It wasn't a tenth of the annoyance Carter was feeling, he'd wager.

"We absolutely did not have a meeting this morning. I'm at work."

Harrison chuckled. "Right. *Work*. I wanted to speak to you about your holiday plans."

"I don't have any."

"I'd like to spend Thanksgiving together, including your stepmother."

Carter let his head rest against the steering wheel. "Any reason why you *wouldn't* plan to include Mom?"

"She didn't recognize me when I walked in this morning until I reminded her who I was. I just thought that might make for an uncomfortable family gathering."

"I'd be more uncomfortable if we excluded her."

"Fine. I'll invite her sister, too. Christopher may join us as well."

"Okay. Anything else?"

"Yes, I can't locate your brother, Chase."

"He's in rehab in Bend."

Harrison scoffed indignantly. "Again? That's disappointing."

"I'm not sure he'd agree. Anything else?"

"Tina Gross contacted me to see if you'd be willing to participate in the bachelor auction again this year for that children's hospital." His mother had planned the event the last few years . . . Tina must be desperate if she was asking him. It could be awkward for his mom, if she realized. Willow hadn't asked to go back to those charity meetings lately, so Martina hadn't pushed her. Carter pulled his phone off the dash to look at his calendar, and his father apparently interpreted his silence as hesitation. "These are the kind of events that will help support your position in the community when you come back to TF-PP."

"I'm not coming back to TFPP, Dad." *Assuming I don't lose my job here because I'm so busy trying to handle what's happening at home.*

"You just didn't give it enough time, Carter. You would've fit in here eventually."

Gosh, I hope that's not true. He'd nearly worked himself to death, and he'd hated every minute of it, everyone kowtowing to him, because he was the boss's son.

"Tell Tina that'd be fine. Go ahead and confirm. Anything else?"

"The nurse you've hired."

"I'm not discussing this with you. Anything else?"

His father's words had an unusual bite to them; Harrison so rarely displayed anger that Carter wasn't entirely prepared for it.

"She's still my wife, isn't she? What right do you have to hire someone—"

"I had the *right* because I was *here*. Where the hell were you?"

His usual detachment was back. "TFPP sent me to San Francisco. You know that."

"Then why are there credit card charges in New York? And Texas?"

"I took some side trips through JFK and DFW."

"A week ago? And the charges were in Galveston."

"I don't have to explain myself to you."

"Ditto. Goodbye, Harrison." Carter hung up.

CHAPTER NINETEEN

MARTINA AND WILLOW ended up staying for lunch and a family counseling session with Chase, then it was time to go back to Timber Falls. Just east of Detroit Lake, flashing red and blue lights in her rear view mirror had Martina squinting to see who was pulling her over, an uneasy feeling crawling over her back. She glanced at Willow, who looked nervous, too.

"Nothing to be worried about," she said, squeezing her hand and letting them stay joined to keep her calm. "We probably just have a tail light out." She peeked at the side view mirror to see who was approaching the car. Lizzie Painter was coming to the window, her hand on her service weapon. *This should be okay. Everything's going to be fine. She just wants to talk.* She tried not to think about a million ways that a routine traffic stop could go wrong for a person of color. Tried and failed. Martina let go of Willow's hand, placing both hands on the steering wheel, like her father had taught her. It didn't hurt to be cautious in situations like this. Lizzie blinked when she recognized her.

"Hey, Martina." Her hand fell from her weapon, and Martina's heart decided to go back to beating evenly . . . but her hands stayed where they were.

"Hey, Lizzie." Her voice trembled, and Lizzie noticed.

"I'm sorry to have to stop you. Can I see your license and registration, please? Then I'll explain why I pulled you over."

"Yes, of course. Let me just . . ." Martina scrambled to get into the glove box for the registration, and retrieved her license from her wallet, both of which were easier said than done with her hands shaking. She handed the younger woman the paperwork.

"You okay? This vehicle was reported stolen a few hours ago."

Shock had Martina's mouth going dry. "Stolen? No, it's not stolen. It's Crash's."

Lizzie's eyebrows went sky high. "You guys are back together?"

"No, no," she said quickly. "I'm—I work for Carter now. I'm providing medical care for his mother."

"Who?"

"Crash? This is his mom, Willow."

Willow waved cheerfully from the front seat, and Lizzie smiled and waved back. She lowered her voice. "And she's not kidnapped?"

"Kidnapped?" Martina laughed, relieved. "No, I just took her to Bend to see her son."

Lizzie went strangely still. "Which son?"

"Chase."

Her face split into a knowing grin. "Oh. That son."

"That son?" Martina asked. There was gossip here, she could just taste it . . . she searched her memory for a trace of it. "Ohhh, you arrested Chase, didn't you?"

"Yes." She cleared her throat and squared her shoulders, scribbling something down on her pad.

"And didn't he write you a letter?"

Lizzie's eyes went wide. "Who told you that?"

Ainsley. Ainsley had told her that. "I can't remember now . . . but is it true? What did he say?"

"Later," Lizzie said, waving away the question as she turned beet-red. "Is that true, Mrs. Carpenter? Did you go visit your son?" Lizzie peered into the vehicle.

"Yes, we just took a little trip. This one takes good care of me," she said, reaching for her hand again, and Martina grasped it gratefully. She sent up a silent 'thank you' prayer that Willow was calm and lucid right now. Things could be going very differently for them if she didn't know Martina. It had never occurred to her that she could be put at risk like that, working with a patient whose memory was compromised. Slaps, bites, and kicks? Sure. But not getting pulled over on a kidnapping charge, unable to prove her innocence. *Carter wouldn't have done this.*

"Can I ask who reported the vehicle as stolen?"

"Harrison Carpenter called it in."

"Probably just a mix-up, then," Martina said, smiling, even though she was seething inside. "He just got back into town after being gone for some time. He probably didn't know that Carter gave me permission to use the car. I can show you the text he sent me, if you'd like."

"Yeah, if you could forward me a copy of it, then I'll have that to show my superiors. Sorry to have to be so formal, but it's part of the job."

"I totally understand," Martina assured her. She fired off a screenshot to Lizzie's sheriff email address and cc'd herself for good measure. "And now you have my number in case you have any follow-up questions. I can give you Crash's number, too."

"Great. Thanks, Martina. Sorry to bother you. You ladies have a nice evening."

The deep relief that washed over her couldn't dull the sharp anger that rose up in its place. She signaled and powered them back onto the highway, mindful of her speed. She was going to kill Harrison Carpenter. In the hands of a different law enforcement officer, that little stunt could've ended very differently. A bitter part of her mind reminded her that he couldn't be expected to understand; an old white guy getting pulled over was only in danger of having his time wasted. There was little at stake for him. For Martina, he'd given a cop a reason to pull her over and for a select few, that would be enough to justify violence or imprisonment if they thought she was resisting. She didn't fear the officers in Timber Falls; her father had taken all his girls down to the police station when they turned sixteen and introduced them to all the officers there. It had seemed so stupid at the time. It reminded her of when they take little kids down to the fire station and show them what a fire fighter looks like with all his gear on so they don't burn to death under the bed, hiding from the big, yellow monster. She only realized in retrospect that he wasn't doing it for her benefit, but for theirs. He was marking her as "one of them," a member of Timber Falls, a status that he hoped would give her some due consideration, should they ever find her behind the wheel, in the backseat, or anywhere else they might be shining their giant flashlights. It made her sad that it was necessary. When she pulled into the long driveway, she texted Carter.

Martina: Are you at the estate?

She literally wasn't going inside if he wasn't. She'd turn right around and take Willow out for really greasy fast food with milkshakes. She'd been doing great on her low-sugar diet, and let's face it, she was dying anyway.

Carter: Yes. Upstairs.
Martina: Your dad called the sheriff and told them I stole your car.
Carter: WHAT
Carter: Where are you

It wasn't physically possible, but she could've sworn she could hear him shouting from outside.

The front door banged open, and Carter flew down the front steps in bare feet. "What the hell? Are you okay?" She was pressed to his chest before she knew what was happening, his clean scent surrounding her, mixed with the smell of what he'd just been eating . . . chips and salsa, maybe? There was no time to dwell on it, because he was pulling back to look her over like she'd been in a car accident, not a traffic stop; his hands wandered into her hair, over her shoulders, down her arms to her fingertips.

"Martina, answer me. Are you okay?"

"Y-yes," she stammered, "I'm fine. We're both fine. Lizzie Painter pulled us over; she was perfectly nice about it."

"But it might've been someone else," he said, pulling her back into a crushing hug, and his voice cracked on the last word. "Someone who would've just arrested you or . . . or . . ." Carter sniffled, and Martina's heart tried to beat its way closer to him through her chest. She wound her arms around him to return his embrace.

"Yes, it might've been. But it wasn't."

"So you've returned to the scene of the crime." At the sound of his father's voice, Carter turned his head without letting her go.

"You." His voice was so cold, Martina shivered. "For your information, Ms. Lopez had my permission to take my car to Bend. How dare you—"

"She took my son's property from the estate; what else was I to assume?"

"You didn't need to *assume* anything! You could've just *asked* me!"

"You blew off our meeting. If you'd been here . . ."

"Are you kidding me, Harrison? I—" Carter stop abruptly and turned to his mother, who was standing in the driveway, wide-eyed and trembling. "I'm sorry, Mom. It's okay. You're safe here, I'm here now. I won't let anything happen to you." He strode over to her, offering his arm like he was escorting her to a ball, and she gave him a shy smile as he escorted her up the stairs.

"I saw your brother today," she said softly. "I don't know if it was Christopher or Chase, but he was happy to see me."

"That's great. It was so nice of you to go visit him," he said, matching her tone, ignoring his father completely as he took Willow inside. Martina stood in the driveway, trying to catch her breath emotionally, wishing she'd followed them inside. Her shift wasn't over for another half an hour, and the night nurse wasn't here yet, based on the absence of her car in the estate's parking area. Mr. Carpenter folded his arms across his chest, watching her from the top step.

She folded her arms and watched him right back. "Do we have a problem?"

He barked out a laugh. "We've had a problem since the first time Carter brought you home."

"Well, this is my place of employment now."

"Looked like more than that to me. I've never seen Carter embrace Mr. Fisher so ardently." That comment had her wanting to bite her nails. Good thing they had a fresh coat of polish on them.

"Mr. Carpenter is my employer. Nothing more."

"Not for long. Not if I have anything to say about it." Fuming, Martina marched up the stairs, but he blocked her path into the house. "I'm warning you," the man said softly. "You're not getting your claws back into my son. The smartest move he ever made was dumping you." *Oh, that's rich.* She managed to keep a smile off her face, amused as she was about how little this man knew about his own family's history.

"No," she said, stepping into his personal space. "The smartest move he ever made was not working for you." She let her shoulder bump his as she went inside, praying he wouldn't follow her into the kitchen. Mrs. Sánchez was there, pulling a slice out of a steaming lasagna.

"Oh," Mrs. Sánchez said, and a cacophony of motherly emotion was poured into that one word. "Here, mi ángel. Eat something. Mr. Carter, he has his mother. Sit, sit. That man won't come in here. He fancies himself a king and rings the bell."

Martina accepted the plate gratefully and sank onto the bar stool at the island. "Thank you," she murmured.

"You're all right?" The older woman was twisting the dish towel she held, clearly distressed. "I heard him make the call. I wanted to warn you, but I didn't have your number."

"I'm okay," she assured her, reaching out to lay a hand on her arm. "It was Lizzie Painter who pulled me over. She's a friend. She knows I wouldn't steal a car."

"It was wicked of him to say so. He's a wicked man." Martina had never seen Mrs. Sánchez's face that shade of maroon; she was shaking, too.

"Agreed," Martina said, taking a small bite of the delicious Italian food. Her appetite seemed to have disappeared, despite not having eaten in hours. Mrs. Sánchez noticed, and her lips made a flat, displeased line.

"They're waiting. Let me go serve, then I'll be back. I'll make you pancakes and bacon. You love my pancakes." Mrs. Sánchez gave her a one-armed hug and a quick kiss on the cheek, then hustled out, her arms full with the crystal salad bowl and an overflowing bread basket.

Martina sat in the silent kitchen, watching the timer tick down on whatever dessert Mrs. Sánchez had going. She wanted someone to hold her. No, she wanted Carter to hold her, like he had outside. It was the first time she'd felt right since she'd stepped back into this house . . . and now, maybe she'd be leaving it for good. Mr. Carpenter didn't make threats unless he could back them up with action. She imagined Willow separated from her and Carter and Mrs. Sánchez, confused, afraid, and she felt grief well up. It wasn't fair of Harrison to punish Willow for Carter's decisions; and really, since he left him de facto in charge, how could he come barging back into their lives and start giving orders? *I should quit.* If she asked Cindy to re-assign her, maybe that would assuage Harrison. It was only her he hated; he wasn't lying earlier when he said he'd had a problem with her since their first meeting. She didn't think he'd come right out and admit to being a racist, but then again, he probably felt safe here. Invincible, even.

"Tini." Carter was watching her warily from the doorway between the kitchen and the dining room. "Go home, honey. We'll talk on Friday."

She shook her head slowly, her eyes filling with tears.

He crossed the kitchen and sat next to her on the adjacent stool. "I'm sorry, Martina. I'm so sorry for what he did. I can't get rid of him, or I would. The good news is that he rarely takes an interest in what we do, so most likely, he'll be gone again soon."

"He's going to put your mother in a care facility. He hates me so much, he'd ruin your remaining time with her, just out of spite."

His hand on her shoulder was warm and firm, and he pulled her against his side. "I'm not going to let him."

"You can't stop him, Carter. I'll just ask Cindy to send someone else, it's not a big deal . . ."

"It is a big deal." He turned his face into her hair. "You walking out of our lives again would *definitely* be a big deal." His gravelly voice had her turning to stare deep into his eyes, and the conflict she saw there didn't make her feel better. "It almost destroyed me last time," he whispered. "I was so sure you'd be back. I was just positive . . . in a few days, I thought you'd flounce back in like nothing ever happened, and we could forget that I suggested something so stupid. I was such a colossal idiot." His hard swallow made her stomach feel hollow. "I went to your house, and your dad told me it wasn't going to happen, getting back together with you. He advised me to move on, try to find someone new to love. And I tried. I tried to move on, but God, every woman, no matter how beautiful or smart or sexy or funny . . . she just wasn't you. So I partied harder and harder, tried everything under the sun, but it didn't help, because every time I sobered up, you were still gone. I don't think I was consciously trying to end my life, but I was sure as hell wasn't trying to preserve it. And then I flunked out, and my mom put me in counseling."

"Why?" she whispered. "Why are you telling me this now?"

"In case I don't get another chance. I need you to know how deeply sorry I am, honey. I was so wrong to ask that of you. I was wrong to *think* it. I was scared; I didn't want to go so far away from home, I didn't want to leave you, but I felt trapped . . . my father had mapped out this life for me that didn't fit me at all, but I couldn't say no to him. I was so scared. I tried to talk to Christopher about it, but he told me I was being stupid." He put his hands on her cheeks. "But Martina, I'm so much more scared now than I was back then. Nothing scares me like the thought of losing you again."

"Carter," she breathed, not knowing what else to say, blinking back tears again. It was all she'd wanted to hear for years. She hated hearing that he'd been so unhappy, but it wasn't like she'd ever managed another relationship half as deep as theirs either, as immature and screwed-up as it was. It's not like she'd ever fallen in love again.

"Please don't quit," he said, dragging his thumbs over the sensitive skin of her cheeks. "Please. Give me time. I'll fix it. I won't let him send her away. Will you trust me? I don't deserve to ask for that, I know, but—"

She put a finger to his lips, if only to keep herself from kissing them. "I trust you. I won't talk to Cindy yet. I just don't want Willow to suffer because of me." *Because of us.*

"I don't want that, either, believe me." He tipped her head down and kissed her forehead. "Promise me."

"I promise." He let his hand drop slowly, like he didn't really want to. She didn't really want him to, either. It was on the tip of her tongue, a burning desire to have his lips on hers, to taste him again; it would be better than any meal anyone could offer her right now. The incident with the sheriff's office had shown his hand; he was definitely still in love. The question was whether he planned to do anything about it.

CHAPTER
TWENTY

"MARTINA, CAN YOU SET the table? Just the napkins and silverware, we'll serve from the kitchen." She'd just finished putting together the ambrosia salad with marshmallows and cherries (gross), so she nodded and washed her hands again. The dining room was quieter than the rest of the house, comparatively. She found the good silverware in the drawer of the buffet and the plaid orange, green and brown napkins in the drawer next to those. Martina got all the way around the table, and she still had two sets of silverware left in her hand. Perplexed, she counted the chairs around the table.

"Mom?" she called. "We're two places short."

"I know," Linda called back. "You and Francesca are eating in here."

What? She can't be serious . . . Martina tried to stem her outrage by clarifying.

"In the kitchen?"

Her mom poked her head through the doorway, drying her hands on an apron with holly all over it. "Yeah, at the kids table. We didn't have room for you at the big table if we wanted to keep the couples together. Sorry, hon." A timer went off, and it was fortunate for the sake of family unity that it did, because

Martina thought she could feel the steam coming out of her ears. She was about to spend her favorite holiday trying to prevent food fights and policing whether her nieces and nephew ate enough vegetables to get a piece of pie, and they weren't even her kids. Arguing would do no good. Exhaling slowly, Martina slapped a smile on her face and went into the kitchen to set the rest of the table.

"Tia Tini," said Daisy, once they'd all been served, "where's your husband?"

"I don't have one. Eat your green beans, please."

The four-year-old picked at the delicious food on her plate, utterly unimpressed. "Why?"

"Because green beans are good for you."

"No! Why you don't have a husband?" Daisy persisted.

George, his mouth overflowing, spoke before she could answer. "Because God didn't send her one, dummy."

"Don't say 'dummy.' We don't call names." Then privately, she leaned over to her niece. "Have you seen the movie Snow White?"

The girl nodded, her light brown curls bobbing. Gus had given her pigtails, and she was looking just adorable. "Well, I'm just waiting for a kiss that wakes me up." Martina expected the girl to ask more questions about how she didn't look asleep now. Instead, Daisy nodded sagely, opening obediently for the bite of turkey and stuffing that Martina offered her.

"I love you, but you're hopeless," Francesca offered from across the table. The seventeen-year-old floated a spoon in front of their two-year-old niece like an airplane, and Émilia reached out and grabbed the spoon to feed herself.

"Gee, thanks, sis."

George got up and began to head back toward the TV before Martina caught him by his collar. "Whoa there. You didn't finish your salad, you didn't clean your hands, and you didn't ask to be excused. Three strikes and you're out, bud. Have a seat back down."

"I don't have to."

"You do, actually," Martina said, steering him back toward his chair by the shoulders. "Your mom said." She could hear the adults in the other room laughing, heard the cork being popped on the wine bottle for a refill. She hadn't even gotten through her first glass. *No time.*

"You're not the boss of me."

"Unfortunately for both of us, that's not true. Now sit your butt down and . . ."

"Butt!" gasped Daisy. "She used a bathroom word."

Martina and Francesca exchanged twin looks of befuddlement. "*Butt* is a bad word?" Martina asked, and the kids nodded. "What are you supposed to call it, then?"

"Mommy says caboose," Daisy offered.

"Okay, sorry. George, please sit your *caboose* back down on the chair." She didn't dare ask how she'd labeled their other private parts; it was assuredly something equally ridiculous. She'd never understood what was wrong with the anatomical names for things herself.

"No!" he shouted, digging his heels into the carpet, and she heard the conversation in the dining room pause. George spun and delivered a swift kick to her shin, then tried to take off, but she still had him by the collar.

"Nice try, kid." Catching him under the armpits, she scooped him up and plopped him back in the chair. Martina handed him a damp washcloth. "Grandma wants you to wash your hands before you leave the table."

Ptooey. His spit landed squarely in her left eye. Martina flailed in surprise, knocking something to the ground that broke with a crash. Eyes squeezed shut, groping for a napkin, she could smell the spilled wine before she could see the broken crystal strewn around her feet.

"Here," Francesca pressed something in her hand, and she took it gratefully, wiping her face gently.

"Everything okay in there?" her mother called.

Martina didn't answer. They obviously didn't care if they couldn't even be bothered to leave the table to investigate broken glass. *My, quite the pity party we're throwing here.* Martina told herself to shove off, and she stumbled toward the kitchen sink to try to wash out her irritated eye; there must have been food still in his mouth, because there were definitely solids in her eye now. She felt a warm hand on her back between her shoulder blades.

"You all right?" Her mother's voice was low. "What happened?"

"Gus's bratty kid happened," she hissed quietly over the sound of the running water, trying to glare fiercely, despite being one-eyed. "He spit in my freaking eye."

"Oh dear." Linda rubbed her back. "I'm sorry. I should've sat with them."

"Why, so he can spit on you instead? I don't think the issue is *us*, Mom . . ."

"Shh, just . . ." She patted her shoulder nervously. "She's coming."

"Why was George crying?" Augustina asked, her voice all sympathy for her son.

"Are you kidding me?" Martina muttered. When her mother didn't respond, Martina tossed her the kitchen towel and marched out of the room and up the stairs before she said or did something she'd regret. At the top of the stairs, on her way to the bathroom to find the eye wash cup, a flash of red out of the corner of her eye made her pause.

"George, you don't belong in Grandma and Papa's room. Get out here."

A furious-faced six-year-old propelled himself at her, fists clenched. George pulled back to hit her, but Martina was faster. She put her hand over his fist and clenched her arm muscles to keep him in place.

"You hit me again, and I'm gonna hit you right back."

The boy's eyes widened, then narrowed. "No, you won't. Grown-ups don't hit."

She grimaced. "You're right. I won't. But I've told you every time I see you, you cannot hit me. And I'm angry that you keep doing it."

George stared at her, apparently speechless at her attempt to communicate with him honestly.

"If you hit me, kick me, bite me, hurt me? There will be consequences you will not like. Do we understand each other?"

He nodded, and she released him.

"Mooooooooom," he wailed, tearing down the stairs, and Martina rolled her eyes. She should probably go talk to them, but she just couldn't right now. Martina closed the bathroom door and threw the lock. Rummaging through the first aid supplies proved fruitless; did her parents not have an eye wash cup? She could've sworn they did. Martina sat down hard on the fuzzy toilet lid. Her phone buzzed, and through her slightly blurred vision, she read the text.

Carter: Happy Thanksgiving.
Martina: Happy Thanksgiving to you, too.
Carter: Having fun with the family?
Martina: Sort of. You?
Carter: Not really.

She hesitated. Her favorite Thanksgiving was the one she'd spent with him. Well, she'd spent the afternoon with him, anyway. Her mom had insisted that she spend the morning and the meal with them (also at the kids table), but she'd been allowed to go to Crash's for dessert. Unlike her family, the Carpenters all parted ways before the leftovers were even cold, so dessert had meant hiding away with an entire pecan pie in the pool house, feeding each other bites and spraying each other with whipped cream. They watched *Home Alone* and kissed and quoted the iconic lines as they came and kissed some more. She touched her lips, just remembering . . . but she wasn't brave enough to ask if he still thought about it, too.

Martina: Your brothers ditch you already?

Carter: Chase didn't get his pass. Christopher called last night to say he wasn't coming.

Martina: So it's just you and your parents?

Carter: My Aunt Sylvia came, and she brought her boyfriend.

Carter: He hates Thanksgiving, because he's vegan. And he hates us, because no one told Mrs. Sánchez, so there's very little he can eat.

Carter: So all around, a crappy day.

Martina: At least you didn't get stuck at the kids' table . . .

Carter: oh no.

Martina: OH. YES.

Carter: Not cool.

Martina: Right? Their parents should be the ones dealing with their tantrums. But I'm single, so . . .

Carter: You should come over here. We don't have a kids' table. But we do have wine.

That was tempting, but her mother would be upset if she bailed now. A soft knock on the bathroom door. "Tini?" Of course they'd send her father up here to deal with her. God forbid that her sister have to deal with her face-to-face.

"I'll be out in a minute, Dad," she said in Spanish.

Martina: Wish I could.

Martina flushed the toilet and ran the sink without washing her hands to make it less obvious that she'd just been hiding. She greeted him at the door with a bright smile. "Hi."

"Hi." Hector grimaced. "Let me see your eye, please."

She stood still as he gently probed the skin around her eye, which she knew was red and puffy, clicking his tongue unhappily. "I'm sorry, Tini. Kids . . . they sometimes don't do what they should."

"I know how kids are, Dad. But I hang out with Starla Miller's kids at the library, and they don't act like this. They're almost the same age as George and Daisy."

He scowled. "You're right. I will lay down the law with them."

Martina's phone dinged, but she put it in her pocked without looking at it.

Carter: Or are you spending time with Dr. Trout today? I shouldn't have assumed.

"No, I didn't mean . . ." *Sigh.* "I just meant that we should be able to talk about things. Every time I start to try to talk to Gus, Mom shushes me. She can't handle the confrontation."

"I will confront her. I will demand that she make her children be polite."

"No, Dad," she groaned, rubbing at her sore eye. "Just . . . never mind." She gave his growing white beard a friendly rub. "Is this how it is now? You've decided you don't care if people think you look old?"

"I don't think I look old. Besides, at the farm, I thought I would play Santa Claus. Give the kids a thrill."

"You'll be a wonderful Papá Noel."

"Will you come help out this year?"

"I'll try. Maybe I could bring Carter and Willow to get their tree, but I think she usually uses a fake one." Her father sniffed with disdain, and Martina smiled. "Don't be uppity, Dad. To each her own."

"But is it flocked? Because that's a crime."

"No, I don't think it's flocked," she lied. "Come on, I need dessert." If anyone noticed her swollen eye, no one mentioned it when they re-entered the kitchen. Martina ate her pecan pie and even tried a bite of the pumpkin chia pudding Francesca had made because it had yerba mate in it, even though she didn't care for pumpkin in general. No one could say she wasn't being a good sport when she played three group games, and no one complained when she claimed she had to go home to feed the cats at seven o'clock. It was only when she saw Carter's last text that she realized she hadn't so much as thought about Greg all day.

CHAPTER
TWENTY-ONE

"THANK YOU, MRS. SÁNCHEZ. That was delicious." Harrison wiped his mouth and got up from the table, a sign to everyone that dinner was over. Ignoring a scathing look from Aunt Sylvia's very unhappy boyfriend, Harrison left the dining room, pulling out his phone as he went. His mom was distracted by her sister, still chatting with her, arm in arm as they went into the library. At least someone was enjoying this holiday.

Seizing the opportunity, Carter stalked after his father. "Hey."

His father paused, then slowly turned. "Are you speaking to me?"

"We need to talk."

"About?"

"About you calling the sheriff on my employee."

"Employee," Harrison mused, swirling the scotch still in his glass. "That's an interesting choice of words." He turned and continued on his path to the study.

"She *is* an employee," Carter insisted, storming after him. "I needed help. I told you that. I told you I couldn't do all this by myself. It's bad enough that you blow off Mom's care and disappear for weeks at a time, but you cannot undermine the choices I was forced to make in your absence, too. Martina was absolutely the best person for the job."

"Oh, I have no doubt she's qualified. The question is whether she's warming your bed again on the side."

Carter barked out a humorless laugh. "Considering Mom was the nanny, you're the last person on earth who should judge me if she was. But I'm not like you whatsoever, so our relationship is purely professional."

Harrison's gaze narrowed. "It didn't look very professional, gathering her into your arms and fawning over her like a lovesick idiot because of a simple traffic stop."

"Over a simple . . ." Carter repeated, dumbstruck. "God. You really don't get it, do you? Do you really not fathom why what you did was wrong?"

"Keep your voice down, Crash. We have guests in the next room over."

"Let them hear!" he snapped, but he did lower his volume. "Let them hear how you've abandoned your family since we stopped making you look good! Let them hear how you tried to use someone's race against them!"

"Enough!" Harrison snarled. "I won't be spoken to like this in my own home!"

"You'd have to *live here* for it to be your *home*!"

"I travel for work, to support this family's fortune! I have a serious job, Carter, not some blow-off position for a joke of a company. If you'd stayed at TFPP, you'd understand—"

"This again?"

"Yes." Harrison sat down behind his desk in the tall leather chair. "I need a successor. Christopher has his own life happening in New York, his own success. Chase is apparently incapable of success, so that leaves you. With some grooming, I'm sure you can meet the task."

Carter put his palms on the desk and leaned forward menacingly. "Pets get groomed, Harrison. I'm not interested. And the next time you threaten to put Mom in a facility or call the sheriff on Martina, we're done. 100% done. No more holidays, no charity events, no phone calls, nothing. Do you hear me?"

Harrison leaned forward, his hands interlocked. "I know I must seem cold and unfeeling to you, but I'm not. I've been young and wealthy, and I know how many people who I thought genuinely cared about me turned out to be leeches, your mother among them. I'm just trying to protect you, son." Harrison leaned back, bouncing lightly in the chair. "And if you need help, then I can arrange to be around more."

No, Carter wanted to whisper. *No, go away. Go do whatever it is you do. Leave us alone.* He gritted his teeth, realizing was going to have to play along for the moment. His father would get bored or restless here eventually. He'd leave again when he figured out that living with a wife who barely recognizes you and definitely doesn't like you isn't so great. Carter just didn't know how long that would be.

"Great. Thanks." Carter had already turned to go when he heard his father's voice.

"I'd like to be hooked into the closed-feed video system, so I can help keep an eye on my wife."

"Password's 'pinkhair,'" Carter muttered. "You can figure it out yourself." He turned and left before his father could prolong their interaction further. This wasn't over, that much he knew. It was only over for now.

CARTER STARED AT HIS last text to Martina again and sighed. No answer. He'd only invited her over because he was currently halfway to drunk on his own personal bottle of 2012 Adelsheim pinot noir in the pool house, watching *Home Alone*, alone. He wasn't brave enough or drunk enough to tell her that he'd kept listening for the slam of the front door all morning, wishing she'd walk through it. Even if she was just stopping by because she forgot something. Even if it wasn't about him at all. Just having her nearby, even for a few minutes, would've been . . . right. Better than being trapped here with all these people he was connected to by blood and shared space, but nothing more.

Carter hadn't turned the lights on in the pool house, and it startled him when his mother suddenly appeared in the doorway.

"There you are," she smiled, wandering into the room. He paused the movie.

"I thought you were with Aunt Sylvia."

"She went home. I didn't want to be alone." Her new-found honesty was so refreshing. His mother had always acted like she didn't need anything, and it made him feel better (and worse) to think that she was just as needy as he was sometimes.

He patted the sofa next to him, and she eagerly sat down next to him. "What are we watching?"

"*Home Alone.*"

"Isn't that a little juvenile?" she asked, her nose wrinkling.

"Yes." *But so is pining for a woman who's not mine anymore, so . . .* "It's a tradition." She wouldn't know better. He started it over, hoping it would help her follow the plot better. He needn't have bothered; she was asleep before the movie mom noticed they'd left without her youngest son. Carter didn't bother with a glass and drank straight from the bottle. He turned on his side, watching his mom's peaceful face, the way her hands pillowed her head. Those hands used to be so capable; now it was like she'd been replaced by an actress who was trying to play her in a movie about her life; someone who was portraying her badly, who hadn't known her at all. He half-expected her to yell out "line!" sometimes, to some unseen script-holder.

"I miss you," he whispered. "I miss you, and you haven't even gone anywhere yet." He took another long drink, and Carter let his body slide down onto the couch. "I am thankful for you, Mom. Even when you're being difficult and can't remember the smallest thing. I'm thankful you're here. I'm thankful we're together." Not caring if he woke her, he reached out and squeezed her hand, letting tears and sleep cover him together.

SOMEONE WAS RUBBING his back. Someone brushed the hair off his forehead, someone with soft fingers. *Uh oh.* He knew the feel of those fingers.

"Carter?" someone whispered, giving his shoulder a little shake. "Wake up." He opened his eyes and what he'd feared became reality. Martina stood next to the couch, her face painted with concern. Looking around, he knew what she was seeing: the TV asking if he wanted to watch *Home Alone 2* now, the empty wine bottles, him still wearing yesterday's clothes. He cursed inwardly, blushing furiously outwardly.

"I . . ."

What on earth could he hope to say about this? What could explain him re-enacting his favorite holiday memory of her? Beyond admitting his undying love, that is. His pounding head and sour stomach were not helping him come up with any kind of logical excuse.

"I guess I was feeling sentimental."

Well, it wasn't the *worst* explanation.

Martina smiled. "We all do sometimes. I know it's been a hard time for you. Nothing wrong with wanting to think about happier times." She gestured toward a still-sleeping Willow. "And it was nice of you to include your mom."

"She crashed my private screening. At least I didn't have to share my wine."

"Thanks for sticking to the rules. Though I know you gave her pie."

"It was a holiday," he said, blushing again. *Get it together, Carpenter.* He groped around for his phone, and Martina held it out to him. Carter took it gratefully. He was surprised it wasn't dead, but alarmed to see there were only thirty minutes until he was supposed to be at work; it was a floating holiday, and he'd opted for more time off around Christmas.

"Shoot, I gotta get to work."

"When?"

"Um, now." He looked around frantically. For what? He had no idea. That's how frazzled he was. After a moment, he felt her pushing him toward the bathroom.

"Here. Shower here, and I'll bring you some clean clothes."

"What?"

"Just go!" Martina hurried out of the room, and he stared after her. Well, it wasn't the worst plan in the world, and he did hate being embarrassed twice in one day. He jumped in without waiting for the water to warm up, and it was better than coffee. In terms of waking him up, not in terms of comfort; that was severely lacking. He was toweling off when there was a quiet knock at the door. He wrapped the towel around his waist and opened the door.

Martina was holding out a pile of clothing, dutifully staring at her toes. "Here you go."

"Thanks." He wanted to make a snarky comment . . . about her unusual shyness, about her blatant kindness, about the nicely-coordinated outfit she'd picked . . . but he came up blank. Because being cared for by her felt good. Was he jealous of Willow? That was a strange thought. He shut the door and got dressed, blasting out of the door, only to find a fried egg sandwich and coffee in a travel mug waiting for him.

He didn't notice the text conversation he'd apparently had last night until he arrived at work.

Carter: Happy Turkey Day.
Christopher: Yeah, you too.
Carter: You with friends?
Christopher: Nah.

Carter: Girlfriend?

Christopher: I don't do girlfriends, man.

Carter: Did you at least have pie?

Christopher: Of course. I'm not a monster.

Carter: What kind, though?

Christopher: Pumpkin. Made from scratch.

Carter: Bet it still wasn't as good as Mrs. Sánchez's.

Christopher: You know what? It wasn't.

Carter: I invited my ex over. She didn't come, though.

Christopher: Are you drunk? Go to bed.

Carter: Okay. Night.

Carter: Wait, are you coming home for Christmas?

Christopher: Maybe, bro. Go to sleep.

Carter groaned, wolfing down the last of the breakfast she'd left for him now that his stomach had settled down. Well, it could've been worse; he could've texted Martina and told her was still hopelessly, helplessly in love with her.

SHE WAS ALREADY GONE by the time he got home that night; the night nurse, Cara, had come early, so she left early. Mrs. Sánchez was washing dishes again as he ate dinner. He'd been thinking about her advice the other night about winning Martina back. He chewed his food for a minute, thinking. *Screw it.* He had no pride left. This troll thing, this game they were playing, it was a good sign. And he'd apologized for his absolute stupidity after graduation night; that was a good start. But they were going to need more. He had a lot of work to do if he wanted her back. He needed help. "Can I ask you something?"

She gestured for him to go ahead with a flick of her wrist.

"What makes a woman trust you again? Like, if you f—uh, if you messed up?" He didn't want to swear in front of Mrs. Sánchez. She always gave him the sternest look, and it made him feel about two feet tall.

"You are thinking of Martina?"

No point in lying. "Yeah."

"It's more simple than it seems."

"Meaning?"

"How do you re-build anything? One piece at a time."

"I just don't even know where to start," he mumbled. She watched him for a long moment, then pivoted to the crystal cabinet and carefully pulled out a vase and a jar of marbles.

"Love," she said, "it is like this. When we start out, the bank is empty. Slowly, we make deposits." She dropped two marbles into the vase. "Little things. Kindness. Respect. Small acts of service. Every day." She let three more fall with a *plink-plink-plink.* "It will tip the scales against what you did, before. When you were young and very stupid."

Carter choked on his dinner, laughing. "I was very stupid, wasn't I?"

"I could not *believe* how stupid. For such a smart young man to say such *stupid* things . . ." She leaned forward on the quartz counter on her elbows. "I thought my English must be very bad to misunderstand you like that."

He poked at his food with his fork, embarrassed. "I knew she was in love with me, and I was in love with her, and I didn't think anything could ruin that. I thought we were rock solid. I just didn't want to be alone, you know?"

"For you to be together, was it impossible? Back then?" Oh, he'd tried. Even filled out an application for Oregon State. His father had been furious when the acceptance packet came in the mail. Shredded it right in front of him and didn't speak to him for a week.

"My father wouldn't have let me go anywhere but his alma mater."

Yesenia nodded slowly. "We don't need to worry about him now. Focus on her. Honor her. Show her you have changed. Show her you are considerate . . . and not for any *other* reason than love." She dropped her chin to glare at him, and he blushed.

"That's not even on the table, so . . ."

"Good. Do not flatter her, do not try to buy her love. She is a proud woman, like me." She toyed with a thick silver ring on her thumb. "With Diego, I did not care if he bought me flowers or chocolate. But if he would pick up the toys the children left out, if he would come home on time, if he would wash my car . . ." She dropped three more marbles into the vase, setting it ringing again. "Real things. Not . . . oh, how do you say it?" She rattled off something in Spanish, but he just shrugged; he didn't recognize the phrase. Yesenia pulled her phone out of her pocket and typed in something with one finger. "Not smoke up her skirt."

That set him laughing and choking again, and she patted his back until he got his breath back. "Okay, I get it. Thank you, Mrs. Sánchez."

"Okay, honey." She patted his hand, then turned, yawning, back to her work.

CHAPTER
TWENTY-TWO

A FEW NIGHTS LATER Martina and Willow were watching the Seahawks game up in the media room when Carter got home. His mother hated football . . . but apparently, she didn't remember that.

"Who's that one, the fast one?"

"That's Luke Wilson," Martina said, munching popcorn.

His mother crossed her arms over her stomach. "He's very good-looking."

Martina snorted. "Yes, yes, he is. They are a fine group of men, aren't they?"

"Oh, yes," his mother agreed, articulating too carefully. "That quarterback, too. Very fine. I see why you enjoy this. Oh, hello, darling."

"Hey, Mom, hey, Martina. How was your day?"

"Excellent," his mother said, not taking her eyes off the screen, transfixed. "We made bread."

"My report is on the kitchen table. You should read it before you do anything else." She dropped her chin to give him a meaningful look, and he raised an eyebrow. Martina pulled out her phone.

Martina: Do. not. eat. that. bread. It is mostly salt.

Martina: She was not in a mood to cooperate today, so we just let her bake whatever she wanted (under supervision). Mrs. Sánchez is going to throw it away once she's in bed and tell her it all got eaten.

Carter: So you're going to blame this on me?

Martina: That's right. Glad you understand.

Carter: I see. Well, I don't know how I feel about that.

With a vicious smile, Martina put her phone away. "There's food for you in the kitchen, Mr. Carpenter. Make sure you get some of that bread. It's really something."

"Okay, thanks. You can head home now, Ms. Lopez."

"We're just going to finish the game first . . ."

He held back a smile. She'd always hated being interrupted during a game. Once, they'd had to race out during halftime to get more snacks, and they'd just barely gotten back to his house in time to see a touchdown. He'd broken the speed limit for her. It wasn't unusual for him at that time. But now? Now he saw risk everywhere he looked; it was his job. And he was good at it, but it was exhausting, especially when your mother no longer had a drop of common sense.

"No, no. Please. I don't want to keep you. And I can't afford your overtime . . ."

Martina glared at him. "I'd really like to stay, even unpaid."

"I don't think that's such a good—"

"Oh, Carter," his mother said, exasperated. "Just go away. Stop flirting and go away." His mouth fell open a little at her blunt words; she didn't notice. She simply reached for more popcorn. He caught Martina's gaze over her shoulder, as she tried valiantly not to laugh. The comment didn't bother her, clearly. He took that as a bit of hope he could tuck away in his heart.

He beckoned to her with one finger, and she got up and came to the doorway, her eyes still glued to the TV.

"Yes?"

"Is there anything I can do for you?"

"Huh? No, no, don't leave Treadwell open like that! No!" she exclaimed, as she watched the Vikings receiver run for a touchdown.

Carter made himself repeat it more clearly. "Is there anything I can do for you today?"

Martina wrinkled her nose at him, then replied with patronizingly slow enunciation, "I work for you. Not the other way around." *That's the hurt talking. Be genuine, tip the balance. No flattery.*

"That doesn't mean I can't try to make your life easier."

"I'm fine, thank you," she said, still watching the game.

"Okay. I'll ask you again later."

She softened a smidgen, tearing her gaze away from the screen. "You will? Why?"

He shrugged, resisting the urge to cross his arms. Why was this so hard? "That's just the kind of boss I am, I guess."

"Uh-huh." Skepticism was dripping off her, and he smiled.

"See you later."

"Undoubtedly." She paused. "You want to bring your food up here and eat with us?"

"I'm not interrupting girl time?"

"Well, you are, but I think we can make an exception for you." She winked. "As long as you don't talk during the offensive plays and let us ogle the players all we want."

He grinned at her, then mimed locking his lips. He got sidetracked in the kitchen by an urgent work email, and by the time he got back with his plate, Willow was gone, and Martina was sitting on the couch alone. *We're alone.* Well, this was a step in the right direction. Though if it wasn't end-of-the-season football, she might still be hurrying off.

"You don't really mind if I finish the game, do you?"

"Nope." He sat down on the couch, near her, but not next to her, trying to give her some space.

On a commercial, she turned to him. "You asked if there was anything you could do for me."

"Yes?"

"Did you mean it?"

He nodded. "Yes. Tell me."

"Your mom asks for you, at dinnertime. That's a very agitated time for her anyway, and I think in her mind, you're still a kid who should be home for dinner. It would be great if you could join us."

"I'll be here."

She pursed her lips. "Okay, but it would be better if you could do every night. If it's a sporadic thing, she'll just—"

"Martina. I'll be here. I promise."

"Okay. Six o'clock."

He rolled his eyes. "Yes, it's my house. I actually do know what time Mrs. Sánchez has dinner ready, since it hasn't changed in twenty-plus years."

"And yet, you can't manage to get yourself here by that time," she teased, pushing lightly at his shoulder.

"I didn't think you wanted me here." *Oof, that was too honest.* She reacted like he'd slapped her, and yet, it felt good to say the truth out loud instead of hiding it.

"I'm sorry I gave you that impression . . ." she said softly. "Forgive me?"

"Of course." *And I'd love it if you'd forgive me, too.*

"And just so you know, I asked for Friday night off, so the night nurse will come a little early."

"Oh. Greg taking you out?" *Please say no. Say you broke up. Say he's boring and smells like old cheese and kisses like a fish.*

"Yup."

The silence was pregnant.

"So it doesn't bother you to see me with Greg?"

"I wouldn't say that."

"What would you say?"

"I'd say it doesn't matter that you're with Greg."

She shifted on the couch, slightly farther away from him. "You're right; as my employer, it shouldn't matter to you at all."

"No, that's not what I'm saying." He moved closer, and Martina held her ground. His voice was soft. "I'm saying it doesn't matter if you see Greg or not, if your heart belongs to someone else."

She likely did the best she could, under the circumstances, but her haughty sniff wasn't haughty enough. In fact, it sounded more like a prelude to tears. "And you think it belongs to you?"

Yeah, he wasn't going answer that. And since they were shoulder-to-shoulder, he didn't have to look at her, either. He'd hit the trip wire on her temper, apparently. *But yes, since I saw the look in your eyes when I apologized for my horrible father and the way I hurt you years ago. Since I see the way you look at me now, when you think I'm not paying attention. Since you put orange juice back in the fridge for me. Yes, since you asked. I do think it still belongs to me.*

"The *ego* on you. It boggles the mind." Interesting. That wasn't a denial.

"This isn't ego. I actually have very little of that left."

"And yet, it's apparently growing all the time . . ."

Carter shook his head. "I see the way you are with Greg. Friendly. Fling-y. Nothing wrong with that, but it's the tiniest shade of what we had. I know what love looks like in your eyes, and I don't see it when you look at Greg."

"Maybe I could. If I gave it time."

"Maybe," he said, bobbing his head. "We'll see, I guess."

CHAPTER
TWENTY-THREE

THE HOURS TICKED BY slowly the next day. She took Willow for a long walk, even though they'd gone for a run that morning, just so she'd stop watching the clock. Because if he didn't show up . . . *Whatever. It doesn't mean anything.* Something had been happening to them, though. Things were . . . good. Warm. It was like massaging a stiff limb . . . she felt the muscles that had been immovable with fear and anger and a deep sense of betrayal begin to move again. Begin to flex—just a little. And that felt dangerous. The anger had been much safer. The betrayal had been a faithful reminder of what she stood to lose. The fear kept the battle lines drawn. And now, checking her phone every minute as the time crept closer to 6 o'clock, it felt a lot more like love than any of those other things.

At 5:58, he walked in the front door, put down his bag in the study, took off his tie, and went to find them. Martina knew, because she was watching on the closed-feed cameras they'd had installed to check on Willow. She quickly hid her phone as he walked into the dining room. Harrison and Willow were already seated at the big dining room table, but Carter ignored his father.

"Smells good in here." He leaned down and kissed his mom's cheek, and she beamed like she'd cooked it. "Eggplant parm?"

Martina nodded.

"With garlic bread?" he asked, his puppy-dog gaze pleading with her.

"With salad," she replied firmly.

"And garlic bread?"

"And steamed green beans with olive oil."

"And garlic bread?"

"And chocolate coconut milk ice cream for dessert; no added sugar!"

When his shoulders slumped and his bottom lip poked out in an adorable pout, Martina covered a giggle behind her fist, coughing to clear her throat. "And garlic bread."

"I knew it!" He rubbed his hands together greedily, then took off for the door. "Forgot to wash my hands. Be right back."

Willow leaned forward like she had a secret, her eyes bright. "He came home for dinner."

"Yes," Martina smiled, patting her arm. "For you."

"No," said Willow, shaking her head. "For *you*."

"For me?" Martina asked, confused.

"Yes, of course," Willow answered, leaning back so Mrs. Sánchez could serve her some of the main course. "Husbands and wives should eat together. I'm glad to see him making time for you." She glared at Harrison, who smirked back at her.

"Message received," he said.

Carter sat down across from her, snapping open his napkin, thanking Mrs. Sánchez in Spanish. "It'll be nice to eat this hot for once," Carter joked, glancing at Martina. She felt her lower lip tremble; apart from the sharp hurt of Carter not being her husband, Martina tried to piece together Willow's line of thinking. Abandoned by her husband, Willow must have concocted a scenario in her head where Martina was also abandoned by the person she loved. Despite the delicious scent of Yesenia's cooking, Martina's stomach was churning and sour. She felt too hot. The tears burned behind her eyes. Because in Willow's mind, she'd fixed it. She'd exerted her influence to get her son to the dinner table on time, to be a good partner to her daughter-in-law. To not make the same mistakes his father had made.

"Martina?" Three of them were staring at her with matching looks of concern; Harrison, at least, was engrossed in his phone and oblivious to her distress. Someone must have asked her a question, but if they did, she didn't hear it.

"I'm sorry, what did you say?"

Carter was frowning. "You okay? You look sick." He reached across the table to press his fingers to her forehead. "Do you feel like you have a fever?" That gentle care; it slayed her. Because he would be a good husband, to someone. He'd never abandon her like Harrison had Willow; look at how he'd cared for his stepmom, even when he could've gone on with his own life. He cared. And right now, her raw heart couldn't take it.

"You know," she said, pushing away from the table with shaking hands, "I forgot to wash, too. Will you excuse me for just a moment? Willow, I'll be right back."

"Martina?" She heard Carter push his chair back, and she grimaced. She didn't want anyone to see her cry, and she couldn't hold it back much longer. She'd be lucky if she even made it into the hallway.

"I'll be right back," she said over her shoulder. "Don't wait for me." She barricaded herself in the bathroom near the kitchen and let the tears come, pressing the fluffy white hand towel into her face to muffle her sobs.

A quiet knock at the door had her holding her breath. "Martina? What happened?"

"Don't leave her alone," she choked out. Harrison did not count as company.

"She's not alone, Mrs. Sánchez is sitting with her. Open the door." His tone was firm, but gentle. "Please."

She threw the lock and he opened the door cautiously.

"Did she hurt you?" he asked quietly.

"Not with her hands," she assured him. She blew out a long, uneven breath. "She thinks we're married. She thinks you've been blowing me off for dinner, that's why she wanted you there. Because she cares about our nonexistent marriage."

Carter tipped his head back to look up at the ceiling. "And we can't correct her, because that'll upset her."

"Right." A shudder made her breath come out stuttered, and he tipped his head down to look at her. "It won't matter what we say. She won't remember." She wiped her face with the towel, leaving black smudges on it.

"Can I give you a hug?"

She nodded, and he opened his arms just in time for her to press her face into his chest. He held her tightly as her tears slowed, rubbing her back soothingly. Then he gasped.

"*This* is where you put it? I've been looking for days!" He pulled the pink-haired doll out from the behind the tissue box, and Martina laughed.

"I thought you were never going to find it! I'd already decided to move it tomorrow."

"Ha!" He said, holding it above his head like a trophy. "I have prevailed."

Martina chuckled a little. "You have. Now let's eat before it's stone cold."

"Nah, I'm used to it." He grinned at her, then before she could protest, he gathered her up again for another long hug. "Plus, I need time to think about where I can hide this that you'll never find it."

She pinched his middle just enough to make him jump. "But the whole point is that it's hidden in plain sight!"

"Are you asking for leniency?"

She leaned her head back to see him better. "No. Bring your A-game, Mr. Carpenter."

"Just remember, you asked for it." Holding her like that, their faces close, it was amazing to her how close two people could be to kissing without actually touching that square inch of their bodies together. Because as long as she didn't kiss him, she was still following the rules, she was still being faithful to . . . to Greg, that was his name. She was still keeping her contract intact. For a moment, staring into Carter's baby blues, she'd almost forgotten. He released her, and Martina could've sworn she felt the brush of his lips against her hair, but it happened so quickly, she thought she must have imagined it.

"Does that work, by the way?"

"What?"

"Tipping your head back so the tears don't get out."

"It does," he nodded, mockingly serious. "You know gravity? It sucks 'em right back in if you put the back of your head parallel to the ground."

"Fascinating. I had no idea."

"You could learn a lot from me," he said, tossing the doll to himself as he backed out of the bathroom with a grin.

"I bet that's true," she whispered, wiping her face once more for good measure.

CHAPTER
TWENTY-FOUR

"IS THERE ANYTHING I can do for you today?" Carter asked. He'd managed to catch her in the morning today. Their dinner last night had been fun, apart from his mother imagining that they were married. *Don't worry, Mom. I'm on it.*

She cocked an eyebrow at him. "When you say 'anything,' do you mean . . . anything?"

He nodded ardently. "Yes. Anything. Anything that would make your life easier."

She twisted her lips to the side in a thinking posture. Then she held out her keys. "I need my tires swapped; I need my snow tires put on. Charlie Miller said they could do it at lunchtime. I was going to go myself, but it leaves the bulk of your mom's care on Mrs. Sánchez, so I felt bad . . ."

"I'll do it." He took the keys.

"And here, let me give you some cash . . ."

His refusal was a reflex; the words just popped out. "No need. Mastercard's everywhere I want to be."

She snatched the keys back. "Never mind."

"Wait. No. I'll do it." Martina pressed the keys to her chest between her breasts, as if she knew he couldn't grab them there, and he held his hands up to assure her that he wasn't going to try. "I'm sorry. I should have . . . I shouldn't have offered to pay. Please?"

"You're begging me to let you do my crappy errand?"

Unashamed, he held his hand out, holding her gaze. "Please?"

Martina looked around, like she wasn't sure this wasn't a set-up somehow.

"I just want to make your life easier. No agenda." *Except making you see that you can trust me again.* Still wary, she tossed him the keys from where she stood, leaving no opportunity to touch her again. But he brushed her fingers a little when he accepted the $100 bill she held out. "Let me know if that's not enough, and I'll pay you back." He would get it washed and detailed, too. And he'd pay for that himself.

"Why are you grinning like that? Is this a trick?"

"No trick. *Doing things for you makes me happy.*"

"Your social life must be really dull," she quipped, turning back to the stairs.

He put his voice in a low register. "Not really." He contained a chuckle, but not a smile when she froze on the bottom step. That was one of the advantages of wooing your ex; you knew her turn-ons. Carter strolled over to her, drawing her hair behind her shoulder to speak quietly into her ear. "Doing things for you makes me happy, Martina. I can't help it." He wanted to do so much more; wanted to kiss her neck, put his hands on her hips, make her do that breathy sigh. He clasped his hands behind his back to ensure they behaved. "I'll have it back for you when I come home for dinner. Is that okay?"

"That's fine."

He stepped away from her, and it was an exercise of pure will; there wasn't a bone in his body that wanted the distance.

"Hey, Carter?"

"Yes?" He was back by her side in an instant, and apparently, it was amusing, because he got a full-dimple smile, bright as a daffodil.

"Just . . . thanks. I appreciate it."

"You're welcome." He backed up now because that smile was damaging his self-control, and he couldn't have that. Not when the scales were starting to shift. "I have to get to work."

"Me too," she teased. She headed up the stairs, but she was still looking at him over her shoulder. *Steady, Carpenter,* he told himself. *It's one thing for her to trust you with her errands and her car; it's another for her to trust you with her heart.* But he couldn't help but grin as he wedged himself into her Corolla on his way to Salem.

CHARLIE MILLER WAS on the phone when Carter walked in, and he waved, as if to say, 'I'll be right with you.' Carter waved back. There were several other people in the waiting room; good thing he'd brought his computer with him.

"No," Charlie snapped into the phone. "No, Starla. You can't—" He turned away from the reception area, prowling into his office. He slammed the door behind him, but it wasn't hard to hear the conversation through the glass door as he continued. "I told you, she's just a friend! There was never any . . .

What do you mean, leaving me? What about the kids? Where do you think you're going to live?" A long pause. "Of course she did. That Buchanan bitch never did know how to mind her own business," he snarled, then stopped. "You can't talk to me like that, Starla, I'm your husband. No, don't—you can't—" Based on the way the baffled man stared at the phone, Carter was fairly sure Starla had hung up. *Good for her.* He didn't know her well, but her struggles with her husband were well-known, and she seemed like a sweet person and good at her job. Starla had suggested audiobooks for his commute, and it was such a nice way to give his eyes a break from screens and still enjoy a good story. A very economical use of his time.

The office door flew open. "Jason!" Charlie bellowed. "Get in here!" He turned to Carter, straightening his tie. "Sorry about that. What can I do for you, Mr. Carpenter?"

"I've got Martina Lopez's car here for you, she needs her snow tires on."

The redness draining from his face slowly, Charlie scanned the computer screen. "Toyota Corolla?"

"That's the one."

"$115." Carter whipped out his credit card. He'd tell her later about the discrepancy. He would, he promised himself. After he paid, he sat down in the waiting area; it was full of people he didn't know. Jason Miller, Charlie's brother, came in from the garage, wiping his hands on his coveralls, and Charlie motioned him into the office and closed the door. Their conversation was much quieter than his conversation with his wife, but Charlie still looked just as mad.

He knew someone who'd like to know what had just happened here.

Carter: Guess who just left her husband?

Martina: Starla Miller.

Carter: What? How did you know? I literally just heard him on the phone with her.

Martina: She's been planning for months. Half the town knows. Interesting that no one bothered to warn Charlie, though...

Carter: I hope she secured her finances first.

Martina: Always the pragmatist.

Carter: Fine. See if I share juicy gossip with you again.

Martina: You will. You can't help yourself.

Carter: And you owe me fifteen bucks.

Martina: Sorry. Price went up.

Carter: I don't mind covering you.

She went quiet then. He pulled out a tuna sandwich, wishing he'd known he was going to be eating it in an enclosed space, regretting it almost enough to break his personal rule against fast food in order to eat alone. Almost.

Martina: Thanks.
Carter: Anything for you.

That's when it happened: she sent back an emoji with hearts circling the tiny yellow face, the one that means, "I feel loved."

"Yes!" He jumped to his feet, his lunch sack thumping to the floor, completing the move with a fist pump. The other people in the waiting room stared. "Um . . ." He adjusted his tie. "My team's winning."

"What's the score?" a middle-aged man with a bad goatee asked.

"Love all."

"Is that golf?"

"No, tennis."

"I didn't think it was tennis season . . ."

"Doesn't that mean they're tied?" an elderly woman queried, and Carter blushed.

"Great save, on the part of my team." He sat back down and tried to finish his lunch without embarrassing himself further.

"Must be a doubles team," the woman muttered.

CHAPTER TWENTY-FIVE

IT WAS A COLD DAY AT her father's Christmas tree farm, but it was dry, so business was booming. Weekends were always busier anyway, and it was only two weeks until Christmas now. The air smelled like the goats in the petting zoo near the live nativity, the scented cinnamon candles in the arts and crafts section, and of course, complimentary candy canes. When Greg texted her that morning, she was knee-deep in twine and dull saws, trying to keep everyone moving through the baling line.

Greg: Got time to talk?
Martina: Not unless you want to come down to the farm.
Greg: What farm?
Martina: My dad's Christmas tree farm. Tannenbaum.
Greg: Oh, I've seen signs for that. That's yours?
Martina: Yeah. Come get a tree, I'll give you a discount.
Greg: Yeah, okay. I'll be there soon.

She put her phone away and forgot about him immediately in the face of a family trying to get a twenty-foot blue spruce on their minivan. "Sir? Hang on, sir, you're gonna scratch the heck out of the paint on your roof . . ."

When she saw Greg, he'd already picked a pre-cut tree, so she took a cocoa break for the sake of her cold hands, as well as privacy.

"What's up?"

His hands were stuffed deep in his pockets again, and he was rocking on his heels. "So I have kind of a confession to make."

"Oh?"

"Yeah. I was kind of . . . using you." He held up his hands. "It's not that I don't find you attractive, I definitely do. And I think you're a really great nurse and really funny and smart and cool . . . but my heart sort of already belongs to someone else."

"I see," she said, blowing on her drink. She wasn't sure what her face was doing. It probably wasn't what her heart was doing, which was freaking out. Not because she liked him, but because she'd just lost her insurance. And without her insurance, she wasn't sure how she was going to get through the holidays with Carter.

"I was trying to make her jealous," Greg went on, oblivious, "but I don't think she's the jealous type, because it didn't work. Now she's just mad."

"We're talking about Tharushi, right?"

He blushed. "Is it that obvious?"

"Definitely." Martina grinned. "But it's cool. I was using you, too. So don't feel bad. And you're a good kisser, so there's that."

Greg laughed, his blush deepening again, his hands stuffed deep into his coat pockets. "Okay. Well, that was a lot easier than I thought it would be."

"Were you tossing and turning last night, trying to figure out how to let me down gently?"

"Kind of. I mean, there was a rumor that you're into Crash Carpenter, and we were just a casual thing, so I wasn't too worried . . ."

Martina raised an eyebrow at him, and he laughed again.

"Okay, fine, yes! I was worried. I didn't want to hurt you. I didn't think you'd find me interesting enough to go out more than once or twice."

"Oh, I wouldn't have. You read that situation right. You're not my type. Like, at all."

He crossed his arms playfully. "I see you had no qualms about letting *me* down easy."

Martina laughed. "Not really. Your residency will be over soon, and I didn't think you were planning to live here in Timber Falls any longer than necessary."

Greg paled a little. "I wasn't. I mean, I'm probably not."

"They offered you a job at Santiam, didn't they?"

"Yeah," he sighed. "I don't know what to do. I know Tharushi won't stay; she can't wait to get out of here. She's said so more times than I can count."

"Maybe she just needs a reason to stay."

He stared at her, then shook his head. "That's a lot to ask."

"No, it's a lot to offer. You offering to share your life with her, that's what's big. And if she can't see that . . . then she should go, because she doesn't deserve you."

Greg stared at her again, then motioned her forward and enveloped her in a big hug. "Thanks, Martina." He paused. "Also, this is the easiest break-up I've ever had."

"Well, it's easier when you're in love with someone else."

He laughed. "I suppose so. What about you?"

"What about me?"

"Are you and Crash . . . ?"

She shook her head, then stopped. "I don't know. Time will tell, I guess." She pulled a wrapped candy cane out of her pocket. "Merry Christmas, Greg. I didn't get you a present yet."

He smiled as he accepted the candy. "Merry Christmas, Martina. I hope you get a happy ending under your tree this year."

CHAPTER
TWENTY-SIX

WHEN CARTER CAME HOME on Monday night, Martina was ready for him. She'd hidden the troll in the gym, and since he always went running outside, she was confident it would be at least a week before he found it. He'd had to stay at work late for an important meeting, but since he'd let them know the night before, she'd been able to prepare Willow, more or less.

"Is there anything I can do for you today?" he asked while he was still taking off his tie.

Martina swallowed. "Yeah, I wanted to ask you something."

"Shoot." He stabbed at his salmon. "Your mom wants to go golfing."

"Okay. That's fine. You've still got my card, right?"

She huffed. "It's not a matter of money. I don't know how to play golf."

"She does. She'll show you."

"No, honey, she doesn't."

Carter's gaze fell to his plate, and he pushed some of the fish around with his fork like he was looking for bones. "Right."

"I mean, she knows how to do it herself; that's the interesting thing about muscle memory. If we put a golf club in her hand, she'll know what to do. But she can't teach me how, she can't explain it. Does that make sense?"

He nodded, still focused on his food.

"I thought maybe you could come with us," she hurried on, not wanting to watch him be sad anymore. "Nurse Dennard had a family event on Saturday, so I'm filling in for her. I thought the three of us could go together, maybe, or . . ."

"Yes." He looked up, the sadness fading. "That sounds fun. Let's do that." He swallowed. "You want to bring Greg along?"

"Oh. No, we're not together anymore." She traced the veins in the quartz countertop with her finger, pointedly avoiding his gaze. She did not want to know what he thought of that.

"I'm sorry." His voice was light, too controlled. It was his fake, parent-appeasing voice. "But we'll have fun, just the three of us."

"Well," she hedged, "I don't know if it'll actually be fun. I'll probably end up chasing the balls a lot."

Unfortunately, Carter was taking a drink, and he laughed hard enough for water to come out his nose. Without thinking, Martina surged forward, concerned, as he coughed over the sink. She passed him a towel and patted his back until he could breathe again.

"It wasn't *that* funny . . ." she chided.

"Yeah, it was. I don't chase balls, Tini. I just buy more." She pursed her lips in a grimace, and he laughed again. "You definitely need my help."

"You're a sucky teacher, though. You got so mad at me when you tried to teach me to drive stick."

"That's because you were burning out my clutch," he said, his indignation loud enough to ring off the cabinets in the large kitchen. "I could smell it. I could *smell s*moke in my car!"

"It wasn't that bad," she said, but her grin was guilty.

"Might have to touch you if I'm going to teach you golf," he said, picking through his food again, pushing the lemon slice off to the side. "You gonna be okay with that?"

"Sure, yes. Of course. That's friendly touching. We'll be in public. There's nothing sensual about it."

Carter nodded slowly, setting down his plate. "You sure about that?" He dusted off his hands as he strolled over to her. "I think you'd better show me what I can do."

"What do you mean?" She felt her cheeks heating. He wanted to touch her? Here? Now? In the kitchen, at night? The household staff was nowhere around, but the pots and pans were still dripping. Mrs. Sánchez would be back to put them away in a few minutes before she went home. And Harrison was probably in the study . . . if he caught them . . .

"I mean, show me what I can do."

"Carter," she glowered, "when I said I don't know how to play golf, I meant *I don't know how to play golf.* How the hell should I know what you can do? Aren't I just swinging a big metal club around? Why does that require touching at all?"

"Well," he said, his voice low. "You might need help adjusting your grip."

"My . . . grip?"

"Yeah, you know, your grip—here," he said, handing her a thin, modern rolling pin from the drying rack. "Here, this is about the right diameter. Now, hold it out in front of you like a club."

She held it in her fists, pointing down at the ground, glancing up at him anxiously. "Like this?"

"No, you've kinda gotta . . . weave your fingers together."

Martina looked down at her hands, then interlocked her fingers as if in prayer. "Like this?"

"No, not all your fingers, just some of them . . ."

She looked up at him, annoyed. "Like I said: a sucky teacher."

Carter fluffed his hair with one hand. "But if I could touch you, I could you show you, that's what I'm saying. I just want to make sure you're okay with that."

"Fine, so just show me with *your* hands. It's not that hard."

He edged closer. "What if I need to correct your posture?"

She blinked at him. "What? That sounds bogus."

"No, no," he chuckled. "It's important. If your posture's bad, the ball's going to go off in some crazy direction." His laughter drew her forward like he'd lassoed her with it.

"How do you do that?" She sounded like a breathy fool. She could hear it, but she couldn't stop it.

"Well," he said, turning her gently, "the easiest way is to just cozy up behind you and help you with the angle. Teach you what it feels like." His voice was rougher than the edge of the fairway. He fit his arms over hers, correcting her hold on the rolling pin, their fingers tangling. Tangling was happening inside, too . . . Martina tried to ignore it, but his strong hands over hers weren't helping, and she could feel the heat from his chest radiating against her back. All she had to do was lean back an inch, and they'd be pressed together. "See how that'll work better? Make sure you keep your head down, even when you swing. Keep your focus on the ball."

"Like baseball. Check."

"Like most games that involve a ball. Let's do a practice swing. Straight arms," he coached, pulling the rolling pin back, then swinging it forward smoothly. "Keep your hips square. Widen your stance a little. And bend your knees."

"You're giving me too much to think about," she grumped, and her bird's nest of confused thoughts was not made better by his nose brushing her cheek for just a heartbeat.

"I'm sorry," he whispered. "You're right, I'm a crap teacher. I guess we'll be losing a lot of balls." She pivoted to see him better, and for a moment, she was sixteen again, flustered by his sideways glances in trigonometry, craning her neck for a glimpse of him on the soccer field, hanging around Annie's, hoping he'd show up.

"You can afford it," she said, giving him a smile she knew would bring out her dimples. Carter's pupils were blown out like he was high, but she knew he wasn't; it was them. It was the way they were together, the highest highs and the lowest lows, mercurial as Oregon's winter weather. A flash of gray appeared in her peripheral vision, and she heard Mrs. Sánchez gasp softly.

"Excuse me, I didn't mean to interrupt," she said, backing out of the kitchen. Carter stepped back quickly as Martina brought up her hand to stop her, still holding the rolling pin. "You're not intruding, there's nothing happening," she assured her. "Really. Please, come finish your work, I know you're tired."

Mrs. Sánchez warily came back into the kitchen, and Carter avoided looking at both of them by finishing his dinner as quickly as possible, shoveling the cold food into his mouth in huge bites, then rinsing the plate himself and putting it into the dishwasher.

"I'm going to take off," Martina said to his back, and he nodded.

"Wear something nice; the club has a dress code." He was already at the kitchen door into the black hallway. "See you tomorrow."

"Yes, looking forward to it," she called after him, but he was gone.

"I'm sorry, sweetheart," Mrs. Sánchez whispered, wiping her hands on a tea towel. "I didn't know."

"There's nothing to know." Martina put the rolling pin away and slammed the drawer shut too hard, wincing at the sound.

"Okay."

"I mean, the agency said there can be nothing, so there must be nothing." Why did Greg have to dump her now? Couldn't they have continued the charade just a few more weeks, just through the new year? She didn't even have a date to Winnie's wedding now . . .

"Yes, I understand, but . . ."

"But what?"

"But when she is gone, surely . . ."

Martina held up a hand. "I can't think about that yet. That could be years away . . ."

"He's not worth the wait?"

Of course he is. But worth sacrificing my career? That I don't know.

CHAPTER
TWENTY-SEVEN

SALEM GOLF CLUB WITH its serene red-roofed club-house, manicured landscaping and perfectly-pressed occupants felt like another world to Martina . . . the Carpenters' world. She'd rush-ordered a white golf skirt, which she now tugged down her legs as they walked into the main entrance. She'd have preferred to try something on first, but there was no time. And she'd underestimated how this was going to ride up on her long legs, especially given that she was curvier than the stick-thin model they'd pictured online.

"You look nice," Carter whispered as they reached the front doors. He opened it for the ladies, then followed them inside. *He has his good manners on today.* Martina let her eyes wander around the clubhouse while Carter paid and arranged for clubs for her and a cart. She was careful to keep Willow in her peripheral vision; she was having a good day, but that guaranteed nothing. The smell of roasted potatoes, eggs Benedict, and smoked salmon mingled with leather. Carved wood and old photos filled the walls, and it impressed upon her a sense of history; it wasn't as stuffy as she'd imagined it would be.

"Well, look who it is. Mrs. Carpenter! It's nice to see you again!"

A man in a green synthetic polo shirt—one of the golf
pros, she'd guess—was walking over to Willow, hand extended,
and Martina stepped quickly to join her at her elbow. Willow
smiled and shook his hand, but didn't seem to be able to start a
conversation with him.

"Hello, I'm her assistant, Martina," she said, reaching out
for his hand as well. "Willow's going to show me the ropes today." She'd already decided in the car that she was going to describe herself in the way that put Willow in the best light. Besides, it was true: she did assist her with many things.

"Well, she always was a natural," he said, smiling. "I'm Stan
Gross."

"Great to meet you, Mr. Gross."

He turned back to Willow. "So what have you been up to?
We haven't gotten an invite yet for the Rotary Club ball; is that
still happening this year? We're coming up on it, right?"

Willow opened and closed her mouth a few times, and
Martina waited patiently until she turned to her with helpless,
slightly desperate eyes. She interlocked their arms, knowing the
contact would help Willow settle.

"You know, she hasn't been involved this year."

"That's right," Willow said, her throat sounding a bit raspy.
"I thought I'd let the younger generation have a crack at it."

She and Mr. Gross laughed, and Martina chuckled along,
but that rasp had her worried. Acid reflux was a common side
effect of her Alzheimer's meds, and she wanted to head off any
problems well in advance. She made a mental note to examine
her throat at the next opportunity to do so in private as Carter
re-joined them.

"Stan, you know my son, Carter."

"Yes, good to see you again," Stan said, giving him a firm handshake. "My wife's thrilled to have you for the bachelor charity auction for Doernbecher Children's Hospital. You brought in a lot of donations last year."

I'll bet he did. Jealousy stabbed at her from behind.

"You still working on that slice?"

"Yes, sir," he said, smiling politely, "when I get the time. I've been pretty busy down at Greenfield lately."

"You're selling insurance now? I've been thinking of adjusting my umbrella coverage . . ."

"No, sir. I'm an actuary. But I'm sure they could take good care of you if you come down to the office." He gave Stan a business card, and Martina tried not to be impressed by his grown-up demeanor. They all shook hands again, and Carter shepherded them toward the carts. She had to try out a set of clubs for size, and she tried to remember what he'd taught her in the kitchen the other night. Then she was helping Willow into the cart for balance, and he was driving the cart along the asphalt path at top speed, all of five miles an hour.

"Why do you get to drive?" Martina asked from the back seat.

He looked at her over his shoulder. "Because I assume your driving is as good as it always was."

"My driving is excellent, thank you."

"If you're on the Formula One circuit, then I agree."

"Ha ha ha," she said mockingly, and his eyes went all crinkly as he grinned at her. They got out of the cart and approached the first hole. "Maybe you could help her pick a club," Martina prompted, touching his elbow. He nodded and handed her a large-headed club.

"The bigger the head, the farther it goes," he explained.
"This first hole has a few closer tees, so that should make it easier."

"A ladies' tee?" She snorted. "Isn't that a little sexist?"

He adjusted his sunglasses, and she recognized the move as
one he went to when he needed patience. She didn't want to
make him regret coming with them.

"I believe they're now colored, not coordinated to one's sex
or gender."

"Oh."

"Is it good exercise?"

"What?"

"Jumping to conclusions like that?"

Martina elbowed him playfully, and he grinned, elbowing
her back. They watched side by side as Willow lined up for her
shot. Martina felt her heart lift, seeing Willow 'just know' what
to do, her body moving with grace and poise as she pulled back
the club and connected with the ball. Her shot was pure poet-
ry; high, long, and straight. They all sheltered their eyes, watching it fly. Then the moment was gone, and she turned to them
with childlike uncertainty.

"Was that a good one?" She knew how to play, but she
didn't know how to win.

In unison, she and Carter both began to applaud her, and
she beamed. She even put the club back in the bag instead of
laying it down on the tee.

"All right, your turn," Carter said, ushering her forward
with a gentle hand at her back.

"Maybe I should watch for a few holes," she balked. She was
going to be bad at this and she was at *work*. She especially didn't

like looking incompetent at work. Yet it didn't feel like work when Carter wrapped himself around her from behind, shielding her from the wind, arranging her hands on the grip of the driver. He adjusted her stance, bending her forward with careful hands, and yet it still felt as intimate as it had when they were alone in the dimly-lit kitchen. At least they were mostly alone out here, and with the weather looking drizzly, there shouldn't be too many other people wanting to play through.

"Just stay loose, try to keep your elbows straight, and look at the ball, not the fairway."

"Okay. One question."

"Yes?"

"What's a fairway?"

Carter laughed into her shoulder, his body shaking behind hers. "This is gonna be great, just great. I can take a video, right?"

"No, you may not, Carter James Carpenter and don't you even—where's your mom?"

They straightened, looking around. The cart was still there. The only sound they heard was the sound of the creek bubbling along between evergreens, and the wind bent the willow boughs. A starling pecked in the grass. Carter cursed under his breath.

"Mom?"

"Willow?" The wind carried her voice away, so she called louder. "Willow!" No answer.

"Shit, shit, shit," Carter said, clasping his hands behind his neck. "What do we do?"

"Okay," Martina said, holding him by the upper arms to keep him from pacing away. "She's gotta be close by; we were only distracted for a few minutes. I'll run back to the clubhouse and see if she went that way, and you try to catch up with her. Call when you find her."

"She's gonna get hit with a golf ball, she's gonna crash a cart into the creek..."

"Crash." She put her hands on his cheeks to capture his worried gaze. "Don't panic. Just go to the next tee. She's probably just trying to keep playing, and she didn't think to wait for us. Hurry. Go." She released him and turned and ran back up the hill toward the clubhouse, suddenly very unconcerned about whether or not her outfit was okay. She slipped into the clubhouse, trying to slow her heavy breathing, so as not to attract attention to herself or the situation. Stan Gross was talking to two men in the lobby, and she quickly went over to him.

"I'm so sorry to interrupt, Mr. Gross, but have you seen Mrs. Carpenter? We seem to have gotten separated..."

He blinked. "Oh. Did you try calling her?"

Geez. That felt so obvious now. "No, I didn't. Thank you, I'll try that."

"I've been standing here since you left, and I didn't see her come back in."

"Thank you. I have to go..."

"Wait," he reached toward her, but didn't touch her. "Is she ...okay? She seemed quiet. Different."

Martina paused. Now really wasn't the time, and she hadn't talked to Carter about disclosing his mother's condition to anyone. So she just smiled and lied. "She's fine. I really do need to go. Thanks for your help. Really."

She dialed Willow's number, and she answered on the second ring. "Hello?"

"Willow, it's Martina, your assistant."

"Oh, Martina." She could hear her crying. "Help me, I don't know where I am."

"You're at the Salem Golf Club," Martina said, trying to stay calm. "Can you tell me what you see when you look around? I'm looking for you, and it'll help me find you if you can give me some clues."

"Sinks. And toilets." *The bathroom.* Martina sighed with relief. That was a fairly safe place to be. "And urinals."

Shit, she's in the men's room. Martina stopped a caddie. "Excuse me, where are the restrooms?" He pointed down a long hallway near the restaurant. "Thank you." Martina heard the beep of an incoming call and realized it must be Carter, freaking out when he didn't find Willow at the second tee. She wished she could answer and assuage his fear, but it was more important to support Willow and stay on the line with her. "All right, Willow, I'm coming. I'm on my way. Just hang tight." She could hardly keep her feet to a walk; she felt like a racehorse at the bell, ready to sprint to her as fast she could.

A man was coming out of the restroom, looking mildly perplexed, still drying his hands on a paper towel. "Excuse me, sir, is there a blonde woman in there?"

"Yeah, I was just about to talk to the manager . . ."

"Oh, please don't. That's my patient; she's got Alzheimer's and she wandered away while I was . . ." *Flirting.* That was the hard truth. This was her fault.

"This lady was pretty young . . ." He didn't seem convinced that she was telling the truth.

"Yes, sir, it's early-onset Alzheimer's. Are there any other men in there?"

"No, just me."

"Okay, I'm going to go in and get her. So sorry about this."
She rushed past him without waiting for a response. "Willow?"

"Hello?" Her voice was small. Martina hung up the phone
and hurried inside.

"There you are," she said, keeping her voice warm. "We've
been looking for you. Is everything okay? I'm so glad we found
you."

Willow's hug felt more like an attack, meant to squeeze
every molecule of air out of her lungs. "You found me."

Martina stroked her hair soothingly. "Of course I did! I'll
always find you when you're lost. I'm going to take good care of
you."

"I was scared."

"That's totally understandable. I'd be scared, too, in your
shoes."

"I don't know how I got here . . . where's Carter?"

"Oh shit." Martina let go of Willow, but Willow didn't let
go of her. She held up her phone and tried to see it over Willow's shoulder as she typed with her thumbs.

Martina: Found W, we R OK.
Carter: Where are you?

Before she could answer, the phone rang. She put it on
speaker.

"Where are you?" He only sounded a little panicked.

"We're in the men's restroom in the clubhouse. Also, Willow, do you think we could leave now? Let the men of the golf
club do their business with a little privacy?"

"Good idea," Willow agreed, letting go finally, getting a tissue to wipe her running mascara. "I don't care for the odor in here, anyway."

"We'll be in the restaurant, Carter; can you meet us there?"

"Yes. I'm on my way."

She hung up and slung an arm around Willow's thin shoulders. "You know, it's a shame you can't be the designated driver. I could really go for a beer right now."

"That's funny. Because I don't drive."

"Right," Martina grinned, and Willow smiled back.

They'd just found a table when Carter found them. He was sweating hard and he collapsed into the leather chair with zero decorum. "That was the longest hour of my life."

"It was more like ten minutes."

"I don't see how that could be true. And you're driving home." He signaled the waiter. "A beer, please. Anything cold." Carter put his head down between his knees for a minute, still trying to slow his breathing.

"He seems upset," Willow noted.

"Yes, he is upset."

"Is it because we didn't get to go golfing?"

Carter's shoulders began to shake, and Martina hoped to God he wasn't crying that hard. She was going to have enough trouble getting the three of them out of this golf club without setting the Timber Falls rumor mill aflame. But when he sat up, he was laughing. He picked up his mom's hand and kissed the back of it. "No, it's not because we didn't get to go golfing. Do you want to know a secret?"

Willow nodded, transfixed by him.

He leaned closer to her and whispered, "I don't even like golfing. I only came because you like it."

"Oh, I don't like golfing. I only play because your father likes it. Where is he, anyway?" Carter and Martina stared at each other in wonder; she couldn't believe her ears. Willow had never mentioned inviting Harrison, not that Martina would have even if she had. But it broke her heart a little that Willow was still trying to play the part of dutiful wife. She was a far better person than Martina would be in her shoes.

"He, uh, he stayed home today," Carter said, and Martina thought it was a good cover.

Willow huffed impatiently. "Then why are we even here?"

"I feel like that's a question we're all asking, Mom," Carter said, straight-faced. Then he snickered.

"Don't," Martina said, giggling for a moment before she sobered. "If you get me started, I'm not going to be able to stop."

He put his fist in front of his mouth, like he was trying to stuff the laughter back in, but it wasn't working.

"Don't," Martina said, laughing again. "Don't. Seriously, Carter." She looked around. "Let's not make a scene in this fancy golf club, all right?"

"Too late. I'm gonna get drunk and make you drag me out of here."

"Welcome back, High School Crash. I did not miss you."

He laughed. "I never did that to you."

"Only because you didn't want to get arrested. There was the time you got drunk at Elk Lake after we took the ATVs up there with the soccer team. Trying to wrangle all of you plus the vehicles back onto the trailer, then drive it down the mountain myself? Not so fun."

He put a hand over his mouth. "Present Me would like to apologize for Past Me, on so many levels."

"Apology accepted." She held his gaze for a long moment, and she knew they weren't just talking about the ATVs.

The waiter brought Carter's beer and Martina and Willow's raspberry kombucha. Carter lifted an eyebrow at her choice.

"What?"

"Nothing," he laughed, but his eyes . . . they had the kind of pixie-dust sparkle that usually preceded a kiss, and in her heart, she wanted that. She wanted his teasing and his kisses and his touch. *I did miss* this *Crash, the one who adored me.* There was no denying it anymore. She needed him back. She needed him.

This was going to be complicated. And there was no way he was doing that bachelor auction.

CHAPTER
TWENTY-EIGHT

"I'M GOING TO WRITE a book on this someday," Carter announced. They were in the kitchen, sitting on stools at the island, eating brownies and ice cream Mrs. Sánchez had made after she heard about their day. Willow had been asleep for an hour; they'd nearly lost her at dinner, when she nodded off so hard she startled herself. Martina had hurried her upstairs, praying she wouldn't hurt herself on the way.

"On employing your ex-girlfriend or on living with an early-onset AD patient?"

"The second one."

"That's the way I'd go, too."

"And today has inspired a chapter called, 'How to take someone with AD golfing.'"

"And what will you write in this chapter?"

"It's a short one," he said, taking a sip of his beer. "'Don't.'"

The laughter started as a tremor in her abs, shaking its way up into her chest and shoulders. She couldn't hope to hold it in, but she slapped a hand over her mouth, even as tears filled her eyes and spilled over. She was completely silent, but her body was wracked with laughter; she hadn't laughed so hard in years. She tipped over, resting her head on his shaking shoulder, unable to support her own weight. Mrs. Sánchez appeared in the doorway.

"Everything is okay?"

They nodded, still laughing, and she smiled at them as she left. "Good night."

"Good night," they called after her, still laughing. Carter lifted his arm and draped it around her shoulders, pulling her against his side. "That was a day."

"That *was* a day," she agreed. And then more tears started coming that tasted like sadness and fear instead of laughter. "But it was my fault."

"Whoa, whoa, whoa. Brakes, please."

"No, it was. I was distracted. I was too focused on—" *you* "—the game, and I should have known better."

"I can't believe I'm saying this, but remember the online classes you sent me? I actually took them. All of them. And do you know what lesson one was about? Wandering. Because people with Alzheimer's wander, at all stages of the disease."

"But I'm a *professional*," she lamented, the tears coming harder now. "It's not supposed to take *me* by surprise."

Carter laughed, wiping the tears from her face with his thumbs. Then he kissed her, like he did it every day. It was the type of casual kiss between long-time lovers that one thinks nothing of; a kiss when leaving for work, a kiss when getting home from the store. A kiss at the mailbox because your tax refund finally came and now you can buy that TV you've both been wanting. Entirely natural. So natural that Martina gave him one back. Carter kissed her again, a little longer this time, the warmth of his lips both calming and exciting. And when he drew back, she followed him; it wasn't even conscious at this point. She felt pulled toward him by his wood sage and sea salt cologne. They both stumbled off their stools to stand in front of each other, the heat of their bodies ricocheting between them as they passed innocent kisses back and forth. He touched her hair, letting his hands drift down the length of it, wrapping his fists in it, even as the kisses increased in duration and intensity. She stayed focused solely on his lips, not letting her gaze stray to meet his. Because if she looked into his eyes, she'd know for sure whether he regretted this instead of just fearing that he did. And if she looked into his eyes, he'd know how badly she wanted this, wanted even more, which she had no right to ask for. He'd know that her soul had finally come out of hiding just now. She wrapped her arms around his neck, and she felt his hot hands on her hips, drawing her closer. Then on her next turn, eyes squeezed shut, she nipped at his bottom lip, and he groaned. Carter's French kisses were even sweeter than she remembered, and she relaxed into his embrace. What had they been talking about before? She couldn't remember. Oh, right. She's a *professional*. Crap.

She'd promised, and she never broke her promises. And that *didn't* feel amazing. Dread pooled in her belly. She could not get fired. But she definitely wanted to do more of this. She wanted to consider her options, but it was very hard to think with Carter touching her like that, so reverently and alluringly at the same time. She'd need to stop kissing him back. That didn't seem likely to happen any time soon without divine intervention. She waited for it. Nothing happened. It seemed that God unfortunately wanted her to woman up and deal with her own choices.

When she dodged his lips, he moved his kisses to her neck. "Carter . . ."

"Yeah?"

She was supposed to be moving back a little, getting some perspective, but her traitorous mouth kept saying things like "yes" and "that feels good" and "missed you so much."

"I missed you, too, Tini," Carter panted. Then, without her having to ask, he stopped. "We should . . . we should talk, right?"

"Yes," she said, nodding. "We should talk." He was still holding her, and she looked up into his ice-blue eyes. They were melting, heated and affectionate, but she saw no trace of regret, and she felt the tension bleed from her neck and shoulders.

"I still love you, Martina." He kissed her again, just a little one, and it felt suspiciously like he was trying to keep her from replying. "I want to be together."

"I . . ." she swallowed hard. "I love you, too."

As if this settled the matter, he beamed at her like she'd just crowned him king and leaned forward to kiss her again.

She put a hand on his chest. "But . . ."

He paused. "But?"

"But this is complicated for me, Carter. My contract is very clear: I am not allowed to fraternize with my boss."

"So quit and come work for me directly . . ." He managed to land a sweet kiss just below her ear.

"Also not allowed. I signed a non-compete. If I take you on as a client and cut her out, she could sue me. I can't afford that."

"I can," he said. "No problem."

"But what if something happens between us and you fire me? Who would I work for then? Go back to the hospital? I don't want to be blackballed in the community." She sat down hard on her stool with a sigh. After a long moment, he sat down, too.

"Okay. I hear you. I guess I didn't think about it how it might unfold for you . . . but those are some serious risks." He let his gaze fall to the wooden floor, and she could almost hear what he was thinking. *And I don't know if I'm worth it to you.*

"You are incredibly important to me. But so is Willow, and I know it would be difficult for you to find a replacement for me." She reached out and took his hand. "I'd like some time to think about this. To figure out what to do."

He nodded slowly, then gave a rueful smile. "I've decided: adulting sucks sometimes."

Martina chuckled. "Why, because High School Crash would be carrying me upstairs like a fireman right now?"

"Adult Carter was tempted, too. But he decided to talk things over first."

She tried to smile at him reassuringly. "He missed his chance."

"I hope not," Carter said softly, then frowned. "Not for sex, for . . . all of it. For a relationship with you again."

"No, I know." She paused, attempting to collect her courage from wherever she'd cast it off earlier. "Let's just press pause here. I'm gonna take a few days off, and then we can talk."

"Martina, what happened at the golf course, it really wasn't your fault. These things happen. Please don't feel responsible."

"It's not just that, it's . . ." She dared to look into his eyes. "Everything."

"I understand." But he looked crestfallen again, and that made her want to kiss him. She put her hands on his chest, and he looked down at her, his eyes troubled.

"Trust me, okay?" she said.

"Yeah, I do. I trust you." He swallowed. "Can I text you?"

"Sure."

"Can I call you?"

She smiled. "Yes, that'd be fine."

"Can I come over?"

Her smile grew. "That's probably not a great idea, especially given that I'm supposed to be figuring out if we can make this work."

"We can." He tangled their fingers and kissed the back of her hand. "I know we can. I'll do whatever it takes."

"Even fire me?"

The puppy-dog eyes were back.

"Ugh. Crash, put those away!"

"Why?" He grinned. "Are they getting to you?"

"Yes!" She pushed at his shoulder, and he laughed. "They always did."

He sobered. "I'm not firing you. Please don't ask me to. We'll work this out."

"Okay." She leaned into him again, looking at his lips long-ingly.

"You want another kiss?" he teased, and she nodded, giving him the puppy-dog eyes, and he laughed.

"Okay, but just one," he breathed, pinning her against the island, and she smiled as his lips met hers again and again.

CHAPTER
TWENTY-NINE

MARTINA WAS IN THE bath. It smelled like peppermint, which reminded her that it was Christmas Eve. She sighed, and the bubbles in front of her went flying. She'd been gone from work for two days, and she was already antsy to get back. But she hadn't figured out any solutions while she'd been out. And Carter was trying to take care of his mom by himself, which was not a great solution for a lot of reasons.

Carter: What do I do when she says she wants to go home?

Carter: I tried telling her she *was* home, and it went over like a lead balloon.

Martina: Listen to the feeling behind the words: she feels scared that I'm not there.

Carter: Okay, so . . .

Carter: Tell her she's safe here?

Martina: That's a good start. And tell her she can go home in a few minutes, then try to get her distracted by something else. A puzzle, a TV show, a nap. Maybe she wants to water the pansies we planted last week.

Carter: We'll try pansies. Thanks.

Carter: Also, when do you think you might be back? She just threw a shoe at me.

Martina: Stiletto?

Carter: No, a ballet flat.

Martina: Aw, that's nothing.

Carter: Also, I miss you. And not just because you're an amazing nurse.

Martina: I miss you, too.

She wanted to hug the phone to her chest, but she was wet. She was just reaching to put it down by her red-and-white-striped candle when she noticed an email notification. **Your contract has been terminated.** She sat up quickly, sloshing water out of the tub and onto the floor, nearly dropping her phone into the bathtub. She didn't want to be naked when she read this; she hurried to get her robe on and get to her bedroom. Snow White, Rajah, and Charming were snuggled up together on her bed, but Rajah hissed and jumped down when she sat down.

Dear Ms. Lopez,

I'm sorry to have to send this on Christmas Eve, but it can't wait. It has been brought to our attention that you have violated the terms of your contract by fraternizing with the person who contracted your employment. We were sent digital evidence of you and Carter Carpenter engaged in intimate physical activity in the home where your patient resides. Since we cannot be liable for such relationships in a place of business, this contract has been terminated by Partners in Care. If you feel this in error, you may contact us at 503-819...

Digital evidence? Who in the world would have digital . . . Harrison. He must have used the closed circuit video feed. He'd been watching them, waiting for her to screw up. She let her chin fall to her chest.

Martina: I got fired.
Carter: Honey, that's not amusing.
Martina: Not a joke.

The phone rang. She answered, flopping back onto her bed. "Tell me you're joking."

"Nope. Just got an email. I think it was your dad. Did you let him onto the closed circuit feed?"

"Yeah, he said . . ." Carter cursed. "He said he wanted to be able to check on Mom during the day. I should've seen right through that."

"Do you think we should put out a hit on him?" Martina asked. It was a joke, but it wasn't funny, and no one laughed.

"I don't know. Who do we know who hates Harrison more than we do?" He paused, thinking. "Wait. I might be able to answer that. I need some time." He paused. "Don't call Santiam for your old job back yet, okay? Just . . . just wait."

"Okay, I'll wait."

"Don't panic, okay?"

"I'm panicking a little bit."

"No, no. I think I can fix this. Just . . . I'll talk to you tomorrow. Don't do anything."

He hung up without saying goodbye and Martina let the phone slip through her fingers and fall onto the bed. She lay there a long time with her eyes closed, eyes burning with unshed tears.

"MERRY CHRISTMAS, SON." Harrison was waiting at the bottom of the stairs the next morning, still in his pajamas and robe, coffee in hand. Mrs. Sánchez had the morning off; he must have made it himself. Nice to know he still knew how. Ignoring him entirely, Carter went into the kitchen and found his mom sitting at the island, eating scrambled eggs and a cinnamon roll. He helped himself to a pastry, wrapping it up in a paper towel for the road.

"Look, I'm sure you're upset about the photos . . ."

Carter scoffed, but said nothing. He gave his mom a kiss on the forehead. "Someone new is coming to be with you today, Mom."

"Who?"

"I don't know yet."

"When's Martina coming back?" she asked.

"Soon, I hope." He glared at Harrison. "Very soon."

"I did the right thing," his father said, his voice low. "She would've used you. It's better this way."

Don't shout. Don't play his game. Don't scare Mom. Just ignore him. Ignore him, and then go fix this.

"What's he talking about?" Willow asked, her eyebrows in a deep V. She was more used to Harrison's presence now, but he still seemed to unsettle her.

"Nothing." The doorbell rang, and his parents both straightened. Carter went to open it himself and winced when he saw Cindy's smiling face.

"I'm so sorry, Cindy. It's really important or I wouldn't have asked."

She waved away his apology. "One of the perils of small business ownership. It's just me and Mr. Hewes today anyway. The grandkids don't come until tomorrow."

"I should be back tonight. Her meds are clearly marked in the cupboard by the microwave," he said, handing her the key.

"Wait, where do you think you're going? It's Christmas morning," Harrison protested, chuckling as if this were a joke. "Don't you want to open your presents?"

Carter turned to look at his father's face for the first time that morning, and he poured all his burning resentment toward the man into his gaze like a lava flow. He had done nothing but screw things up ever since Thanksgiving, and this was the final straw.

"The only thing I want is for you to leave me alone." To his credit, Harrison actually took a step back before he caught himself; apparently, even a snake like his father could recognize when he was in physical danger. Turning his back on the man, he put on his tattered running shoes and his wool pea coat. He hoped the rehab center didn't have a dress code, because this was the best he could do today.

The drive to Bend felt longer than two hours, despite the traffic being light. Carter put on an audio book, a thriller he'd gotten from the library, but he couldn't concentrate. He wished he'd been more proactive about planning out what he was going to say to his brother. The huge evergreens gave way to smaller, scrubbier juniper as far as he could see as he left Sisters. He liked Bend; if he was being honest, it appealed to him more than Portland. It was smaller, less industrial, less corporate, and more cowboy. And if he moved here with Martina, she'd probably die of happiness when she saw all the places she could get tempeh. He chuckled into the quiet air of the car at the thought. It wasn't too early to be planning a future. Mrs. Sánchez had been right; he didn't give himself enough credit. He had good instincts. He wasn't the same person who'd screwed up with her before. Fear wasn't his MO anymore. That was funny, too, because anyone examining High School Crash and Adult Carter side by side would definitely ID his younger self as the confident one. But he was learning to reach for his own opinions instead of spouting what he knew would be popular or socially acceptable. So much of their high school years, for both him and Martina, had been about their image, their "friendships." His father had always been talking about making connections . . . the kind of schmoozy behavior he now left to the salesmen at work. But following that advice, he'd lost that connection with himself that he craved, that sense of what he knew was right in his gut. He felt it when he was with her. He felt strong, like his truest self was outlined in black instead of its usual fuzzy gray.

As Carter drove up to the rehab center, which was actually closer to Redmond than Bend, nestled along the Crooked River, he admired the amazing view of Smith Rock. He wondered if he'd still like rock climbing, now that he wasn't constantly chasing a high just to feel something. He parked in visitor parking and walked up to the big front door, nervously adjusting his baseball cap. He felt weird showing up here on Christmas Day to ask for a favor, especially with so many other families here to celebrate. He hadn't even brought his brother a present. A woman in a long, white flowing skirt with hair to match greeted him. "You must be Carter; you're just in time for lunch. Chase just hopped in the shower, since he was out with the horses this morning."

"Great. Thanks." He sat down on a bench made of twisted wood, raw and strange, yet functional. Chase came down a few minutes later, finger-combing his wet hair.

"Hey, man!" He greeted him with a bear hug.

"Hey."

"It's great to see you. Merry Christmas."

"Yeah, Merry Christmas. Great to see you, too." He looked around the lobby of the huge house, searching for something to talk about. "So you were out with the horses?"

"Yeah."

"I didn't think you liked animals."

"I didn't used to." Chase led him down a hall, out the back door onto a porch with heaters. "I felt weird being in here by myself with everybody else's families. I'm learning all kinds of things about myself here. The horses help my anxiety."

It was strange; Chase had never shared that diagnosis with him before, but as soon as he said it, Carter felt like he had all the corner pieces to the puzzle that was his brother. His nervous stomach, his sweatiness, his restlessness. The way he never seemed to sleep well, the way he snapped at people.

"Huh." He couldn't think of anything else to say. "Look, I came here to ask you something, and I kind of need to get it out before I change my mind."

"Shoot."

Carter took a deep breath. "I need you to take over the payments for Martina."

His brother's eyebrows dipped in concern. "Your trust low?"

"No, my trust is fine. But they canceled our contract, since she's not allowed to date her employer, and Harrison sent them a picture of me kissing her. So I need *you* to be her employer."

The happy smile that had been spreading across Chase's face fell immediately. "Dad did that? He sabotaged you?"

"Yeah, he's never liked—"

"I hate him. I hate him so much."

"I know." Their interaction this morning was still weighing on him. He liked to think he was an even-keeled person, but Harrison brought out all the storminess in him. His brother's jaw was still clenched, and he closed his eyes for a long moment, breathing in and out slowly. When they opened again, he was smiling again.

"Well, we won't let him win. I knew you two would patch things up."

"Well, they're not patched yet, but we're going to try. And this is a big responsibility, Chase. If you don't pay her, Partners in Care will cancel our contract. They had a very strict policy about on-time payments."

"I can handle it."

"I'd be depending on you. We both would."

"I want to do this for you. I'm not gonna screw it up this time. I swear. And I'm sure as heck not going to let Harrison win."

"I'm not trying to be a jerk, but you said that before. You looked right into my eyes and lied to me." Carter steeled himself for dramatics: yelling, pushing, turned over tables or chairs, stomping off.

Chase scooted his chair closer. "I know. You're right, that's true. And I'm sorry. I really am. But all I can do is be a better person from here on out. And I'd really like this opportunity to prove it to you." Since he was the one who'd asked, he had to agree, but it didn't help the wormy, uncomfortable feeling in his gut. He wanted to trust him, but Chase's track record was . . . bad. And this felt too easy. Yet there was definitely something different about Chase. He'd always had kind of a frantic way about him, an edge, even before he was using. That wasn't there now. His hair was longer, and it looked like it was by choice. He wasn't in constant motion, wasn't dominating the conversation or being belligerent and overbearing.

"Okay. I'll wire the money to you on the tenth, and it's due on the fifteenth."

"No." Chase was forceful. "I want to help. My trust is just sitting there. Seriously. Let me do this."

"You're sure?"

"Yes."

Carter paused. "Really sure?"

"Dude! Yes! Come 'ere," he said, pulling him into a hug. "I can't believe you got your girl back. That's amazing. I'm so happy for you."

Carter felt his lower lip trembling, but he couldn't stop it. They'd been fairly close in the past, but up until recently, this warm kind of brotherly affection had been absent. But it still fit just right in the hole in his heart. One of them, anyway. "Thanks," he whispered, hugging him back, burying his face into his brother's shoulder to hide the tears. He wiped his face with the heel of his hand as they parted. "Don't screw this up."

"I'm not going to. You think I could live with that? Damaging three people's lives instead of just mine? No way. I've got all the incentive I need."

"Okay."

He tugged on Carter's shirt sleeve. "Come on, let's go eat."

He started to follow his brother into the house, but then stopped. "And hey, when you get out . . ." That sounded like he'd been in jail again. "I mean, when you're better . . ." That sounded like he needed fixing. Shit.

Chase laughed lightly. "It's okay, man. Just say it."

"If you need a place to crash, you can stay at my condo. It's empty right now, anyway. Or at the estate, of course, but I know you and Harrison don't really get along . . ."

"Yeah, I don't think the estate's an option. But maybe your place. I'll check it out; it'd be closer to my NA meetings."

"Yeah, that'd probably be . . . that'd be good." He swallowed. "Do you need, like, a sponsor or something? Is that something I could do for you?"

Chase stared at him, wide-eyed, for a long minute. "Um, no. It has to be someone who's in recovery. But I didn't think you'd even . . ." Chase cursed, pinching the bridge of his nose, like he was trying to stave off tears. "I thought for sure you'd want nothing to do with me. You're a better brother than I deserve."

Carter balked at that, kicking at the porch post. "I don't think I really . . ."

"Yeah, man. You are. Believe it." Now Chase was swiping at his face, too. "Have you heard from Christopher lately?"

"He texted me a little on Thanksgiving. But he didn't come home for Christmas. And he never returns my calls."

"See, that's what I deserve. Not you, though. I don't know why he ghosted *you*." Carter couldn't cover his surprise; he'd assumed Chase and Christopher were still in contact. They'd talked daily for years, lived together in college; he'd assumed it was a twin thing that he didn't understand.

Carter took a breath to tell him that he didn't think he deserved to be ghosted either, but Chase went on. "It was probably easier to trash all of us than to try to pick and choose. Don't take it personal, man." He sighed, but he was still all energy. "Man, I like your visits. I'm all pumped now about possibilities. Let's go eat and we can talk some more. I know you have to get back on the road, but the food here isn't half bad. We can at least get you something before you have to go . . . oh! They made Christmas cookies!" Carter smiled as he followed his brother's voice back into the house.

IT WAS AFTER SEVEN o'clock when he pulled back into the garage at the estate. He threw his keys onto the desk in the kitchen and, yawning, he poked his head into the fridge to see what they'd had for dinner. As usual, his plate was wrapped up in aluminum foil, labeled with his name by Mrs. Sánchez. He was just about to put it in the microwave when she hurried into the kitchen.

"Oh thank God, you're back. Please. Please, come."

Her tone was urgent, so he quickly followed her out of the kitchen and up the back staircase. He heard the tantrum before he saw her: they were in the music room, and it was a disaster area.

"Please, Mrs. Carpenter," Cindy was pleading, and she sounded on the edge of tears. A thick red book went flying through the doorway and nearly hit Carter as he tried to go inside. Unsurprisingly, his father was nowhere to be seen.

"Mom?"

"Carter?" She froze mid-throw, another volume of a music theory text in her hand, poised to try to take someone's head off with it. "You're back."

"Of course I'm back," he said, approaching her slowly. "How are you feeling, Mom?"

She covered her face with her hands. "Martina. I need Martina. She was supposed to come today. She comes almost every day. And when she's not here, you're here. Where is she?"

"Martina will come by to see you very soon. I promise. Do you want the cat she gave you?" It was a stuffed animal that looked like Charming, her tortoiseshell cat. He'd seen a lot of pictures. A lot. Willow nodded vigorously.

"I think it's in your bedroom, shall we go get it together?"

"I don't know the way," she sobbed. Stepping carefully over a bent flute, scattered sheet music, and a violin bow that would need all new horsehair to ever be functional again, he wrapped his arms around his mom and held her as she cried.

"I'll show you. It's okay. I'm here for you," he whispered. "It's going to be okay." Carter glanced around. Cindy stood in the corner by the door; defeated didn't begin to describe her posture. She ran a shaking hand through her short hair, brushing her fingers over a large ketchup stain on her polo shirt. At least, he hoped it was ketchup.

He gave her a little wave without releasing Willow, and she waved back, swaying a little on her feet.

"Don't leave, please. We need to talk," he murmured as he ushered Willow out of the room, and Cindy nodded in agreement. Carter found the stuffed cat, laid out two sets of pajamas, and helped her brush her teeth, then tucked her in. Reducing risk was what he excelled at: he just needed to convince Cindy that she could trust him. That Martina was trustworthy; he at least needed to get her job back, even if she didn't want to be together. He found Cindy in the kitchen, staring at Martina's daily report form.

"Thank you for taking care of my mother today."

"You're welcome," she said faintly, then she shook her head. "All I heard about all day was Martina. From your mother, from the rest of the staff, especially Mrs. Sánchez. They seem to think she's some kind of miracle worker."

"I'm inclined to agree. That's why I've asked my brother to re-hire her."

Cindy looked up sharply. "Which brother?"

"Chase."

"The *drug addict*?"

"He also plays a mean game of Scrabble. Beat me twice today." He pulled a beer out of the fridge, then offered her one. She accepted it immediately and downed half of it on her first pull.

"I don't know, Mr. Carpenter . . ."

"Were you planning to let her sign another contract with another family?"

"Yes. I mean, this was an unusual circumstance. I shouldn't have let her sign the first one with you, not with your romantic history . . . we're a small company. A family company. I can't have people going around accusing us of misconduct."

"I understand. But there's no chance of misconduct with my brother; I'd kill him if he tried to kiss the woman I love."

Cindy's gaze softened. "What about your dad?"

"What about him?"

"I think he left; I saw him with a suitcase earlier, but..."

"He's the one who sent the evidence?"

She nodded. "Pictures. Sexy ones, if you don't mind me saying so."

"Oh, I don't." He smiled. "You see, those pictures were actually a video, and if I showed it to you, you'd see that I kissed Martina first. So really, I'm the one who violated the contract. She should be suing me for sexual harassment. Thankfully, we're in love, so I don't see that happening. Willow and I will sign anything you want, releasing you from all legal responsibility. I can have our family lawyer draw up an agreement tonight."

Cindy sighed deeply, then let her elbows rest on the quartz counters. "This was not covered in my business classes."

"I imagine not," he said dryly, taking another sip of his beer. "But I promise you, the last thing I want is to screw you or Martina over. I just want good care for my mother, and I just want Martina to be my girlfriend. But she's less likely to agree to that if I can't get her job back, so . . ." He leaned forward onto his elbows, too. "Will you help me be her knight in shining armor? Please?"

She gave him a hard look. "She'll be on probation for six months."

"Fine."

"And if this happens again, she's absolutely done."

"Mrs. Hewes, I don't plan to give her any reason to stop seeing me. There shouldn't be an opportunity for it to happen again." He held out his right hand, and begrudgingly, Cindy shook it.

"You're really an actuary? Not a lawyer?"

He laughed. "Really."

"You missed your calling, young man . . ."

CHAPTER THIRTY

IT WAS CHRISTMAS NIGHT, and she'd spent the day with her family avoiding Augustina and George and checking her phone for messages from Carter. She'd made herself a cup of tea, forgoing dinner, and around nine, she'd gotten a cryptic text, asking if he could come over. Since she was now fired, she couldn't see any harm in it.

"It worked." Carter pushed into her apartment and shook his wet hair, leaving Martina sprayed and confused.

"What worked?"

"Here's your new contract with *Chase* Carpenter for Willow's care." He slapped the stack of papers down on the kitchen counter. "Just needs your signature." Carter took her face in his hands and began devouring her, lavishing her with hungry kisses. "Love your Christmas tree, by the way," he breathed as he moved lower to suck on her neck. Her head was spinning; guilt stabbed at her.

"I didn't ask you to do that . . ."

He straightened, searching her face. "Is this not what you wanted?"

"No, it is! It is. I just feel bad that you had to clean up my mess."

"It was my mess, too. It was my fault you got fired. And it's not like you could ask Chase to hire you." He went back to kissing her. Martina's head was still troubled, though. These few days had done nothing to help her muddle through the mess in her heart, either. Because Carter had asked her to trust him. She wanted to; she wanted to be together. But she needed assurances. A guarantee that it wasn't going to end the same way, that they weren't going to end up right back where they started.

"Let's go to Vegas," she whispered. "Tonight."

Carter slowed his kisses. "Why?"

"To get married, silly."

He scowled. "You're still scared?"

"N-no," she protested. "I'm not scared."

"What are you scared of?" He pulled her over to the couch and settled her on his lap. "Talk to me."

"I'm not scared!" She crossed her arms, putting a tiny amount of distance between. Just the right amount, in her mind.

"Then why are you trying to rush things?"

"Dude, I'm not the one who came blasting in here, pushed a new contract into my hands and tried to swallow my neck whole."

Carter chuckled. "I'm sorry if I came on strong." He kissed her again, lightly this time. "I just missed the heck out of you. But I want to actually date this time. Like, talk about hopes and dreams this time, now that we're in control of our own lives. Take time to get to know each other."

"And having waited nine years for this, *I* want to stop wasting time and go to Vegas." She pressed gentle kisses along his jaw. "You can get to know me later. The rest of our lives."

"Getting to know each other is not a waste of time, Tini."

"Well, I guess we're at an impasse then," she said, standing up. The bereft look on his face was almost comical.

"But we're still together, right?"

"Of course!" She smiled down at him as she ran a hand through her hair, shaking it out.

"Tangentially, what are you wearing?"

Martina looked down. "My pajamas?" They were the new set she'd bought herself for Christmas morning; she liked to look extra cute in the inevitable pictures, and these pink unicorn pj's were just the thing.

"Those are adorable."

"I know, right?"

"Just like you." He leaned forward and caught her hand. "Want to watch *Home Alone* and make out?"

"Yes, please," she grinned, sitting on him so hard he grunted. He didn't seem to mind as much when her lips met his again, and they spent some time breaking in her couch.

After a while, Martina wanted ice cream, so they took a moment to catch their breath.

"You start Monday. Again. Mom is very excited. So is Cindy, who wasn't able to find someone to fill in for you on such short notice and had to do it herself."

"Oh? Did she get the ballet flat treatment or the stiletto?"

"Stiletto. Also a flute, I think?"

"Oh boy. That's a really bad day."

"You can say that again."

"Did your brother take much convincing? Was it weird to ask him?"

"Nah, he hates Harrison." Carter stretched out on the couch, and Rajah jumped up onto his belly. "Well, hi there." Martina's mouth dropped open as Rajah pushed against Carter's hand, demanding to be petted, and he obliged. "Who's this?"

"If I say his name, he'll hiss and take off. Are you enjoying this moment?"

"Well enough, I guess." He scratched the calico behind his ears, and Rajah started to purr. "Hey there, No Name Cat. Merry Christmas."

"And here I thought he hated everyone. Turns out, he just hates me. Rude, Rajah."

He looked at her sharply, then seemed to decide she wasn't worth the effort and rolled over onto his back for Carter to scratch his belly.

"Rude and shameless."

His bowl empty, Carter stuck his spoon into hers, angling for a chocolate chunk, and she gasped in faux shock.

"Mr. Carpenter, this is my *personal* ice cream," she said, but she didn't move the dish away from him. Crash ate the bite slowly, looking deeply into her eyes, his tongue darting out to lap at the spoon. Oh, how she wanted that tongue against hers again . . . she licked her lips just thinking about it, and her heart rate skyrocketed.

"Tease," she breathed, and he grinned at her, unrepentant. Fine. Two could play at that game. She dipped her own spoon into the bowl, finding the drippiest bite she could. Tipping her head back, she let the minty liquid drip into her mouth, catching it on her tongue, and a little dribbled onto her chin and onto her chest. She laughed and swiped at it, then glanced at Crash.

Crash wasn't laughing. To call his gaze heated was like calling an active volcano a little warm. Never taking his eyes off her, he reached out with his spoon and caught the ice cream dripping down her face. Then he lifted the spoon and touched it gently to her bottom lip, his eyes still smoldering. Her mouth fell open automatically, like he'd discovered a secret button. His spoon felt warm in her mouth, but the ice cream was cold as she sucked it from the metal. Forget the ice cream; *Martina* was melting. And it only got worse when he went back for another bite in her bowl, then brought that one to her mouth, too.

She opened for that one, too. Why was this so hot? Was it because it was his spoon in her mouth? Was it because he was treating her like she was some princess who couldn't be bothered to bring her own spoon to her mouth? Her imagination began to run away from her . . . Crash, her doting servant, her the spoiled royal, languishing on a cushion while he spoons sustenance into her waiting mouth . . . it was hypnotic, really, him just feeding her, getting closer to her with every bite. All her focus was trained on him. At any moment, she expected him to throw the spoon over his shoulder, push the bowl aside and lay her back onto the couch . . .

"I should go. It's getting late." *Wait, what?*

"No," she said. "Stay. Please. I want you to." Abandoning the game, she kissed him, and he groaned.

"I have to go. Really."

She moved to kiss his neck, caressing his chest, and he grunted. His voice was shaky. "It's very romantic and all, with the tree, and the dessert, and the cute pajamas, but I don't want to screw this up the minute we get back together. We can't do this."

Martina sat up. "You're serious?"

He nodded. "Can I see you tomorrow?"

She didn't know what to say. This had been a weird day and an even weirder night. She suddenly thought sleep might be a really good idea. "I guess so."

"It's not that I don't want you. Trust me."

Trust me. He kept saying that, like it was easy. Like she wasn't going to be measuring all their present interactions against the past. Like she wasn't holding her breath, hoping he wouldn't let her down this time.

"I'm trying," she whispered. "Kind of hard when I don't know what to expect."

He nodded slowly. "Let's talk that over soon, okay?" He took her by the shoulders and looked into her eyes. "I'm really glad we're back together. Believe me?"

She didn't doubt that. She nodded, and he kissed her on the forehead. She watched him jog down the steps back to his car, concern and confusion and hope warring in her chest. *Weirdest. Christmas. Ever.*

CHAPTER THIRTY-ONE

AT 7:59, MARTINA KNOCKED on Carter's bedroom door.

"Come in," he called, and she crept inside, closing the door behind her. She'd been back to work for two weeks, and this was becoming their nightly ritual.

"She's asleep, and the night nurse is here..."

"Hang on . . ." He checked his watch. "Five . . . four . . . three . . ."

"You're really going to count down the seconds before my shift is over every night?"

"It's a rule your new boss made. I'm allowed to kiss you, but not to make out with you on work time."

"I thought that was a joke!"

"No. Chase is all about boundaries now, apparently." He pulled her down onto his bed, and she landed on top of him, giggling in spite of herself. She kissed him, putting all the pent-up energy she'd collected all day from all his flirty touches and glances into it.

"My last boss was better."

He chuckled. "Speaking of which, is there anything I can do for you today?"

"I want to go flying."

"I'm not night current."

"It doesn't have to be today. Maybe Saturday?"

"Saturday," he agreed with a happy sigh, nuzzling her neck, curling his body into hers. "Have I told you how much I missed you?"

"Just once or twice."

"And how much I love you?"

"You might've mentioned it." She kissed him. "What do you love about me?"

"Your eyes. Your smile. Your chest."

Martina smacked him, and Carter put his arms up to protect his head.

"Hey! You *asked!* Ow!"

"You're supposed to say something romantic!"

"I said the face stuff first!" he laughed. "That's a little romantic!" He caught her wrists and rolled them so he was on top of her. "I love your intelligence. Your confidence. Your fanciful imagination."

"Speaking of which, how do you feel about a Prince Charming costume for our wedding in Vegas?" She'd gone alone to Winnie's gorgeous wedding last weekend since the weekend nurse had called in sick, and she still had their own potential ceremony on the brain.

He pressed slow, open-mouthed kisses down her chest. "Notice I didn't put 'patience' on the list . . ." Pinned down on sheets that smelled like Carter, his weight pressing into her, his lips making desire spiral hurricane-like in her blood, she had to admit that she didn't feel patient in the slightest. She bucked her hips under him, and he kissed her harder.

"I was thinking," he said between kisses. "I don't think we could get my mom to Vegas."

"You're considering it?"

He rolled onto his side, lying on the bed next to her. "Maybe, I just . . . I want her to be there. She and Chase are the only family members I really care about, even if she's not going to remember . . ."

"She may. The brain is a funny thing."

"I want her in the pictures, you know? I want her there for me."

"Me too," she said, brushing the hair off his forehead. "I wasn't trying to exclude her."

"Okay." They talked about their days, touching and kissing in the dark room, until Martina couldn't finish a sentence without yawning.

"I should go home," she said, rolling to sit up.

"If she thinks we're married, doesn't it strike her as odd that you don't sleep here?" Carter pulled a sweatshirt on.

"Maybe she assumes I do. She goes to bed pretty early. Also, see my earlier comment about brains being weird." Now he was putting on his shoes. "What are you doing?"

"I'm walking you out to your car."

"Really?" Was that little gesture really making her heart beat faster?

"Of course. This was a date. How else am I going to get a good night kiss? Honestly, hon, you're ridiculous sometimes."

"You know," she whispered, "there are other goodnight things I could give you, too."

He paused. "I don't mean to sound like a broken record, but . . . no." Carter gathered her into his arms. "I need you to trust *me*. Not this," he said, waggling a finger between their two bodies. "That part was always easy for us."

"I've learned lots of new things," she whispered, and Carter's arms tightened around her. "We won't be two kids fumbling around, not knowing what they're doing . . ."

"Still had plenty of fun," he murmured, and she felt him shiver. Then he set her away from him gently. "No. I want you to trust me. I haven't asked for a lot, but I'm asking for this. You're trying to take shortcuts. We're taking the long way, Tini. The scenic route."

They'd been together for two weeks, and she'd suspected he felt this way. She expected to feel disappointment, so that part wasn't a surprise. But the delight? That shocked the socks off her. Because it was true; he hadn't asked for a lot. But the fact that he was refusing her because he thought it would make their relationship stronger? That meant something to her.

"You're so sexy when you're putting your foot down," she whispered, trailing her fingers over his pecs.

Carter rolled his eyes. "Nice try." He kissed her with a grin. "Shoes, lady. Let's get you home. I hear that family you're working for is very demanding, and you need to get your rest."

Driving home in the dark was a good place to think. His words rang in her mind about trust and relationships . . . honestly, it wasn't something she'd had to practice much. And when she'd tried, like with her family, she'd often end up shutting down. But avoidance wasn't really getting her what she wanted. In a weird way, she thought, it was a bit a like a football team. When they weren't communicating, the play broke down, and they couldn't move the ball the needed yards. But when they worked together, it was a thing of beauty to watch; nothing could stand in their way.

"I will figure out how to trust him," Martina said out loud into the quiet car. "I can be part of a team without sacrificing who I am. I'll be someone he can trust, someone he knows will be there when he needs me. We'll make our plays together. We'll get our wins together."

By the time she got home, it was past midnight, but she felt wide awake. She felt at peace. She felt real hope.

CHAPTER THIRTY-TWO

ON SATURDAY, HE PICKED her up and took her to the private air strip where the Carpenters' airplanes were hangared. It was overcast, but not rainy, and the layer was high . . . or so he said.

"172 or Bonanza?" Carter asked, focusing on his flight plan.

"What's the difference?"

"Smaller with a better view or bigger and faster?"

"Smaller, please."

He smiled. "Good choice. Cheaper on the fuel, too."

Martina snorted. "Like I care about that. You're paying."

She helped him push the small plane with a blue stripe out of the hangar, then climbed into the right seat. She felt that familiar thrill when he shouted for non-existent bystanders to stand clear of the propeller and the rumble of the small engine made her seat vibrate. There was just something about flying that she adored; despite the engine noise, it felt quiet up high. She watched Carter's black SUV get smaller and smaller as they climbed, until it looked like an ant sitting next to the hangar.

"How far would it be to Vegas?"

"This again?"

"I didn't bring an overnight bag, but I don't think we'd be spending much time clothed, so . . ."

He didn't laugh, and when she turned her head, his gaze was concerned.

"I'm just kidding. I know we already decided against it."

"Martina. Talk to me. For real, this time. What's this Vegas thing about?"

"I don't know. I guess . . ." She paused, trying to formulate her thoughts as she watched the patchwork of fields and farms far below. "I guess sometimes I just envy Willow."

"Why?" he asked softly.

"Because she doesn't remember. In her mind, we've been married all this time, together all this time. I wish I didn't remember what you did to my heart last time. I wish I didn't remember how it felt to have to walk out on you. How it felt to ignore you, when all I wanted was to run back into your arms, self-respect be damned."

He took her hand, intertwining their fingers. "But honey, don't you know how much it means to me that you do remember? That you're choosing to believe in me, despite my massive screw-up? That you're giving me your forgiveness, day by day, for all my mistakes, old and new? If you had AD, I'd never win you back, because I'd never get the chance to show you I've changed." He lifted her hand to his lips for a kiss. "I want you to know me. And I want to know you. And if that means a long list of things I love about you and a long list of things I've forgiven you for, I'm okay with it."

"I did burn your clutch out that one time."

"That's at the top of the forgiveness list," he agreed, grinning.

"Could you please kiss me?"

Carter closed the distance between them with a sweet, lingering kiss.

"Now could you please fly the plane?"

"It flies itself, look." He took his left hand off the controls. "See?"

"Hands on the steering wheel, Carter!" she yelled. "We do *not* want to bring that nickname back."

"It's a yoke, not a steering wheel."

"Yolk, egg white, whatever you want to call it, just keep your hands firmly on the part that guides the plane, please!"

He laughed so hard, the vein in his forehead popped a little, but he obeyed. Martina glared at him. "It's not funny."

"It's kind of funny." He snickered, then sobered. "So. No more Vegas talk?"

"No more Vegas talk," she agreed.

"You want to fly it?"

"Stop."

"I'm serious! Just put your hands on your yoke."

"No!"

"I won't let us crash, I promise." He put her hands on the u-shaped controls in front of her. "Just keep it level, no sudden movements."

"Do you remember how badly golf went? This could be waaay worse."

Carter laughed. "Martina, you think I'm going to let anything happen to you when I just got you back? No way. Never." She couldn't look at him, because when flying an airplane, it didn't seem wise to gaze into your boyfriend's eyes, but she knew that tone: his pixie-dust sparkle was back.

"Can I stop now?"

He laughed again, and she realized he'd been doing that a lot lately. *I made him happy. I fixed Carter. We fixed each other.*

"Yes, beautiful. You're *so* brave. Flying the plane for *sixty whole seconds.*"

"Shut up, *Crash.*"

"GOT PLANS TOMORROW?" she asked, as he pulled up in front of her apartment building. "I have a brunch thing in the morning, but my afternoon's free."

"I've got that bachelor auction in the afternoon, but I'll be around all morning if you want to come over after your brunch. Mom would probably love—"

Martina felt like someone had dumped a bucket of cold water over her.

"I'm sorry, what?"

He cocked his head. "I said I'm free all morning?"

"Not that—the bachelor auction."

"Right."

"But you're not a bachelor. You're . . ." she gestured between them, "you know. Not single. Attached."

"But I didn't know that when I signed up."

Hot anger flooded her senses. *No way.* This was just like before; he wanted to have his own way, and what she thought didn't matter.

"Carter, you cannot go on a date with anyone else."

He ran a hand through his hair. "I can't back out on them now, Tini, the organizers would be furious. And it's for a really good cause. Doernbecher is an amazing hospital. They help so many kids—"

She held up a hand. "I'm a nurse. Believe it or not, I am familiar with Doernbecher. But good cause or not, you cannot go on a date with anyone else," she repeated firmly.

"Martina," he said gently. "You can trust me. I promise. It'll be completely platonic."

"No."

"It's only one night," he cajoled.

"I don't care!" she yelled. She slapped a hand over her own mouth; she never lost her temper anymore, but if she said one more word, she was about to erupt like Mt. St. Helens.

"I'm sorry, honey," he murmured, reaching for her hand, but she snatched it away. She stormed up the stairs to her apartment, startling the cats when she slammed the front door.

Unbelievable. She threw her purse on the couch. *Not again. No. Not this time.* She'd just have to convince him to quit, and that was the end of it. Martina was done sharing Carter Carpenter. She pulled out her phone.

Martina: You said I could trust you, but you're not listening. This is important to me.

Carter: I am listening, Tini. But you don't have to be worried; nothing's going to happen.

Martina: I don't want you to do this.

Carter: I'm sorry. I have to.

Carter: It wouldn't be right to quit.

Martina: But it's right to cheat on me?

Carter: I'm not cheating on you! I swear.

Martina: Well, that's what it feels like.

Martina threw her phone onto the couch in a huff, and her gaze fell on her dried-out Christmas tree. This felt like the perfect day to take off the lights and ornaments and haul it out back for the birds. She'd work on him again later. A little voice in her head asked what she would do if she couldn't change his mind, but she drowned it out with the sound of the vacuum, sucking up pine needles like it was her mission in life. Maybe she wouldn't leave it for the birds. Maybe she'd just burn it.

CHAPTER THIRTY-THREE

GOING TO HER PARENTS' house was the last thing Martina wanted to be doing on Sunday. She spent most of the morning sulking and playing with the cats. She texted him again as soon as she got up.

Martina: You're seriously going to do this?
Carter: I can't cancel. I promised.
Carter: You can trust me. Nothing will happen. It's just dinner.

It wasn't about them. It wasn't about him. It was about her. He didn't want to elope and go to Vegas? Fine. But she wasn't sharing him anymore. Not with Jennie Wallace, not with some random girl whose dad won a charity bid. She did trust him, but . . . but she couldn't bear the thought of him with anyone else. And it was worse than last time, because now he knew better. They weren't kids anymore; he should be able to see how hurtful this was. It was like she'd found a shipwreck deep in her heart, damaged and decayed, where her insecurities had made a home like a school of fish. She felt tense, worked up. He couldn't change his mind about them, not now. Not when

they'd worked so hard to get back together. She started another
text, but it was immature, manipulative, and she deleted it with
a sigh.

That wasn't who she wanted to be, wasn't the kind of partner she wanted to be. Because they were a team. She hadn't
signed onto this goal, but if he needed this, if he needed to ful-
fill his commitment, she would give him the space to do so.
If he said nothing would happen, she would believe him. She
would believe him if it killed her.

She was quiet at her parents' house, and her siblings and
their children seemed to notice; everyone was giving her a wide
berth where she'd parked herself in the recliner. Everyone, that
is, except George.

"Tia Tini, play a game with me."

"No, thanks."

He held up a football. "Mama says you like football. Here,
catch." He threw it directly at her face; her hands flew up, but
she wasn't quick enough. The stiff leather hit her directly on her
left cheekbone, and the pain had her cursing before she could
stop herself.

"Martina! Language," her mother chided, and Martina
slowly got to her feet, livid. She went to the freezer to get an ice
pack, then turned to her mother.

"How long until the meal?"

"About twenty minutes. The breakfast casserole is almost
done."

She nodded. "I'm calling a family meeting in the living
room." Her mother froze for a moment, then wiped her hands
on her a dish towel, shaking her head.

"Dear, I really don't think . . ."

"Mom. It's time."

Within ten minutes, they were all assembled on the couches. Augustina and Stephen, Lola and Patrik, her mom and dad and Francesca.

She stood in front of the fireplace, still icing her face. "This won't take long. I need to apologize to you. All of you. I haven't been honest with you, because sometimes, you make me so mad, I just don't know what to say. But I'm realizing that I need to work on trusting people, and this is a start." She turned to her older sister. "Augustina, your son hurts me on purpose. I don't like that. I'd like you to work on it with him and give me authority to discipline him." Wide-eyed, Gus nodded. Martina turned to her mother. "Mom, I hate being at the kid's table just because I'm not married. I'm more than ten years older than Francesca, and it's kind of insulting when you lump us in the same category. And I want you to put some faith in me that expressing my anger to my sisters isn't going to break us apart. Please stop trying to sweep everything under the rug." She made eye contact with each of the others. "I'm sorry for how my anger has kept me from really participating in family stuff. I'm sorry I've been so . . ."

"Grumpy," Francesca finished, and Martina nodded.

"Yes. Grumpy. I apologize."

"Martina." Her father sat forward, his elbows on his knees. "Is this new job too stressful for you?"

She laughed. "No, Dad. My new job is great. And since I have you all assembled, let me announce that Carter and I are back together. He's convinced me not to elope in Vegas, but we will likely be getting married at some point." Every person in her family was wearing the same matching expression of disbe-lief, and Martina snickered.

"Aren't you working for him?" Lola asked.

"No, I got fired."

The living room erupted in chatter in Spanish and English, and she held up her hands.

"I got fired for kissing Carter. His dad caught us. But I have a new contract with his brother, Chase."

"The drug addict?" Linda gasped.

"Yes, Mom, the drug addict," Martina said patiently. "He also plays a mean game of Scrabble."

"Do you love him?"

She turned to her dad. "Yes," she answered softly. "I do. He's apologized for what he did. He's a different man now. We're getting to know each other again, but he's proven himself reli-able. And caring. And faithful."

"Isn't he in the bachelor auction?" her mom asked. "We got tickets in the mail; he was spotlighted as one of the main at-tractions . . ."

Oh boy. "Yes, he is."

"Then why aren't you there bidding on him?" Francesca asked.

"Because I'm trying to trust him."

"Girl," Augustina said, laying on the attitude thickly, "there's trust, and then there's foolishness. If you can donate to a good cause *and* keep your man out of someone else's hands, why wouldn't you?"

Her other female relatives chorused their agreement.

"I-I'm not dressed right," she said, looking down at her jean skirt and polyester lace blouse.

"Oh, Cinderella," Lola said, "don't worry about that. Your fairy godsisters are here. We've got you." She paused. "Not that you're dirty or poor or anything. Dang, girl, with the bank you're making at the Carpenters', I bet you're the richest person here."

"Not if you factor in the value of my Christmas tree enterprise," her father muttered.

"And not if you account for my school debt," Martina added. Then her sisters were pulling her upstairs to try on their prom dresses (they didn't fit) and into Mom's closet (her basic black would have to do).

"I have stuff at home," she protested, but her sisters wouldn't hear of it. Within an hour, they had her eyes smoky, her hair up in a chignon, and her ears, wrists, and neck sparkling with nicer jewelry than she knew her mother even owned.

Augustina pulled out a pair of silver stilettos and handed them to her. "I'm sorry, Tini. I knew he was misbehaving sometimes, and I should've done more about it. Forgive me?"

She kissed her cheek, leaving a rosy lipstick print behind. "Of course. And I'll forgive George, too, if he asks."

"He will," she promised. "And I'm taking a parenting class at church that I hope will really help . . ."

Martina smiled and gave her a hug. "Me too, sis. For your sake more than mine."

CARTER CHECKED HIS phone; it was almost time. Since he was the headliner, he'd had to go last. He just wanted to get this over with. If she hadn't been mad at him, he could've spent the morning with Martina. Now he was stuck undergoing this demeaning ritual; how was it okay to auction men off, but not women? He didn't like being looked at like a piece of meat. It was for a good cause, but . . . it was going to be difficult going on a date with someone else, even if it was purely platonic. He peeked out at the edge of the curtain to check on his mom; he'd seated her with Mrs. Durand, figuring they knew each other from the hair salon. She seemed to be happy, chatting with other people at the table . . . including Martina. His heart stopped for a moment, and when it started beating again, it was pounding out an anthem of victory. Carter had no idea what she was doing here, but she clearly wasn't pissed at him, and that felt like a win. He could only sort of see her, through the crowd of people, and he craned his neck to see her better, see what she was wearing. Whatever it was, it was hot. He texted her quickly.

Carter: What are you doing here?

He enjoyed her perplexed look as she glanced around, trying to see him. When she gave up, she texted him back.

Martina: Just here to support a worthy cause.
Martina: If I see anyone I like, that is.

Carter chuckled to himself . . . that old confidence surged through his veins like a drug. She hadn't seen him in a tux since their senior prom, and this one was custom made. It fit him like a glove.

Carter: Oh, I think you'll like what you see.
Martina: You think so?
Martina: Hmm. I'll be the judge of that.

"And now," Evan Durand, the MC of the event, announced, "the final bachelor in our auction this evening, Carter Carpenter!" He walked out on the stage, hands in his pockets, grinning . . . at Martina. Even with the hot lights in his eyes, he could pick her out easily.

"Be prepared, ladies, Mr. Carpenter always fetches a high price. What's more, he's informed me tonight that this will be his final auction, so this is your last chance to make him yours for the night!" A ripple of speculative whispers passed through the attendees, and Carter winced.

"Sorry," he mouthed to Martina, and she laughed. He hadn't meant to drive up the price; how could he have known that she was going to show up and bid on him? But Martina didn't seem to mind . . . her dark eyes were warm, forgiving, and he suddenly felt that they were the only two people in the room. Dr. Durand was still talking about his merits, but she had him transfixed. She was here, supporting him. Loving him.

"We'll start the bidding at $100," said Evan, and Martina lifted her paddle. So did thirty other women. Carter felt his mouth go dry; he felt helpless up there, standing alone. He didn't want her having to pay thousands of dollars to get him. Everyone knew their history; it was going to make headlines in Timber Falls when the news got out that they were together again. If people knew she was the one bidding, maybe they would let her win. He saw his mom lean over and whisper something to Martina, who turned to her and smiled. Then she stood up. He watched the other women's eyes go wide, and he listened to the whispers race across the tables like the sound of a rushing river. Every time Dr. Durand upped the bidding, someone else dropped out. $200, $500, $600 . . . by the time they got to $750, everyone had realized what was happening and put their paddles down. The room still rolled with whispers, but it was paired with smiles.

Martina didn't appear to see any of it: he knew, because he never really took his eyes off her. And she never took her eyes off him. *Mine. She's mine now, and I'm hers.*

"Well, folks, I guess it's good that he's bowing out, because our headliner has officially made less money than any of the other bachelors tonight," Evan joked. He looked down at Martina. "And it seems there's a good reason for that. Ms. Lopez, please come claim your bachelor." Martina, ever comfortable in sky-high heels, hurried up the stairs and whispered something in Evan's ear on her way to him.

"Sorry, I'm being corrected: Mr. Carpenter is no longer a bachelor." The crowd got to their feet, cheering and whistling, as Carter took her in his arms. He dipped her and gave her a kiss that would leave no room in anyone's mind whether he was happy to be leaving with this woman tonight.

CHAPTER THIRTY-FOUR

EIGHT MONTHS LATER

IF SOMEONE HAD ASKED High School Martina to describe her future wedding, not much about the ceremony that was about to begin would've been similar. Oregon's mercurial summer weather had dictated that her beautiful backyard wedding was rained out, and there was currently a small army of friends and volunteers re-arranging the cream and gold chairs in rows in the ballroom of the Carpenter estate. Her in-recovery almost brother-in-law Chase was directing the flower arrangements that were being delivered. Her nephew George, who less than a year ago had spit right in her face, was practicing his walk down the aisle with her niece Daisy as ring bearer and flower girl. Her future father-in-law and her dad were trying to get the white, rose-covered portico through the garden doors without destroying it.

Even her groom was not exactly the same man she'd fallen in love with back then. Oh, he had the same name, the same stunning blue eyes, the same sandy blond hair . . . but this man was calm, considerate, and competent in a way High School Crash never was. It had been his idea to bring down the piano bench to keep his mom calm amidst the activity of the day, and now he sat chatting with her as Willow held her stuffed cat. He winked at Martina across the room, and she beamed at him. Her hair was already done in a side-swept mermaid braid, and she played with the end a little, enjoying the sight of him in his black Tom Ford tuxedo. *So. Freaking. Handsome.*

"I thought it was bad luck for the groom to see the bride before the wedding," Gus teased, elbowing her.

"We don't believe in luck." *We don't need it. Some things are meant to be.* Her gaze drifted back to Carter, and he was still watching her, too, his smile as heartwarming as ever.

"Go get dressed," Lola said, pushing her toward the stairs. "We've got this."

Martina looked around, taking in the rush of caterers, decorators, musicians, and photographers, and she threw up her hands a little desperately. "Okay. I'm going." She'd mostly done what she could do down here without ruining her nails, anyway. If she didn't get started on her makeup, it wasn't going to be the rain that ruined things; it was going to be the tardiness of the bride.

She hurried upstairs to the media room, which looked like a bridal boutique where a bomb had gone off: there were shoes, clothing, jewelry, makeup, nail polish, safety pins, and snacks everywhere. Winnie was already waiting to help her get into her dress. She wolfed down a yogurt, knowing she wasn't going to want to eat once she was dressed. Martina stared up at the Vera Wang champagne strapless ball gown hanging on the door . . . if she didn't feel like a princess in this thing, then it was not possible. It fit perfectly, as did the tiara Carter had gotten her. She even had gloves; she had shamelessly gone full fairy tale.

Her phone had gone missing, so she sent Francesca to go find it; guests were already arriving. She hoped everything had come together, but if it hadn't, at least she had the essentials: Carter, their families, and the pastor.

Francesca popped her head into the media room. "Found your phone. Oh, and Pastor Kellen's truck got a flat, so he's gonna be a little late . . ."

Winnie look at her sideways, and they both started to laugh. There was nothing else to do. They found a stool so her dress wouldn't wrinkle and she turned on the pre-season game.

Martina: What are you doing?

Carter: Just waiting around. Wedding coordinator won't let me eat. And Christopher finally showed up.

Martina: Ask me.

Carter: ?

Martina: You know. Ask me.

There was a long pause, and she wasn't sure if he'd been put to work or if he really didn't know what she was asking. Then three blinking dots appeared.

Carter: Is there anything I can do for you today?
Martina: Marry me.
Carter: Gladly. That's much better than putting snow tires on your car.
Martina: I know, right?

Martina: Just wait until tomorrow when we get to Hawaii . . .
Carter: Not tonight?

She could feel his puppy-dog eyes like he was standing right in front of her. They were driving to Portland right after the reception to stay in a hotel near the airport before they caught their early-morning flight to Kauai, but she expected the party to go late. The wedding didn't even start until 3:00.

Martina: Won't you be too tired?
Carter: I cannot state this emphatically enough: NO.
Martina: Thank you, by the way.
Carter: For what?
Martina: For changing my mind.
Carter: Love you, Tini.
Martina: Love you, too.
Carter: Pastor's here! Showtime, baby. :wedding ring emoji:
Martina: But there's still twenty minutes until half-time!
Carter: Man, I hope that's a joke.
Martina: Should've gone to Vegas with me when you had the chance.

"Here's your bouquet," Lola said, handing her the bundle of pink, white, and red roses. "And the florist really looked at me funny when I told them your special request."

Martina gently pawed through the flowers until she found what she was looking for, then grinned. "Then everything's ready. Let's do this."

EPILOGUE

FOUR YEARS LATER

"SEE, WILLOW? THAT ONE'S the daddy duck, because it has a green head," Carter explained to his three-year-old, holding her on one hip.

"I'm Willow," his mother corrected him from the picnic table where she sat, holding her tortoiseshell stuffed cat.

"I know," he smiled. "We named her after you."

"You did?" Willow smiled back. "Isn't that nice?" She paused, looking out where Martina was pretending to chase their six-month-old son, Nicolas, who was crawling around in the grass. "Do I know you?"

"Yes," he said, taking her hand. "I'm your son, Carter. And that's your daughter-in-law, Martina."

"Oh, I know her. That one takes good care of me."

He grinned. "She sure did. We miss having you around the house, Mom." He'd convinced Martina to let him move her into a care facility eight months ago, since he didn't think she should have to change three people's diapers.

"Hmm." She watched them play quietly, lost in her own mind. He put his Willow down and let her run to Martina and

Nick. Then his mom turned to him suddenly. "Your wife had a doll with pink hair hidden in her bouquet, didn't she?"

"That's right!" he said, laughing.

"It was small, but I saw it . . ."

"That's right," he repeated, kissing her temple. "You remembered."

"Of course I did."

Martina came over carrying Nick with a crying Willow loping pathetically behind her. "We fell down and wanted to be carried, too," she explained. "We did not care that we're too big to be carried, since Brother was being carried." She handed Nicolas to his mom, who took him with delight.

"What a big boy you are," she cooed, and Nicolas grinned his two-tooth smile, spit dribbling down his chin. "Carter, my sweet boy."

He ignored the mistake and answered, "I love you, too, Mom." Nicolas did bear a striking resemblance to his baby pictures—everything except those dark eyes. Martina paused in getting out the picnic she'd packed, the fermented carrot sticks still in the jar in her hand. She tipped her head back, as if she were scrutinizing the scattered clouds above them. Then she began to wave at her face with one hand.

"Is my gravity trick working?"

Lizzie and Chase and their kids were getting out of a gray mini-van, sippy cups and pacifiers falling out of the car alongside them, bouncing onto the pavement.

"Nope." Martina let her head fall forward again, and the tears were obvious. "Sorry." It wasn't something he'd gotten used to, either, having Willow be so here and yet so absent.

"Oh, don't apologize. I've got my favorite people in the world right here; I'm just fine." He gave her a long kiss before hurrying to catch little Willow before she stuck her hand in the giant mud puddle she was heading toward, her injury forgotten.

And with that, they all sat down to eat.

Would you write a review?

Martina and Carter, they make quite a pair.
If you agree, do you think you could share
on Goodreads or Amazon, wherever you lurk?
I'll tell you a secret: it so helps my work.
And getting to hear that you loved them, too?
Well, it makes my whole week. It's totally true.

There's a reason why I'm a novelist and not a poet, but in all seriousness, I would be so appreciative if you could spread the word about this new series! It's a huge help to my business. Thanks!

Don't miss a moment of Timber Falls fun!

Could Be Something Good (Daniel and Winnie)
Must be a Mistake (Kyle and Ainsley)
Right Back Where We Started (Martina and Crash)

Coming Winter 2020...

More Than We Bargained For (Starla and Sawyer)
Never Say Never (Lizzie and Chase)
Maybe It's Just Me (Maggie and R.J.)

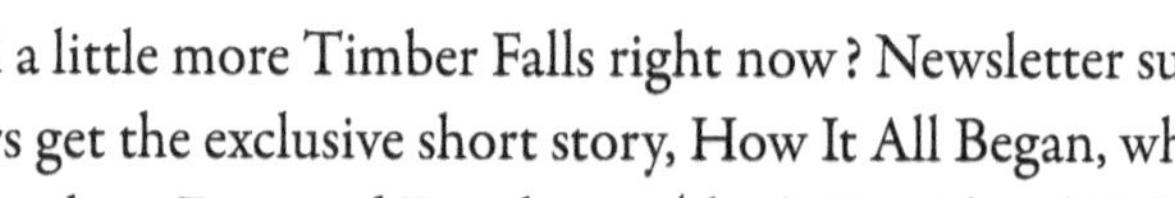

Need a little more Timber Falls right now? Newsletter subscribers get the exclusive short story, How It All Began, which tells us how Evan and Farrah met (that's Daniel and Kyle's mom and dad). Sign up now at https://www.subscribepage.com/timberfalls.

Also by Fiona West

The Borderline Chronicles (sweet fantasy romance)
The Ex-Princess: a chronically-ill princess who fled from her responsibilities is forced to face the fiancé she abandoned and journey across a magically-unpredictable continent. Can she keep the life she's given up everything to build?

The Un-Queen: a king caught between love and legality...can Abbie and Edward's relationship survive engagement and the opposition who wants to tear them apart again?

The Jinxed Journalist: a single mother gets her dream job as a journalist, only to find herself caught in royal scandal, opposing her son's new mentor. When forced to choose between love and her career, can she still come out a winner?

The Semi-Royal: a doctor takes an expedition with her brother's best friend that has life-changing results. Can she resist the underlying attraction that's been there for years?

The Almost-Widow: a security professional finds herself paired with a shy, sensory-sensitive man on the night watch. Can their friendship blossom into something more?

Acknowledgments

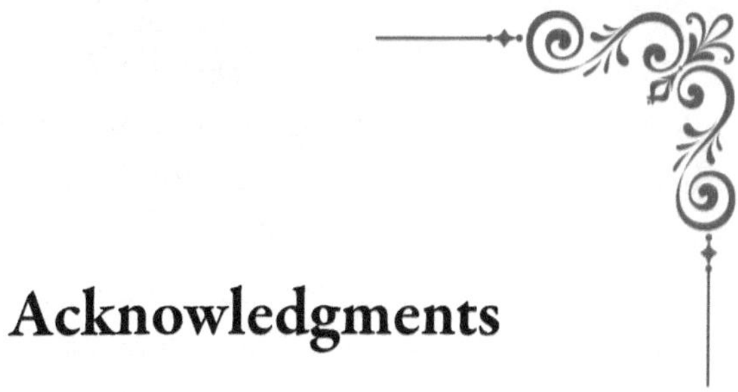

TO MY EDITORIAL TEAM at Salt and Sage: you all rock. I can't say it enough: your professionalism, straight-up knowledge of your genres, and kindness make this so much easier.

To my critique partners, Angela Boord and Rebecca Hopkins: thanks for being my sounding board; your honest feedback helps so much! Thanks also to the Delmas 75 Writing Group, who have persevered through the COVID difficulties and emerged still intact; you ladies light up my life.

To my copy editor, Kristin Houlihan: I'm so thankful to have a professional who's invested in making my work perfect! Thanks for cleaning up all those little details for me.

To my proofreaders, Liz Schandorff: You add so much more than grammar to my books. Thank for donating your time and talents to my books!

To my cover artist, Erin O'Neill-Jones: So lovely. You're such a talented artist and genuinely kind person, and it's a joy to work together.

Gratitude also to my beta readers, Lane Luckey, Tara Johnson, Jennifer Stout, Nancy Kay Bowden and Sheri McPhee for their insights.

And last, but certainly not least, thank you to my CFO, Mr. West. You are the lime to my coconut.

Connect with Fiona!

Thanks so much for taking the time to sample my work. I hope you enjoyed reading it even more than I enjoyed writing it, though I doubt that's possible. Being an author is a dream come true, and getting to share my books with delightful, thoughtful readers like you just adds to the sweetness. Drop me a line and let me know what you thought or leave a review on Goodreads!

Sign up for my bi-monthly newsletter, The West Wind, for freebies, deleted scenes, book reviews, and insight into my writing process at https://www.subscribepage.com/timber-falls.

On Twitter as @FionaWestAuthor

On Facebook as @authorfionawest

On Instagram as fionawestauthor

On Goodreads as Fiona West

Or email me at fiona@fionawest.net.

I love talking to fans!

www.ingramcontent.com/pod-product-compliance
Lightning Source LLC
Chambersburg PA
CBHW051652180726
48284CB00006B/1962